The Heart Of Texas
Texas, Book 1
RJ Scott
Copyright © :
First printed e
This edition: N
Cover design l
Edited by Silve

Dedication

This is Phil's book. Mr Cooper, you rock. Your ideas rock, and I am so very thankful for the day you won me in the auction.
And always for my family.

Trademarks

The author acknowledges the trademarked status and owners of the following wordmarks used in this story:

Dallas Morning News: A.H. Belo Corporation
Jack Daniels: Brown Forman Corporation
José Cuervo: Tequila Cuervo, S.A. de C.V. (all other countries)
Wikipedia: Wikimedia Foundation
iPod: Apple, Inc.
Lego: Lego Group
Quarter Horse News: Morris Magazine Network
Chanel: Alain Wertheimer and Gerard Wertheimer
Black Sabbath
Band-Aid: Johnson and Johnson
Jimmy Choo: J. Choo Limited

Chapter 1

"Sit down, boys," Gerald Hayes said firmly, his back to the Dallas skyline and his arms folded across his chest. They complied with his request since it was more of a command, both sliding into the leather chairs opposite the desk. They wore different expressions, though both were his sons.

Jeff was the mirror of his father, six-five, strong, not averse to getting his own way through means others might consider somewhat underhanded or devious. He'd achieved good things for Hayes Oil, very good things. Under his control, the company had grown in strength due to some well placed deals and some serious, if somewhat questionable, pay-offs to just the right people.

It was how Hayes Oil had gotten where it was today; the second largest oil company in Dallas, billions passing through their coffers on an annual basis, with a staff of over seven hundred in the head office alone. Jeff was a chip off the old block; he knew when to deal, and when to back off, when to buy off. It was a joy for an old man to watch. Jeff was sitting in his chair, his back straight. He was calm, with a virtually inexpressive demeanor, and his eyes were like chips of ice. He was dressed in dark gray Armani, perfectly groomed, his shirt crisp and white, and his tie a deep maroon. His hands were placed on the material of his pants, his nails perfectly manicured. He had an air of expectancy layered about him in palpable waves. Gerald couldn't have been prouder of his eldest son. Jeff was the right choice to form part of the new era of Hayes Oil, his student, and his success.

Riley, his middle child, only an inch shorter than Jeff and nearly as cold, was sitting just as calmly. Nearly. He too was wearing Armani, this time a charcoal black with a black silk shirt and no tie. He exuded the same confidence as his older brother, but with a subtle difference. He was an untamed version of his brother. His middle child had his mother's way about him and enjoyed the money the Hayes family had, way more than was really necessary. But to give him his due, under his guidance, Research and Development had flourished, and Gerald was as watchful of Riley as he was of his oldest— but for very different reasons.

Riley made decisions driven by his heart, by immeasurable instinct, too many times to make Gerald entirely happy with leaving Hayes Oil under his control for any length of time. Still, Riley deserved a place at Hayes Oil; after all, he supposed, whatever his thoughts, and whatever decisions were made, it *was* his legacy too.

Riley looked tired today, and Gerald glanced down at the *Dallas Morning News* on his desk, knowing what was on page seven, the gossip page, knowing what was in evidence before him, and knowing it made his decision easier.

"How is Lisa?" he asked Jeff conversationally, glancing over at the pictures grouped on one side of his desk— his family, Jeff with his arms around his perfect blonde wife, with his two grandchildren posed just so. It filled him with pride to see the Hayes Oil generations all set to carry on the Hayes name. He glanced at photos of his youngest, Eden, and at Riley, both in their photos alone, both for very different reasons.

Sighing, he unfolded his arms, wondering if what he was about to say would change the face of Hayes Oil forever.

* * * *

Jim Bailey was furious. He could only imagine what Riley was going through at this very minute, and he knew someone had to go and find him before the middle Hayes boy took a gun to his father's head. He had watched as Gerald and the favored son had left. The older man's arm was loose across Jeff's shoulders, their heads close in conversation, and it cut him to the core. It was Jim who had prepared the legal papers, Jim who had argued against the idiocy Hayes Senior was proposing. Someone had to be on Riley's side in this whole freaking mess, even if it meant this was the end of his tenure at Hayes Oil, and he knew where to find Riley. Taking the elevator, he left at the sixty-fifth floor, following the darkening corridor to the map room. It was the one place where Riley could always be found if the stress of his family got too much, sitting cross-legged on the floor poring over his beloved maps. He would spend hours with the geological surveys, the statistical results, his instinct for oil leading R&D to make decisions that had quadrupled Hayes Oil's output over the last two years. It astounded Jim that such a young man, only twenty-seven, had such an instinct. It reminded him of the old days, when Gerald and Alan would fly by the seat of their pants to locate new oil reserves based on nothing other than instinct.

Jim hesitated outside the door, steeling himself for what he would find within. Riley was rightly going to be furious with him for withholding the legal changes at Hayes Oil from him. He considered Jim a friend and, as such, probably had the right to expect more. Breathing deeply, he pushed open the door to find the large room echoing and in darkness, the only light from the closing Texas evening and the growing glow of the city outside. It wasn't difficult to locate Riley. Jim could almost touch the anger radiating from the tall man standing at the window silhouetted in the increasing gloom. Jim said nothing, just closing the door behind him and leaning against it. He loosened his tie and focused hard on the dark form. Riley was locked into silent stillness, looking out through the glass.

"Twenty-two percent," Riley finally said, his words clipped and tense. Jim could see himself reflected in that same glass, hesitating, lost, just waiting for the explosion. Jim had known. He had known as soon as the figures hit the desk. For fuck's sake, he was the company's lawyer. He was the one to write up the contracts for handover, the one who'd known the full details for three days longer than Riley.

His anger at what Gerald had forced him to do was manifesting itself as guilt. God knows he had wanted to say something. Every time he looked at the young man who worked so damn hard for this company, he had wanted to tell Riley what Gerald was planning. Never the right moment, never the right reason, and now… now he was paying for the betrayal. "Riley?"

Temper snapped and spat from Riley. "Fucking less than a third, the same as my sister!" He started pacing, gesturing with his hands, frustration in every exaggerated movement. Jim grimaced, because he knew that the percentage Eden got wasn't the point of Riley's temper. Riley was close to his sister, loved her and her shopping ways, and didn't begrudge his Paris Hilton wannabe sibling anything. No, the point was that it hadn't been fair at all. His brother, his acknowledged bastard of a Stepford brother, had just been handed forty-eight percent of Hayes Oil, and effective control of the company.

In a flurry of sudden but controlled movement, Riley spun on his heel, throwing whatever was in his hand across the room, missing Jim by inches. It was a map-reader, fifty thousand dollars of technology smashed into fractured pieces against the glass wall, and then it began. The words that Jim had been expecting.

"He sat there, in his fucking throne room, and he took everything away from me and gave it all to Jeff!" The temper in him was high and rare, and Jim flinched as Riley stalked around the tables that separated them with no direction other than just to walk. "And do you know why?" He stopped, grabbed at the newspapers that were lying in a tangled mess on the final map table by the door, and in one motion, Riley swept everything other than one sheet to the floor. He jabbed at the picture that had been snapped the night before, Riley and Steve at a club, arms around each other, Steve with his usual wide smile, Riley looking somewhat worse for wear from his brush with Jack Daniels and José Cuervo. "This."

It was the usual blurred image from the paparazzi who followed Riley, the playboy prince with a bottomless pit of money, everywhere he went. He shook his head. Now he was really confused and couldn't understand what Riley was getting at. Gerald had explained very clearly that his eldest son was the best for the company, the one switched on to commerce, the one with the business brain. He hadn't listened when Jim had pointed out the amazing upturn in R&D, the increase in oil locations, the way Riley was so committed to Hayes Oil. He had just shaken his head as if he couldn't believe, or didn't want to believe. "The photo?" Jim wasn't stupid; the picture didn't exactly show Riley in his best light. There was the blur of his smile and an unwarranted amount of skin on display as he tumbled half in and half out of the cab, stopping obviously to pose with his best friend.

"He said," Riley paused, a sneer on his face, "that the friendship I have with Steve is unhealthy— unhealthy, shit. He was *concerned* by Steve's association with Campbell!" The name *Campbell* came out on a spit and a sneer, the perfect takeoff of how Gerald Hayes would have said it, how Jim knew he would have said it. "Oh, and also, because I haven't got myself a brood mare like my *oh so fucking perfect* brother, then of course I must be confused about my sexuality."

Jim winced, both at the description of Jeff's wife as a brood mare, and at the whole confusion statement. Steve Murray, Riley's best friend since college, was openly bisexual, but Riley, despite having a history of mixing it up with men as well as women, was a lot less defined by a label. He had a different woman every night, younger, older, richer, poorer, it didn't matter, and neither did the boys he did on rarer occasions in the bathrooms of wherever they were. However it panned out, Riley always had tail.

"Said I should look at him and Mom." Again came the sneer, and Jim saw how the temper twisted his normally calm face. "Fuck. Like my mom had the perfect husband in my dad, like Jeff had the perfect fucking marriage with Lisa and her drinking." His voice trailed off, the venom in it spitting and harsh as he dismissed the marriages of his closest family as society based, financially arranged facades.

"Riley," Jim started, thinking maybe a time-out here, some down time, might be good.

"No, Jim. No," Riley interrupted, his hands clenched in fists. "Know what he said?" Riley stopped. Of course Jim knew what Hayes Senior had said. After all, it would have been Jim who had written the damn contract. Riley bowed his head, his face revealing disappointment at his friend's betrayal. Jim prayed that Riley could see that Gerald had forced him into this position. "He said it would be okay if I just got myself married in the next three months—if I found myself some stable brood mare time, and stayed married for a year. Then he would hand over more of Hayes Oil. Not based on the work I do, or the fact that, without me, Hayes Oil would have been landless for the next eighteen months, but based on a marriage. I mean, what the fuck, Jim? This is the twenty-first century, not the nineteenth."

"I know," Jim said simply, holding his hands up in his defense. "I tried, Riley, I tried to get him to see sense. I'm so sorry." He knew his voice sounded exhausted, sad. All the emotions that were trapped inside at what he'd had to do came swimming to the surface, puncturing the civility he had to show to the world whenever he was at the office. It was almost as if his words pushed through Riley's temper as suddenly and as finally as the thrust of a knife, and Riley visibly deflated in front of him. His head was bowed, his short blond hair disheveled. He looked calmer, but Jim knew this man well; his temper was clearly just below the surface.

"How do I do this, Jim? How do I fucking show the bastard that he can't win, that he can't push me to marry just to get what was rightfully mine anyway?" He looked up at him, the dim light from outside the window casting shadows across high cheekbones and green-hazel eyes. His lower lip was caught in his teeth, and the pain on his face was something Jim had never seen before. "I work fucking hard for this company. What more can I do?"

"So we find someone for you to marry, Riley, some quiet Texan debutante who will agree to a pre-nup, yeah? Someone who ticks the boxes, and then after this prescribed year is up, you can quietly divorce."

Jim could see that Riley wanted to say he couldn't do that, wanted to say that no woman in her right mind would agree to this, but they both knew it would be easy to find a bride. Both knew that the chance of marrying Riley Hayes was going to bring everyone out of the woodwork, fairly begging for the chance.

"I can't do that," Riley said simply. "I won't give Dad the satisfaction of winning like this."

Jim sighed. "So you let him win by not doing it, then. For him it's a win-win situation. Let's face it, you either let him win by doing something, or you let him win by doing nothing. Either way, Riley, you're fucked."

Chapter 2

Steve climbed over Riley's long legs to settle himself in the corner. His face twisted in concern. For yet another night, Riley had pushed it so far with the drinking that he was nearly unconscious. Riley had told him the whole sorry mess, even to the point that he knew his own very fluid sexuality had been brought into play, as well as his less than liked friendship with Elizabeth Campbell. He was sorry. He'd even said so to a clearly drunk-under-the-table Riley and gotten himself verbally bitch-slapped for it. Then he'd been hugged until he couldn't breathe, with undying promises of forever friendship carried on vapors of neat whisky into his ears. So here they were tonight. With just one more day added to the list of days where Riley didn't go to the monstrosity in the sky that was Hayes Oil. One more day where alcohol pushed him to unconsciousness in Steve's company. Steve had kind of reached the limit of how much more he could watch his best friend go through.

"I saw ya, in' parkin'," Riley mumbled, his eyes half closed with exhaustion and whisky, his hands gripping hard on Steve's arm. Steve blinked carefully, not sure where this was starting, but pretty sure it was going to end up with a pity party for one. "With tha' Campbell girl." Riley seemed proud of himself that he had managed to string those few words together and smiled. But the smile didn't reach his blurred and fatigued eyes.

"Beth is my friend," Steve said. It was the easiest way to defuse the comments Riley would start making about his dad and the Hayes-Campbell feud.

"Sheessa Campbell," Riley slurred, nodding to emphasize the words, spilling half his whisky over his jeans and downing the rest in one heated swallow. Steve sighed. So, this evening was going to be one of the *Why does my family hate the Campbells?* evenings. Instead he was surprised when Riley suddenly lifted his head, fire in his eyes. "Thas' it, I'll marry Beth Campbell." Steve's felt his stomach churn at the casually thrown out words. *Riley and Beth?*

"Riley, man, Beth just turned twenty."

Riley looked momentarily confused, blinking steadily. "I'll marry Josh 'en," he declared carefully.

"Josh is already married." Steve was seeing where this was going. That only really left—

"Jack," Riley muttered under his breath. "That'll fuck'em. He's gay. J-ack."

Steve carefully prised off Riley's fingers from his arm, opened his cell and called for a cab. When his friend started talking stupid like this, it really was time to get him home.

* * * *

Riley grimaced as Jim stared at him with a horrified expression on his face.

"Are you sure that's even legal?" his friend demanded.

"Isn't that *your* job to find out, Mr Legal Person?" Riley asked simply. "I looked on Wikipedia." Jim snorted, clearly offering his succinct opinion on *Wikipedia* as a resource. "You do the research then, but I did mine, and one thing I know is this, if you believe what is being said, then the Campbells are in deep shit since Alan died."

"Riley." Jim apparently wanted to stop this particular train of discussion. Riley wasn't going to let him.

"Jim, this could make it a win-win situation for me *and* for Campbell."

"Riley."

"You've been with Dad since before I was born. You gotta know all there is to know about the Campbells and this whole feud we got going on. Talk to me." It was a plea rather than an order, but Riley could still see Jim flinch. Placing his best and most earnest expression on his face, he added the one word guaranteed to get anyone to do his bidding. "Please?"

"Hell." Jim rubbed his hands over his face. "They had money to begin with. From the early oil days. Alan and your father made a pretty damn good team, back then. After the split… Well, Alan always had schemes and dreams and carried his family along from one money-making idea to another. Then there was the lawsuit with your dad— trying to prove he deserved part of Hayes Oil. Somehow, through a combination of gambling and shady deals, Alan Campbell managed to lose what was left after the lawyers had their cut. He liked to live fast and paid the price. You know the story. He died while the kids were still young. Drunken fool wrapped his car round a telegraph pole. Jack was just about finished with high school, Josh was away in Berkeley, studying law, and the little girl was in and out of the hospital, sick. She wasn't much more than kindergarten age I guess."

Jim walked to the window and stared out. Riley waited patiently, wondering if perhaps the other man wasn't seeing the towering office blocks of downtown Dallas, but a much older vista. "Beth had been born prematurely, a late baby. She had a congenital cardiovascular defect." He didn't need to tell Riley what the hospital bills would have been like once the insurances had played out. "It would have cost a fortune to get Josh into law school and keep him there. Alan didn't leave a will. Just debts a mile high. The ranch was mortgaged to the hilt— still is. So Donna carried on, selling off the best of the stock."

"Shares?"

"Horses. She owns the Double D ranch. Inherited it from her daddy. That's where its name came from— Derek Campbell and his only kid, Donna. Derek had some of the best quarter horse brood mares in the state and had a fine young stallion at stud. He trained 'em as well. Prize winners. Cutting horses that could turn on a dime and stop dead. Could get you close enough to a steer to kiss it on the nose." He shook his head. "Donna sold them. That's what put Josh through college, and young Beth through her surgeries. But Jack has been building up the stock again. Last I heard he'd raised a pair of very good brood mares as well as some horses in training for other owners."

"How come they've still got the ranch?" Riley wondered aloud. A memory was stirring in the pain-ridden sludge that currently passed for his brain. He squinted, trying to concentrate on it. "I find it hard to believe that Alan didn't get to use it as surety against loans."

"Couldn't. If I remember rightly, all eight hundred acres of it were tied up in Donna. She'd taken out the mortgages, but Alan couldn't touch it. I guess Derek read his son-in-law right and made sure it was watertight fixed to his daughter and grandkids."

"Watertight. Yeah. That's what I need." A drunken conversation, whispered in confidence, and it could prove to be the lever he needed if Jack Campbell refused to play ball. His stomach churned uneasily. "Get me everything you can on the middle Campbell and the ranch. Then write up the marriage contract, and we'll call a meeting, get Campbell here to…" Riley's voice tailed off. He swallowed, standing to look out of his office window, his head thick with hangover, finding it hard to string sentences together with the whisky-scarred thunder in his head.

"To propose a same sex marriage that probably isn't even legal?" Jim offered helpfully. Riley grimaced. When Jim put it like that, it did sound kind of bad.

"Yeah," he said a little uncertainly, twisting one hand in another and then he dropped his hand and squared his shoulders, sudden steel where his spine had been.

"If your dad finds out I had anything to do with you and this stupid idea…" Jim winced as Riley stood tall and leaned down to his old friend.

"I will get my share, and I will fuck with my dad. I will get Jack Campbell in, and I *will* get him to agree to marry me."

Chapter 3

Jack Campbell pushed his way through the revolving doors of the tower, the dust of Texas on worn jeans, a battered Stetson in his hand, and denim stretched tight across his shoulders. He paused on the threshold and scanned the foyer, stamping stable dirt off his boots onto the pristine carpet with calm deliberation and cast his eyes down the list of offices held in the tower. It wasn't difficult to spot Hayes Oil on the list, given that they covered floors forty-five to seventy-three. His walk to the elevator was blocked by a security guard who casually looked him up and down and then placed a strong hand on Jack's arm. Jack tensed. He'd been ready for confrontation, but had assumed he would at least make it to the sacred altar of Hayes Oil before he was turfed out.

"Sir? Can I ask you to book in at the front desk?" the guard said quietly, in a clearly non-confrontational I-do-this-all-day kind of way. Jack shrugged off the touch and turned on his heel, slapping his Stetson against his jeans and releasing a small cloud of dust into the rarefied air-conditioned coolness.

"I sure can," he drawled and strode towards the long front desk and the section marked with the Hayes Oil logo. The woman behind it was young, no more than twenty, and clearly a little shocked by the man standing before her. Jack imagined she was used to urban style; city suits, perfect hair, and clipped tones that bordered on rude. Not, for want of a better word, the dirty just-off-the-range Texas cowboy leaning down on her counter. He knew there was three days' worth of stubble on his face, and he was redolent with the smell of the outside. She traced his face with her gaze, and he smirked inwardly as she had to push her professionalism to the front to force out the standard words. He was used to shocking these city types on his rare visits to town. He made a damn fine cowboy, if he said so himself. It wasn't that he was bigheaded, but he knew he looked good, confident, and just a little on the rough side, a little bit dangerous.

"Welcome to Hayes Oil. How may I assist you?" she finally managed to say.

"I have a meetin', darlin'." He intentionally played up his Texas accent, his voice verging on a drawling growl and his g's getting lost in the translation.

"Can I ask your name?" she asked, her fingers flying over the thin keyboard.

"Campbell," he informed her, "Jack Campbell, C. A. M. P. B. E. L. L." She typed the letters in without hesitation, and Jack smiled wryly. She was apparently new to Hayes Oil if she hadn't been privy to the office gossip around the Campbell/Hayes state of affairs.

"That's fine, sir." She scanned and handed him a security badge with the Hayes Oil logo and a code. "If you take the elevator to the sixty-fourth floor, someone will be waiting for you, Mr Campbell."

"Thank you, ma'am," he said softly, clipping the security pass to his shirt, brushing at dirt he spotted on one cuff. He moved past the guard, nodding in polite acknowledgment and receiving a cautious nod in return. Waiting for the elevator, he wondered not for the first time what the hell had made him come here today. Jack Campbell knew he was the personification of a fish out of water and so did the guard.

The elevator arrived, pulling him from his introspection. Ever the southern gentleman, he moved to one side, letting other people in, before joining them inside and selecting his floor. The elevator was all glass and moved upward along an external wall. Uncomfortable with this, he moved to the middle of the small box. He had never really liked heights, and the single layer of glass between him and a fall to his certain death was enough to get him humming in his head to refocus himself. The haze of afternoon sun was glinting from mirrored glass everywhere, the rush of people a fluid river below. Jack was convinced this was some form of technological trauma on all who visited the tower, wearing visitors down until they broke. The girls who had gotten in the elevator with him were laughing and giggling behind him, talking in hushed whispers so as not to be heard. But he did catch the words *cute* and *ass*, and *dirty cowboy*, and assumed they were talking about him.

Jack smirked. Hayes was not going to be expecting a man hot from half a day's work, come straight to the city with the dirt of honest labor on his body and sweat dripping from every pore. There had been absolutely no way Jack was going to make a freakin' effort for any Hayes, much to his mother's disgust.

"You're as good as they are," she had said as he climbed into his battered Ford truck. "Going as you are, what are you trying to say?"

"That I work hard and I don't have time for their bullshit, Momma," he'd said tiredly, pulling her into a final hug as she tutted and fussed with his shirt, fastening more buttons and hiding his chest from view.

They had looked at the letter again this morning as he considered the final decision whether to go or not. It wasn't even direct from Hayes Oil, but was a private letter from a Jim Bailey, inviting him for a discussion with one Riley Hayes at 2 pm on the next Tuesday. Today. The letter had said they hoped he could make it, and that the reason for the meeting couldn't really be detailed in the letter. It was a sensitive subject and one that might well be to Jack Campbell's advantage.

"I don't like it." Donna had looked concerned when she read it. It was a perpetual expression on her face these days, and Jack hated that there was seemingly nothing he could do to help, or to make her life easier.

"I'm just going to see what shit they're trying to stir. I'll be there and back in an afternoon."

"Don't agree to anything. Don't sign anything."

"Momma, I'm not Dad."

They had no secrets, not a single one between Jack and his momma. Jack was more than aware of the kind of deals and plans his dad had made that had pulled the D lower and lower every week. Sunk into depression and drinking, Alan Campbell was far from ideal parenting material, and not very much of a husband. Jack was the unofficial man of the house from the minute Josh had left to go to the University of California's Berkeley School of Law. That didn't change when his father died or when Josh returned. Josh didn't stay long. He moved out to practice law in Fort Worth. Jack and Donna juggled the ranch, the only thing left to the Campbell family now, and that only because it had remained outside of his father's involvement altogether.

"You will never be like your dad."

His mom's words resonated in his head, and Jack held on to them as the elevator lights indicated each floor. The whispering girls got off on thirty-nine, Jack inclining his head politely as they left. This left him and a suited guy on his cell phone tapping furiously at tiny keys and muttering under his breath. Business guy got out at fifty-seven, which left Jack with, he guessed, thirty seconds to prepare himself for whatever was behind the doors when they opened on the floor he needed.

Casually he turned away from the glass and to the mirrored wall that was at the back. What he saw made him smile wryly again. He was the epitome of cowboy rancher, from the dirt under his nails to the Stetson that was worn for practicality and not for fashion, to the scruffy leather boots on his feet. He didn't know what Riley was expecting, didn't really know much about the middle Hayes at all.

"Riley is the middle child. I don't hear much in the way of bad things about him, but you got to know he's a Hayes."

"I know."

"He's different than Jeff, but still—"

"Stop worrying, Momma. He's a kid with too much money and no sense to back it up. I can handle this."

Sure he could handle this, he thought wryly, and sighed as the elevator indicated his floor and he turned to face the front. He stood waiting for the doors to open, blinking at the man who stood on the other side of the glass door. He looked to be in his late forties, with a neat beard and a sharp, clearly expensive, pale gray suit. His hands were in his pockets and his face prepared with a practiced smile. The doors slid open, and he extended a hand to Jack in immediate welcome.

"Mr Campbell," he said politely as they exchanged a firm handshake. "Jim

Bailey, personal lawyer for the Hayes family," the man continued, inclining his head for Jack to walk with him. "I guess you got my letter." It was a rhetorical question, and if he was expecting Jack to be so stupid enough to answer it, he was swinging in the breeze. "Mr Hayes is waiting for us in the map room," he finished carefully, stopping at the door marked with a simple room number and nothing else. He knocked, listened for the "Enter" and opened the door, standing aside to allow Jack to go in first.

It was brightly lit inside the room this Bailey guy called the map room, and Jack's first glance showed him charts adorning walls, large papers rolled in piles to one side and others spread out on tables alongside PCs. Each table was under-lit, for seeing small details on the topographical maps, Jack guessed. No sign of the elusive Riley, he thought as he scanned the room, then started as a face suddenly appeared from behind one of the map desks. Bizarrely, the man had been sitting on the floor hidden from view. Now, he unfolded long legs to stand tall in front of him.

"Campbell," Riley Hayes said simply, and he extended his hand in greeting. Not much Texan in that voice, it seemed.

Jack moved forward, cocking his hip against the table and leaning. "Hayes," he replied, his voice deliberately redolent of the south. He grasped the outstretched hand and shook it firmly.

"You got our letter." Riley released Jack's hand quickly and eased away.

"I got the letter from Mr Bailey," Jack agreed carefully, his eyes trailing across every inch of the man in front of him. It was the first time he'd met Riley. Their social circles were very different. Beth's friend, Steve, though, moved cheerfully between both. The Murray family had money and standing, and Steve had a lot to say about the older Hayes brother, none of it complimentary. Jeff, it seemed, loudly expressed the same hate for anyone with the Campbell surname as Hayes Senior did, and he wondered if Riley felt the same way.

"It was deliberately vague," Riley began, "because there is something, well, quite a few things, we need to discuss."

"I'll leave you both," Jim said abruptly and left. Jack had the feeling the man wasn't one hundred percent behind his boss on whatever this was.

He was curious, but he was not going to show it.

"Is your daddy joining us?" he finally asked, cataloguing every expression that crossed Riley's face at his words. Disbelief? And was that anger? Interesting.

"What we talk about here has *nothing* to do with my father," Riley said firmly, and pressed his lips together in a determined line. One of his hands moved to touch his hair and then dropped. Jack followed the action, taking in the perfectly gelled spikes pushed back off a high forehead, the hand that hovered uncertainly and then dropped. It was telling to see an unconscious habit that maybe Riley was trying to contain, along with any hint of personality in his thousand dollar suit and his carefully knotted sapphire blue tie.

"So why am I here, Hayes?" *Cut to the chase, always the best way.*

"Riley. Please… call me Riley."

Jack narrowed his eyes. This was altogether far too friendly. No Hayes ever approached him, let alone asked him to call them by their first names.

"Jack," he finally offered, then followed Riley as he walked through a side door and into an office. There was no name on the door, but it was a plush, thickly carpeted corner space, shiny and wooden-smart, with a stunning view of the city.

"Coffee?" Riley offered, gesturing towards some kind of coffee machine that had possibly been made from bits of the space shuttle, going by all its gleaming silver shine.

Jack was not going to be pandered to. "Let's just get on with whatever Hayes scheme is gonna screw with the Campbells this time," he stated almost tiredly. He owed it to his family to find out what they wanted, but playing games was not on his list of priorities. Riley stood motionless by the desk, just stood there, his hands in his pockets, and Jack stared back, for the first time actually looking at his nemesis. Riley looked to be younger than him by three or four years, was maybe a couple of inches over six feet, definitely taller than Jack himself, who was just shy of an inch below six. The middle Hayes was very handsome in a smooth urbanite way with his tailored suit, silk tie, and clean-shaven face, and his complexion was the light tan of a man who was mostly indoors and only had the Texan sun on his face during weekends.

His eyes were a mix of autumn brown and green, and he was worrying his lower lip with his teeth, a sure sign of nerves if ever Jack had seen one. His blond hair was short and spiky, in a structured style. They hadn't talked before, never had occasion to, and despite often seeing Riley's photos in magazines and papers, Jack had never actually seen hazel eyes so clear or cheekbones so defined in a man. He was certainly easy on the eyes, Jack couldn't discount that, well-proportioned and almost poured into his dark suit, definitely someone who would catch his eye if he were out looking.

"Not wanting to screw with you, Jack, just want to talk," Riley finally said, sitting down on one of the sofas to the side and indicating Jack should join him. He took his time, sliding to sit across and almost opposite, hands and Stetson on his knees. "I know about the ranch," Riley started cautiously.

"The ranch?" Jack kept the tension out of his voice. He hadn't been expecting that to come up. He'd assumed it was some shit about his dad again. The ranch had been nothing to do with his dad. It was his mom's, *his*, no one was gonna mess with the ranch.

"I know you have financial difficulties there, that times have been kind of hard. The mortgage is a hell of a drain on your resources." Steel shot through Jack's spine, and he sat up from his relaxed slouch, suddenly and oh so very straight. "I want to offer you a way of getting out of that, of not losing the ranch," Riley finished, nodding, probably expecting Jack to say something positive back to him.

Jack blinked steadily. *What the fuck?*

"We are not for sale," he answered coolly. His heart was thumping in his chest, belying the calm on the surface.

"No, I'm not looking to *buy* the D," Riley reassured instantly. Jack frowned. That playboy Hayes even knew the name of his family's ranch was a shock. "I'm looking for another way that maybe I can help you. Pay off the ranch debts, the death taxes, and release you from the burdens of it all so you can make the place pay for itself again." Jack scooted forward, his temper starting to build in the base of his spine. *What the fuck is this man on?* Riley hesitated, standing and crossing to the window to stare at the city far below.

Jack didn't push. He remained sitting, dusty and temper-tight in worn denim, watching Riley who was clearly struggling with whatever he had to say.

"A year," he finally started. "I would need your help for a year, with a contract. In return I would agree to pay off every debt, and pay you on top of that."

"A year of what? Working for you?"

"No." Riley sucked in a huge lungful of air and then let it out in a noisy exhale. "A year of marriage. I want —need— a partner, to be married for one year and for many reasons. Not the least of which is giving me a win-win situation with my father."

"Marriage." *What the hell?* "You— and me?" Jack managed to form that simple question on sheer shock alone as Riley nodded earnestly. Jack couldn't bring himself to move. He just sat there, stunned.

"So what do you think?" Riley finally asked as Jack rose to his feet.

For several beats, Jack neither moved nor spoke. Tension coiled in his body, what he imagined to be a combination of shock and disbelief.

"I'll tell you what I think, Hayes." Riley's surname dripped acid as Jack snarled the single word. "Your family has fucked with me and my mine one too many times."

"It would be beneficial to us both."

"Fuck! What kind of planet are you living on?"

"I don't understand."

Jack shook his head, Riley looked confused. He clearly couldn't see that he was crazier than a cat hill coot.

"This crazy shit is a fuckin' bad dream and a waste of my time." He'd had enough.

"Jack, please, can you just listen?"

Jack paused with his hand on the door handle.

"Fuck you." Distaste and furious anger dripped from his voice as he turned the knob.

"I know what you need. I know about Elizabeth." There was sudden steel, and a sly superiority in Riley's words. Clearly the younger Hayes was finally showing his true colors.

Jack stopped, the door half open. Grief and a sudden anxiety twisted in him before calm returned and he analyzed Riley's words dispassionately. Anyone who read the *Dallas Morning News* knew about Beth. It was open knowledge she suffered from a congenital heart problem, had been ill on and off for most of her life, and had spent more time in the hospital than out. But Riley's tone, the sly use of the words "I know about Beth" set Jack's teeth on edge. Something didn't sound right.

Medical bills had piled up, but the Campbell family had worked their way through. It was what they did. They dealt with the crap, pulled together, and made a difference to their lives through sheer single-mindedness. It left them near broke, but it didn't matter. Beth had gotten her medical treatment, the operations, and the drugs she needed. They managed, and they certainly didn't need any help, financially or otherwise. So if Riley freaking Hayes thought that bringing up Beth was gonna swing things his way, he had another thing coming.

Jack laughed low in his throat. "Hayes, after the *Dallas Times* spread, everyone knows about Beth," he said over his shoulder. That article had hurt. It must have been a slow news week, because some low-life journalist had decided to dig up the old feud story and focus on the next generation. It had headlined as *The Campbell Curse Strikes Again*. Josh was portrayed as abandoning his family, Jack as the useless high school dropout, Beth as the poor little innocent, suffering nobly under her death sentence. "There is nothing you can give her that is better than what we can. That was lame and kinda sad." He turned back to the door ready to walk away. Game over.

Riley's next words froze Jack to the spot. "My money can't help make her better, Jack, but it can help her get through her pregnancy."

What pregnancy?

Emotions flooded through him—shock, disbelief, pain, and anger at the blatant lies. He turned slowly, willing the panic, the fury, to stay behind his mask. What did Riley mean? She couldn't be pregnant. The doctors had said carrying a child full term could kill her. They had warned that her heart couldn't take it.

Riley visibly winced, and Jack knew his mask had cracked. He tried damned hard to regroup, to settle his disbelief.

"Fuck you, Hayes!" he hissed. "Pregnant or not, we'll manage. She'll have an abortion." That was the only solution. If this was true, then she'd just have to terminate. He wasn't going to lose his sister after trying for so many years to keep her alive.

Riley hesitated, clearly measuring his words, his expression carefully blank. "All you can hope is that she lives through it. It's too late to abort now, far too late." Riley's words dripped like ice, and Jack's eyes widened even as he tried to tell himself this fucking bastard was lying. The thought of his sister pregnant, close to killing herself, not telling him… Skepticism shot through him. No. She wouldn't have kept it a secret. She would have told him or Josh, if not their mom. Wouldn't she?

The overwhelming force of what Riley was saying hit Jack in the gut, exposing an unexpected vulnerability. He knew then he would do anything to protect his sister, and he prayed Riley couldn't see it. Jack straightened his spine, shoulders back, armor reinforced.

"Marry me," Riley blurted out suddenly. "Marry me and I will get the best doctors. I know people, my money can *buy* people. I can get the best for Beth and have medical help on call twenty-four seven. All you have to do is say yes. Just one year, and your debts are paid, the ranch is free from mortgage and death duties, and your sister lives. Just one year."

Jack blinked steadily, his head spinning, his heart pounding in his chest. He couldn't focus on the monologue Hayes was spouting or register what the other man was saying. He needed to see Beth. She would tell him this was all wrong, that Hayes was lying.

Without another word Jack left, pulling the door shut behind him. He hesitated only briefly, getting his breathing and emotions under control, before heading to the glass elevator. He wasn't aware of what he was doing, or where he was going, he only knew that Hayes didn't follow. He thanked God for that, because he knew he would have likely killed him.

Chapter 4

The journey back to the ranch was torturously slow. The cacophony of horns and swearing was deafening, and streams of tangled rush hour traffic impeded Jack's progress home. It was a good two hours before the D was in his sights, and he had thought of nothing other than betrayal and fear. She hadn't told him. *That's because it isn't true.* His beautiful sister was dying. *It isn't true.* His beautiful baby sister, the very person who had shaped him as a man, was hiding something so vitally important from him? *It can't be true.*

He found her sitting quietly in the sun-room, the early evening light putting an ethereal light about her head as she bent over her book, her lips moving soundlessly to the music in her iPod. She looked impossibly young, heartbreakingly beautiful, fragile. But it was as if a veil had been lifted from his eyes, and Jack could see how much more pale she was than normal. His eyes instinctively went to her belly, looking for a sign, anything, that would prove Riley Hayes wrong.

He moved closer and Elizabeth started at the sudden intrusion into her space. She pulled the ear buds out and smiled up at him. The smile turned to a frown as she saw the expression he could not keep from his face. She watched without word as he fell to his knees next to her chair, his hands curled into the hem of her dress, pleading silently. And he saw when the realization hit her that he knew…

"Beth—" His voice broke, and tears blurred his vision, but not enough that he couldn't see the tears beginning to track down his sister's pale cheeks. He didn't need to ask if it was true. He could see it in her face, see the pain there, the guilt. "Why— why couldn't you tell me?" *You tell me everything…*

The book on her lap dropped to the floor, the noise breaking into her own sobs, and she caught Jack's hand tight, pushing it against her stomach. She was only just starting to show.

"I couldn't kill my daughter," she said unsteadily, and winced as Jack's hand pressed harder against her soft belly, his head suddenly bowing. But not before she would have seen his pain.

"A daughter?" he finally managed to push out. He wanted to yell, to rail at her, to call her stupid, and an idiot. His anger stilled at the touch of her hand over his.

"Please, Jack." Her voice was broken. "Please. I'm so scared. I don't know what to do."

She bowed her head, her dark blonde hair falling across her neck. Jack tilted her chin with his fingertips and gazed into cerulean eyes so like their mother's. For the first time he recognized the exhaustion bracketing her face. How had he not noticed? Not seen her with a boyfriend, not noticed how ill she was looking? After all those years of reading his sister, how had he failed her so badly this time?

Guiltily he looked away, lowering his eyes. The ranch, the money, balancing the weariness of twenty hour days, especially recently with foaling so close, with juggling the finances of debt repayment against the day-to-day running of the ranch. It had all served to take him away from the one thing that was important in his life— his family.

"Why didn't you tell me?" he finally asked as calmly as he could. He didn't want her spooked at his question, but he needed to know.

"I didn't want to kill my baby, Jack," she whispered. "I knew you would want me to."

Jack blanched. The taking of life, especially that of a tiny defenseless baby… To Jack, it was a baby from the moment of conception. He may have thrown the idea at Riley, but he couldn't condone abortion, didn't believe in it for so many reasons. But this was his sister, his beautiful gentle fragile sister, and the baby inside her would kill her, take her away from him as sure as murder.

"Elizabeth—"

"You would have made me see it was the only way. I couldn't let you do that. Jack, I couldn't."

"Who is the father? Why didn't I know you were seeing someone?"

New tears sparkled in her eyes, and she shook her head, obviously unable to form the words.

Jack looked at the tears, fear sudden in his heart, "Beth, tell me, who is the father? Who did this to you?"

Beth lifted her head. "Please, Jack, don't make me tell you. I'm not ready to tell you, please." Her voice shook with despair, one hand on her belly, the other on her heart, where, Jack knew, the scars were hidden under her thin summer dress.

Panic rose in him. For so many years, he was the brother, the father figure, the one she always ran to, the one who held her hand as she slept after her last surgery.

"Did he… force you?" he demanded.

"No, he— I—"

"Shh, it's okay." He couldn't do this to her. What would it achieve? Forcing her to face who the father was wasn't going to solve the problem. "Hush, darlin', it'll be okay…"

She started to rock, not listening to him. "I can't— I can't," she whispered between sobs, turning away and closing her eyes to hide her grief from him. "Please don't make me, I can't. I'm so scared, Jack! I don't want to die, and I don't want to lose my little girl!"

She was the four-year-old in a hospital bed. She was the ten-year-old sobbing because she couldn't go to normal school like her brothers, and she was the fourteen-year-old who was told she would never carry a baby to term. She was his beautiful baby sister, and Jack could deny her nothing. Leaning up, he eased her into a hug, rubbing soothing patterns on her back, his words slow and careful.

"It's okay, shhhh, we'll do this together. We'll do this. It'll be fine. Shhhh, baby girl."

Chapter 5

Riley glanced once more at the clock. It was three hours and forty-three minutes since Jack had left, and his head was still spinning with the enormity of what he'd done. God! Maybe he was more like his father than he'd ever imagined. This wasn't him. Lost in thought, his fingers curling at the corner of a map, right then he wouldn't have heard if the ceiling had fallen in. Jim was suddenly standing next to him, his hands in his pockets and a concerned look on his face. Riley startled like a spooked deer.

"How did it go?" the older man asked sympathetically. Riley sank deeper in the couch in a dejected slump. "I'm guessing he didn't agree?"

Riley was silent, his head down, not wanting to look Jim in the eyes. Guilt was eating away at his insides.

"Not at first, but I think maybe he will," he finally answered. He flinched when Jim sighed, knowing what was coming next.

"You used it, didn't you?" There was fury in Jim's voice, and a very present disappointment. "Riley, for God's sake! You said you wouldn't go that far!"

Riley looked up. "I didn't have a choice, Jim."

"I'm so disappointed in you, Riley Hayes."

"Jim—"

"You went ahead and did exactly what you promised you wouldn't do. You are a better man than this. Much more than your God-damned daddy or your pissant brother."

"Have you ever thought that maybe I'm no different than them?"

"You're a good man, a hard worker. Look at what you've done at Hayes Oil."

"Exactly. Look at what I've done, and look at it being snatched away from me."

"Your father and the whole break-them-then-make-them shit. You can't let him destroy your self-respect."

"I had to," Riley said firmly. "I had to use it. Campbell was going to walk."

Jim moved closer. "You know Steve is never going to forgive you."

Riley lifted troubled eyes. He knew Steve would disown him if he ever found out it was him who had done this. Steve had talked to Riley in confidence. He snorted. What did he mean, *if*? That was where Campbell was now, checking on his sister, asking her if it was true, finding out she had kept secrets from him.

Steve had needed a friend, had talked to Riley in confidence. "Beth is pregnant and I am so scared for her. What do I do?" he'd asked, a hand over his own heart where he wore matching scars to Beth's, a victim of the same fragile pulse as Beth herself. For all that there was ten years between them, Beth was important to Steve and had been since they'd met in the hospital when they were under the same surgeon.

Riley had been drunk, another night where his failures chased him to drink. He had felt sorry for the Campbell girl that night, given a shoulder to Steve, said all the right things. Then he had forgotten it all as he fucked a blond girl in a backroom, up against paper towels and bleach until she screamed his name, and he lost it with his face buried in her neck. Steve had been hurt that night, had needed a friend, and instead had got something-to-prove-Riley. Riley had apologized the next day, they'd hugged, and nothing more had been said. Not until he'd blurted it out to Jack today, with no remorse but just one purpose. To get him to agree.

Jim touched him on the shoulder. "I hope it was worth it."

"Yeah," Riley muttered. "So do I."

Riley's secretary's voice echoed in the silent room. "Mr Hayes, I know you said no calls, but I have Jack Campbell on line three." Riley said nothing. His teeth worried his lower lip again, and he tasted the metallic tang of blood as he lifted the receiver.

"D ranch, now. Bring the contract," was how Campbell started, and then he added almost too quietly to hear, "I have terms."

Chapter 6

Riley was aware that his coming to the D ranch had to be akin to the enemy at the gate. No one actually knew what had happened all those years before when Donna and Alan had married and Gerald struck oil on his own. But the bitterness, the anger, that Gerald and Alan had filtered to Jeff Hayes, was being carried on with all the delicious enmity that Jeff seemed to enjoy as much as Riley's father. Riley didn't hold the old grudges and couldn't really see why he should. It had all happened long ago and was nothing for him to worry about. Still, if he could use it against his dad, then that was a good thing, however he managed it.

As Riley's low car bumped and scraped over the rutted and potholed track, he cursed that he hadn't thought to drive one of his off-roaders instead. The damage he was surely doing to the red sports car as each hole shook the frame didn't bear thinking about. He felt like a fish out of water, seeing the rough edges of this growing horse operation, and he wondered at the customers who had to traverse the way to get to their horseflesh without damaging their cars.

He would need to talk to Jack about that one. Maybe they should improve the road. No wonder the Campbells were struggling if this was how prospective buyers were introduced to the ranch.

He finally reached the main house, a modest two-story L-shaped spread. It curved around a dusty courtyard where several beaten vehicles stood their ground. He switched off the engine, grabbed the folder and climbed out of the car, looking around with a cautious eye. He could see disuse and disrepair juxtaposed with tidy and clean. The house itself was tired and worn, but the windows were bright and clean. The road behind him may well have been pitted and stoned, but the fencing around the paddocks was pristine and white. The horses grazing there were sleek and glossy in the sun. The two barns to one side looked old, but the corral for the training was a match for the paddocks. There were strong contrasts, and it was easy to see that the Campbell money was being ploughed into the horses where it mattered. It smelled of hard work and cut grass, of Texan heat and stubborn courage. Unbidden and unlooked for, the thought suddenly arrived— it was like Jack. Just like Jack.

* * * *

With a bottle of beer in his fingers, Jack watched from a kitchen window as the sports car drew up in front of the main house. His eyes narrowed as he saw the tall man leave the car and stare unabashed at the ranch about him. Jack knew what he saw —disrepair, lack of funds, miles of untended land— and he could almost sense Hayes's contempt from here. Jack knew what the Hayes spread was like. He'd seen photos of the mansion, for want of another word, spread low and white on acres of land, knew what he had here was nothing compared to that.

Jack steeled himself. The Jack that Hayes was meeting now was the Jack he was going to have to live with, and this Jack… Well, this Jack wasn't gonna make it easy.

If he was going down and doing this thing, it was going to be on his terms. He was sick of the Campbells being played like pawns in these little Hayes power trips; first his dad, then his mom, who he'd held as she cried her tears of loss when his father died, and now his sister.

He blinked as Riley turned to face the house, and he was forced to admit to himself that the man was one piece of prime Texas flesh. If he wasn't… If he hadn't… Jack sighed, pulling himself together. Riley Hayes might be gorgeous, might be everything Jack normally looked for in a man physically, but all that lay at the center of him was a black, dead heart, and that was far from appealing.

Jack might be agreeing to this for his sister, but if Riley was expecting Jack to bend over and give him an easy ride then he was surely mistaken. It was time a Hayes learned exactly what a Campbell was made of.

The lesson started here.

Chapter 7

Jack opened the main door, looming large into the day from the cool interior of the ranch. "Hayes," he said simply, hesitating momentarily and then finally moving to one side to let Riley into his house.

"Jack," Riley replied, nodding, his eyes intent on discerning Jack's facial expression and his body language. He sighed inwardly. If he wasn't mistaken, it was a very different man who stood in front of him now from the one who'd left his office a few hours ago. This man was rigid, angry, focused, someone who was not going to roll over without a fight. As Riley followed him to the large airy kitchen, he could see iron in his spine in the way he held himself. Jack stopped, holding out his hand for the papers in the folder Riley held, and Riley handed them over without a word.

"There's coffee. Stay here," Jack said, his southern hospitality forcing its way through his icy demeanor. Riley nodded and moved to the counter, exploring the years of scratches and ridges under his soft fingers, his back to Jack. He didn't hear Jack leave, but when he turned to face the man, he was no longer there.

Jack sat in the sunroom, staring at the pages in his hand, twelve carefully drawn forthwiths and herewiths, all in a different language. He knew it was just a bargain as far as Hayes was concerned to get what he wanted. Money. It was the schedule attached that was the interesting part. Simple sentences, like someone else, not a lawyer, had written them. Perhaps even Riley?

The schedule was entitled *Riley Nathaniel Hayes and _____; clauses*. He had to smile. Whoever had prepared the draft contract had left the space clear. Jack guessed Riley had a list of people he was going to ask, and he wondered how far down the list he had been. He scanned the list of clauses. Most of it seemed straightforward.

No partner shall give cause to make other people think that the marriage was not entered into for anything other than love.

Both parties to act like a married couple in public.

New partner entering into marriage to have no sexual or physical encounters outside of this marriage.

Partner to reside at the Hayes home.

Partner to attend all functions where needed, suitably attired, and with reference to previous clauses on appropriate behavior.

Partner to change surname to Hayes.

Partner to sign a pre-nuptial contract as stated in main contract.

In return, there was a *not specified at this time* financial settlement on this new partner and space for details. Jack wondered what it would finally say, and there was a sudden sorrow, tight and constricting in his chest. He imagined the words there— a promise to save his sister, to give the Campbell family a chance to stay whole.

He stood, stretching tall, the papers creased in his hands. Drawing in a deep breath, he went back into the kitchen, his own terms and clauses in his head. When he walked into the room, he found his nemesis facing the window, staring out over the ranch.

"For a start…" he began. Riley spun on his heel, coffee splashing on his expensive suit. "It will be Campbell-Hayes, not just Hayes."

Jack didn't move, his jaw set. He could almost see the thought processes in Riley's head, and the moment when the other man obviously realized it was a small battle he could afford to lose.

"Okay," Riley finally accepted.

"The money for Beth's care is signed over in trust so there is no backing out. It's set up so that Beth doesn't find out where the money is coming from. In addition to this, no one, and I mean *no one*, ever finds out about the contract or its implications for the year. There will be no big wedding, just a quick ceremony in Canada, well away from here, and back, simple rings, quiet."

Jack paused. *So far so good*.

"I need an even six million for the ranch, and you will at all times respect my day-to-day work here. It is, and will remain, my family's legacy. The contract will be written so it is out of your reach. End of story."

Riley nodded. "Agreed."

"I will move to your home. I will stay there for the one year, on two provisos."

"Which are?"

"There'll be occasions when I am needed here overnight for days at a time on ranch business. You will not give cause for me to be unable to fulfill those obligations."

"Why do you need to be here? Don't you have people to cover you?"

Temper rose in Jack in an instant. Fucking playboy thought he had *people* to take over the ranch if he wasn't here?

"When the mares are foaling, I could be needed here three, maybe four days and nights. At those times you will come here and live at the D with me."

"Within reason," Riley tossed out quickly. Jack chose to ignore that hasty defense.

"Secondly, I have contracts to honor, horses to train, and my mom can't run the place on her own. So while you're doing your thing at Hayes Oil every day," and he couldn't keep the sneer away, "I'll be here." He could almost hear Riley's brain working. "Not only that," he continued, on a roll now, "as part of this contract, I want you working on the ranch for exactly…" He paused, throwing together quick calculations in his brain and then doubling the number, just because he could. "Twenty-four days out of the three hundred and sixty-five of the contract." Riley's mouth fell open, his shock almost comical. "It can be weekends, Sundays, whatever. I don't imagine it will interfere in whatever you do or don't do at Hayes Oil, but your working with me will add authenticity to the whole shitfest. Agreed?"

"Say again?" Riley's voice dripped with disbelief as he cast a quick look around the kitchen, and that there, that disbelief coupled with the wrinkle of Riley's nose in disgust, was enough for Jack's temper to start to rise.

Riley finally nodded clearly deciding this was a battle he couldn't win. It was all he could apparently do, obviously not trusting himself to use actual words.

"So, there is a no-sex-outside-the-marriage rule for your new partner." Jack was starting to feel tired. He had been up since four a.m., and this was pushing even his levels of alertness.

"Of course there is, it needs to…" Riley paused, clearly sorting out the right words. "No, em, for you no… men." He stumbled over the words, plainly not sure of the etiquette in situations describing what Jack had with other men.

"You, too," Jack said simply, leaning back on the scarred wooden counter and crossing his arms. He had a great deal of satisfaction hearing Riley so screwed at placing the boundaries so firmly around his concept of gay sex. "'Cos you know, man, if I believe everything I read, you get way more than me, and I'm not gonna be taking that in this convoluted idea of a marriage."

"Taking it?"

"You horn-dogging around on me behind my back. You will agree to abstain for the year too. I won't be made to look a fool. We'll be married. I know what you're like, I've heard the shit you pull. So there will be no affairs, nothing, no girls and no boys. Agreed?"

"Nothing?" Riley sounded almost lost.

"Nothing."

Riley frowned. "Do you think I can't go for a year without getting off using nothing but my right hand?"

"Evidence suggests otherwise."

"Fuck you."

"Not likely."

"Shit. Okay." Jack watched as Riley raised a single eyebrow. "Is that it?" He was clearly aiming for sounding bored, and Jack really wished he could think of more terms and conditions to screw with the younger man. Just out of sheer spite. He watched as Riley's expression changed from one of consternation to one of relief and then quickly to one of satisfaction. It was interesting how easily Jack could read his prospective husband.

"You know something, Hayes? You're as cold as freaking ice. Do you have no emotion in you? You sign away your life like this… Do you feel anything?" Riley said nothing in reply. "I am doing this for my sister," Jack added, obviously getting back to what he had really meant to say. "And for my family. They mean everything to me. I don't give a rat's ass why you're doing this, but I swear if they ever find out—"

"I have just as many reasons for it to be a secret," Riley snapped.

Jack arched his back and stretched a yawn, smirking inwardly as Riley's gaze slid southward. Given the way his eyes seemed fixated around Jack's crotch area, he wondered if maybe Riley was a little more bi-curious than he even knew.

Chapter 8

Even as he stood at the private airport Jack knew it wasn't too late. He could tear up the contract. He had lawyers, the deal had been made under duress, and no court of law would uphold it, surely. His brother was a lawyer— he'd fight it for him. Images of Beth were at the front of his mind, tears on her pale cheeks, and her hand protective on his unborn niece. That pushed Jack's feet to move those final few yards.

He couldn't even tell her he was going, or what he was doing, but dammit he wanted to. As he held her close for a hug last night, a reassuring, *Don't worry, it will be fine* hug, the words to describe what he was doing were on the tip of his tongue. Instead he took the coward's way out, leaving a message on her cell.

Don't worry. I've just got a potential buyer, and I'm going to havta schmooze. Back day after tomorrow. Love ya, Beth. Look after yourself. He left a similar one for his mother.

Jack put the cell in his pocket, hefted his backpack over his shoulder, and looked up at the red Hayes Oil logo emblazoned down the side of the jet parked up on one side of the runway. It figured Hayes would have his own plane. Jack seemed to remember Beth commenting on it when she was reading some glossy spread about Dallas pseudo-royalty. As he stood at the bottom of the steps, he realized the next footfall he took really would seal his fate. He'd be leaving the Texas he knew and entering the world of Riley Hayes.

Steeling himself, he climbed the steps and automatically ducked his head to enter the cool interior, stopping on the threshold as images assaulted his senses. Luxury. Leather. Carpet. Someone stood to take his carry-on and usher him to a seating area complete with large flat screen television and two different gaming machines. The Hayes Oil logo was embroidered on everything from belts to seats. Jack rolled his eyes and sat down. He fumbled with the seatbelt, glancing up when Riley slid into the seat opposite him.

This was the first time that they'd seen each other since the meeting two days before. The paperwork had been exchanged by courier. There'd been no phone calls, just one text to state that everything had been arranged, with simple instructions that Jack should make his way to the airport.

Riley was wearing jeans and a black T-shirt and a worn dark leather jacket across his broad shoulders. It was something of a shock to see him dressed so casually. He welcomed Jack aboard with a half-smile, and to Jack's eyes, he looked mostly tired but also nervous and restless.

They didn't talk until the jet was in the air and heading north.

"You can shower, freshen up, and take some time," Riley offered hesitantly, indicating two doors at the end of the large cabin.

"Shower?"

"You brought the suit?"

"I brought the suit."

* * * *

It was funny how the grand total of eighteen words lasted the whole seven hours in the air. Or maybe not funny at all. The flight to Canada was long enough, each man lost in thought for one reason or another. It was not a comfortable silence.

Riley kept focusing on the whole sex thing. It was all that filled his head. He had never even experimented with men. Well, apart from that time at the Christmas dance with Luke Evans—admittedly under the influence of alcohol. But that was nothing. It had meant nothing but a hurried hand job against the outside of the gym, a fumble touch between horny teenagers. He didn't have an issue with the whole gay thing, though. His daddy might, but Riley had hung around Steve long enough to appreciate the benefits Steve found in sleeping with men versus women. *You'd never have to worry about your height, Riley, or your muscles, or your strength. You find someone strong like you and you just fucking go for it.*

The differences between men and women were never more obvious than with Jack freaking Campbell. He was naturally muscled, from his work Riley assumed, hard muscles that bunched and released when he moved to do even the smallest of things. Riley could see why men would want Jack. He wondered if Steve had been there— wondered what other men had been there. Added to that Jack had the clearest, deepest, sky blue eyes, the tightest ass and those *kiss me right the fuck now* lips, the lips Jack was biting on as he closed his eyes and laid his head back with his iPod buds in his ears.

Riley just stared, unable to concentrate, the last two days slipping past his contemplation of bitten lips. What his brother had said to him that morning spun in his head.

He had avoided Jeff all week, especially now with the whole wedding thing filling his waking hours, but today he had gone to the office. He had memos to pass on, reports to collate, and never trusted the details of what he did to his secretary.

"Lisa wants you to stay at home on Saturday."

Riley looked up. It wasn't often that his brother even came to this floor, let alone actually visited the map office itself.

"Saturday?" He blinked up at the only man he knew who was taller than him. Jeff was slick-sharp in a gray suit, even at six-thirty on a Monday morning. They had never been close, but gut-churning anger flew through Riley, just as it had every day he'd seen his brother since that fateful meeting with his dad.

"Alex's birthday. He says he wants his Uncle Riley there."

"I'll be there." Riley paused, climbing to his feet, brushing imaginary dust from his jeans. "Question is— will you?" Jeff didn't even begin to reply to that one. It was doubtful he would be there. He always had just the right excuse to be missing for one of Lisa's family parties.

"Why were you scrabbling on the floor?" Jeff finally asked, although he wasn't expecting a reply. He simply laughed softly as Riley sent him a look of disgust. Jeff knew Riley spread the maps on the floor, knew sitting cross-legged gave Riley the chance to look at the land layouts and the geo data that much easier. It was a constant source of amusement to Jeff that Riley spent so much time on the floor.

"Fuck you, Jeff."

"Whatever, little brother. I have things to do, people to fire, deals to finish… Later."

Deals to finish. Those three words soured Riley's already grim mood. The deals sitting on Jeff's desk included geo searches and advised land purchases that Riley had sourced, from research and work that Riley had undertaken. All of that was to be signed off by a man who, by virtue of being freakin' married to the lush that was an ex-Miss Texas, was now holding the majority stock in the family firm. Well, he had a deal of his own, all signed and sealed and about to be delivered. But it wasn't his proudest moment.

Bile rose in Riley's throat as he sat back in the seat and closed his eyes, the drone of the jet engine annoying, not able to even look at Jack when he had these self-destructive thoughts in his head.

* * * *

Riley had promised him this whole
marriage business would be quick. He
already had the marriage license sorted
in British Columbia, one of the places in
Canada that didn't demand any kind of
residency, and Jack was determined not
to let this pass in a blur. He had never
considered marriage, his life choices
kind of precluding it, particularly in
Texas. But he always imagined that one
day he would find a life partner. He
wanted a life partner, but only after the
ranch was paid off, after his mom was
happy, after Beth was well and safe—
just after.

Still it was difficult to remember it
all as they hurried from flight to rooms
and back again. Jack remembered parts
of the simple service, the words he'd
exchanged, blinking down at the plain
platinum band that sat on his ring
finger, and up at the man beside him.
Riley had looked alternatively calm and
then solemn, and then just this side of
panicked. Jack didn't have time to
wonder what the emotions meant as
they passed over his new husband's face
as the taller man bent his head to place a
chaste kiss on his lips. Then they moved
out to a small park to pose for the

necessary photos. Jack knew he probably looked shell-shocked in the pictures, and hoped that he acted the part convincingly enough to give the photos the authenticity they required for this charade. He had to keep up his end of the contract.

Riley wasn't making it easy. All through the car journey, the service and the photos, all Riley was capable of doing was providing a running commentary on the shit weather, the shit photographer, the shit venue. You name it, Riley had a problem with it. Jack, though, might as well have been invisible. It was just as well, he reflected bitterly, that there wasn't any love lost between them, or this marriage would be ending in divorce a whole lot sooner than Riley intended. As it was, he'd managed to force a smile for the pictures, digging his fingers as hard as he could into Riley's side whilst posing, just to let him know he was there. That worked. Riley pushed back equally hard as he wrapped an arm around Jack. When the photographer had finished, Riley handed over money, they signed what they needed to sign, took compliments when given, and left as quickly as they could.

All too soon they were back on the plane. Riley attached the camera to a laptop, and downloaded the twenty or so shots of their wedding as they sat waiting for clearance to take off. He turned the screen to Jack as he took his seat opposite.

Jack fastened his seat belt, loosened his tie and sighed. He didn't particularly want to look at the travesty, but he supposed he should. Reluctantly he scanned the pictures and was surprised. Some of them actually looked like genuine wedding photos. They were smiling, posing, and he had to grudgingly admit that, despite the almost childish anger he had felt at the time, they looked good together. There were some, though, where it was obvious there was irritation and distrust between them.

"The whole marriage thing, it's like some sick joke," Jack muttered. "We're fucked if anyone actually sees these."

"Well, they do need to be seen. We'll just select the best ones. It has to be irrefutable that we married for love and for no other reason. Agreed?" Riley was brisk and to the point, his eyes narrowing. He turned the laptop back and proceeded to delete at least half of the rushed photos, growling under his breath. "Jesus, would it hurt to have cracked a smile in these, Campbell?"

"What the fuck was there to smile about?" Jack instantly retorted. He wanted to say, *I said I'd marry you, and I did. I would be smiling, why?* But he didn't. This was for Beth and the ranch and for his family.

"The photos just don't look real." Riley worried his lower lip with his teeth as he scrolled through the photos.

"Then maybe you shoulda got married for real," Jack snapped. "Or maybe used some of your fucking money and hired a better fucking photographer, instead of using a shit camera and that Britney wannabe who was hanging around us."

Riley looked taken aback at the snarky comeback, his lips tight, and his fingers flexing on the edges of the laptop. His frown deepened with instant anger at the way Jack was talking to him. Jack guessed no one talked to Riley Hayes like that, especially not impoverished cowboys he now owned, lock, stock and barrel.

"We're both tired," Riley began with what was obviously hard-won patience. He sounded as if he was talking to a small child who needed a nap. "It's been a long day. When we get in the air, you should go an' get another shower or something, maybe calm down."

"Excuse me?" Jack was deceptively quiet, his fingers hovering over the fastened belt, just needing the excuse to release it and slap this guy down after his day from hell.

Riley scowled at him. "I just said—"

"I heard what you said. I'll have a shower when I want one, not when I'm told to."

"No one is going to believe we are married for real if you keep bitching back at me like some kind of—"

"Some kind of what? Husband?" *Score one for Jack.*

"Look, Campbell—" Riley started

"That's Campbell-Hayes," Jack snapped angrily. "At least get that in your head, because if I'm doing this, then you'd better be the fuck behind it."

"I won't forget the name again. I have as much to lose as you do if this goes south," Riley said, suddenly looking very tired of this whole mess.

"What? What do you stand to lose?"

"My share of what's rightfully mine."

"Money." He dismissed the reason instantly and out of hand. This was a tired and very old argument. "I've had enough honeymoon, thanks. Wake me when we get back." He pushed the earphones of his iPod into his ears and closed his eyes. As the music washed over him, he couldn't help but focus on what had happened today. Not for the first time he wondered what the hell he was doing.

Chapter 9

The plane landed after lunch, the Texas sun hot and welcoming after the cold Vancouver air.

"What now?" Jack said carefully as they hurried towards the chauffer-driven car waiting for them. His nerves were on edge, the start of a headache lurked behind his eyes, and he just wanted this to be over.

"I emailed the best photo and the report on the wedding to the *Times*," Riley replied quickly.

"You did *what?*" Jack's temper rose quicker than the sun heating the back of his neck, and Riley backed away, his hands up, placating.

"We need to announce it somehow. I just did it anonymously."

"My family doesn't even know!" Panic laced Jack's voice and fear clenched in his stomach. Why the hell had Riley done something so stupid, and without discussing it with Jack first. His family should hear it from him first. "I need to tell my freakin' family, you idiot! They are gonna go crazy when they see it, and you just— shit." He had no words for the stupidity that was Riley freakin' Hayes. Biting his tongue, Jack climbed into the chauffer-driven car and spat out directions to the ranch.

He looked out at Riley expectantly. The man was standing there, unmoving, bags at his feet. His expression was thoughtful, and he was twisting his new ring nervously.

"Yours first, then mine," Riley finally said, and Jack nodded, eager to be doing *something*.

* * * *

"Momma, you know Riley." Jack had planned and practiced the whole way home: *Mom, I'm married. Mom, I fell in love. Mom, I am trying to save Elizabeth. Mom, Beth is pregnant.* Nothing worked in his head. Nothing.

"Riley," she said, smiling prettily. Her hands were covered in flour, cake mix sat in a porcelain bowl, and Jack's heart swelled with pride. His mom was so beautiful, so quiet, and serene and he was so proud of her. She would understand what he'd done. He only had to tell her. Tell her what he'd agreed to for the sake of the family.

"I have something to tell you," he said softly.

"What, darlin?"

"I'm married, Momma. I met Riley a while back. We didn't tell anyone because —Momma— Before I knew it, I was married."

Silence.

Jack reached for Riley's hand, and she watched as Riley looked down at Jack with something in his eyes, something that might almost be gratitude, and she knew. She closed her eyes, tears spilling from them, her hands clasped. A soft sigh left her parted lips. "Jack, what did you do?"

"Momma."

"Tell me." Her voice caught, and she swallowed. "Tell me you married for love."

Jack leaned into Riley, who rested a hand on Jack's hip in a small gesture of support. "I married for love, Momma."

Donna was still crying, but she pulled both men in for a hug, leaving flour on their shirts. Jack watched Riley, who seemed nervous and unsure where to put his hands when his momma hugged him. "Welcome to the family, Riley."

They stood there for a while, until Jack coughed and looked to somehow change the subject.

Jack broke the silence. "Where's Beth, Mom?"

"In the sunroom, sweetie. She's tired, looks very tired." She pursed her lips, worry creasing her brow, and she turned back to her baking.

"Should we not disturb her?" Riley asked softly.

"No, I need her to see. I need you to see her."

They moved into what was euphemistically called the sunroom— a brick built extension to the main ranch house, spilling with hothouse flowers and the smell of summer.

Jack crouched next to a dozing Beth, taking her hands into his own.

She blinked awake, her eyes red. Had she been crying?

"Jack?" Her voice was drawling tired, but her smile glowed. "Did it go okay?"

"Hey, Beth, I need to talk to you. You all right with that?" Jack waited for her to nod and then just jumped in with what needed to be said. "I lied to you," he said gently, watching her expressive eyes widen with questions. "I wasn't on a business trip. I was away with my boyfriend," he added. Beth looked up and past him to the man standing at his back. Jack had never seen her pale so quickly.

"Your—" Her voice faltered. "That's Hayes, Riley Hayes. Jeff's— Steve's friend."

"Riley was… my boyfriend. We've been seeing each other quietly for a while now."

"Riley?" she said wonderingly, looking back at her brother's face. "*Was* your boyfriend?"

"He's my husband now," Jack said. It was like ripping a Band-Aid off a wound. It was the only way. Just get it out there, in the open.

"Jack?"

"We were in Canada, and we got married." He kept his voice soft, and he winced as her fingers tightened on his and she pulled herself to stand. She was a small woman, no more than five feet two. But she drew herself up to her full height and leaned away from her brother's support. Her back straight and her face blank of emotion, she faced Riley with a challenge in every inch of her.

"Are you your daddy's boy?" she asked plainly, easing farther away as Jack reached for her. Both men knew what she meant, and Jack sent a pleading look to his new husband. *For god's sake, lie to her.*

Riley inclined his head, moving a step closer

"No, ma'am," he finally said. "I am not my daddy's boy. I am my own man."

She closed her eyes briefly, and nodded almost imperceptibly. It seemed that Riley had said the right thing.

"How long have you been seein' each other?" she asked. "Momma and Josh— do they know?"

"About two months," Riley said smoothly, again reaching for Jack. They had talked about this in the car on the way over. Jack hadn't been with anyone for nearly six months, and Riley's flings could maybe be written off as cover-ups if really questioned, if they were pushed.

"That's quick," she commented, moving back to the chair and sitting down with a small sigh.

"Momma knows. We just told her, and Josh is next."

"He won't take it well. He has little respect for the Hayeses."

Jack felt Riley stiffen beside him, and Riley's hand felt hot entwined with Jack's, his fingers flexing.

"He holds nothing against them," Jack said calmly, although that was perhaps a small exaggeration. Neither of the brothers hated the Hayeses family in general in the truest sense of the word; they just hated what had happened to their dad and how he had let the more prominent Texas family tear down almost everything they owned.

"It won't be easy," she said, nodding. "But for what it is worth, Riley Hayes, I love my brothers, and the kind of men they are. They won't make your life miserable for the sins of your father." Jack smiled, dropping Riley's hand and leaning down for a kiss from his sister.

"When did you get so wise, Elizabeth Ann?"

"About the same time you and Josh told me the tooth fairy took teeth even if they hadn't fallen out, Jackson Robert." They chuckled quietly, and Jack touched his fingers to Elizabeth's stomach, feeling the soft roundness of it. He wanted to scoop her up and protect her forever.

"I'm guessing we have stuff to do now," he whispered low in her ear, indicating her belly.

Beth grimaced. "Hospitals and stuff," she replied just as softly, wrinkling her nose in disgust.

"Tell me when, and I'll take you."

"I will, though Steve said he's gonna come to every one with me." She gave that secret smile only Jack had ever seen, the affection she had for her friend Steve shining in her eyes.

Jack dropped a small kiss on his sister's nose and stood, stretching tall. Then he reached for Riley's hand, anything to keep the charade alive. They said their goodbyes, and after leaving with another hug from his mom, he handed out the address for his older brother, knowing that this was going to be the hard one.

Chapter 10

Riley sat back in the car, massaging the hand Jack had held. He was quietly shocked at how natural it had seemed for Jack to bask in the approval of his mom and sister. He wondered if his mom would even care, or if his brother would have anything but derision for what he had done. And whether his dad was actually going to let him leave the building alive when he revealed his latest life decision.

Surely they had something in common, this Riley and this Jack. They both had older brothers, so Jack must know what it felt like to be bullied and bossed around and treated like the lesser man.

"So your brother? Is he a bit of an idiot as well? Do you argue a lot?"

"Josh?" Jack looked at him in frowning surprise. "Hell, no. Why would we?"

"Your sister said…" Riley's voice trailed off.

"Oh. Yeah, well, he won't understand why I married you. You. A Hayes."

"Because?" S*tupid question but best to get it out there.*

"Usual shit I guess." Jack shrugged. "But no, Josh and I —and Beth— we're close. Always have been. After our dad died, we got closer. Josh is living and working away, but that makes no difference. He's married, got two kids," he added awkwardly.

"Same as Jeff."

"His wife, Anna, and his kids, Logan and Lea. they're a good family."

"He's a lawyer, right?" Riley remembered something Jim had said in their final meeting for the contract, something about how he knew Josh would have a fit if and when he read some of the clauses.

Jack smiled proudly. "Yep, worked his way through college and law school, and is at a law firm in Fort Worth. Does a lot of pro bono work. Doesn't make a lot, but enough to support his family and do good with his skills and his education. Anna was his childhood sweetheart."

"Aaah, the American dream." Riley tried to keep the cynicism out of his voice "Two point four kids, the picket fence, the station wagon and the dog." Jack glared but didn't answer, and Riley subsided into silence, watching the pastures of the D pass by until they reached the main road and turned left, away from the D and away from the city.

* * * *

When they reached the outskirts of Fort Worth, the chauffeur took a sharp right and stopped at a cluster of single story buildings, each distinctive in shape as if a small child had mixed and matched Lego pieces into a colorful huddle. Jack jumped out of the car, and walked up to the one with the sign proclaiming Selkirk & Unwin, Attorneys-at-Law, waiting until Riley caught up. He opened the door and walked into a small reception area, Riley on his heels.

Jack paused. His brother's office door was open. Josh's back was to him, the phone cradled between his neck and chin, and a folder was open in his hands. "Okay, I have instruction that, on this occasion, we will settle, but it's gonna be for the full amount… Not if I have anything to say in the matter… I don't care how big they are… My client will sign off on that…. Agreed."

He placed the phone and the folder on the table and sighed, pushing hands through his hair. It was longer and darker than his brother's, but the reflection in the glass-fronted bookcase in front of him told Riley Josh's jaw had the same stubborn jut. Riley tensed in anticipation of an upcoming confrontation.

"Hey," Jack said loudly. Josh jumped and turned, hand flailing and smacking Jack on the arm.

"Shit, J," he spluttered, blinking as he took in not only his brother, but also Riley behind him. He frowned, looking back at his brother cautiously. "What's wrong?"

"I wanted to introduce you to someone," Jack started, and Josh glanced past Riley, as if expecting a third person to appear.

"I know him," Josh said warily. "We've met before."

Riley extended his hand, and Josh took it in a firm grip. "Josh," he said carefully.

"Hayes," Josh replied, just as carefully.

Jack put out a hand to grasp at Riley's. "Actually," he began, "it's Campbell-Hayes."

Josh didn't even blink. "Riley," he said evenly. "Would you please give us a moment?"

Riley nodded, and the moment he walked out of the room and closed the door behind him, the shouting started. He tried not to listen, but that was impossible, given that two pairs of healthy lungs were doing the yelling.

He also wanted to be inside, where he should be, if only for appearance's sake.

"He's not even gay for fuck's sake!"

"Josh—"

"Have you seen the papers? He's got a different woman every freaking night!"

"He's bi, Josh."

"And he's settled on you, the son of his dad's enemy?"

"He hasn't settled; we're in love!"

"Love. You love him? Jesus, J!"

"What? A gay man can't fall in love?"

"Jack, that has nothing to do with it! He's a Hayes, for fuck's sake! Don't you remember what they did to Dad? Falsifying records, lying about land purchases, buying his way out and leaving Dad in the cold? Don't you remember some of the shit Gerald did to Mom?"

Riley had heard enough. He opened the door to see the two brothers in an angry face-off.

"As I answered your sister, Josh, I'm not my father," was all he said. He waited until Josh visibly relaxed. "Your brother and I… We're happy. We want to make this work. Do we have your support?"

Josh closed his eyes briefly, but not quick enough for Riley to miss the battle that warred in them. He finally opened them again and nodded, pulling his younger brother in for a hug. "Shit. I'm happy if you are, kid. If you're really happy?"

Riley watched the brothers embrace, and something inside him twisted. Jeff had never held him like that— supportive, protective, caring. The way brothers should be.

"I'm happy."

Chapter 11

The ride back to the city was quiet, each man on his side of the car, both lost in thought. Riley watched the outskirts of the city begin to build from his side of the car, a store here, a house there, a mall. It wasn't truly dark. It never was. The night sky was alive with the lights from the skyscrapers in the beating heart of Dallas. They were mirrored in the river, starkly, majestically beautiful, and Riley loved it. The magic of the city was, as always, running with the blood in his veins.

He made a decision. He would not tell his family today. Every time he thought of the Campbells and how they had welcomed him into the family, with questions, yes, but with acceptance, Riley's heart clenched. Jack was not going to be as lucky with his family, he knew that, and despite the whole point of the marriage, regardless of wanting to rub his dad's face in what Gerald didn't want for his middle child, he did not want to see them tonight.

They passed the outside edge of the city and, after fifteen minutes, were at the main Hayes house, home to Gerald and Sandra and their perfect kids. It was quiet and dark. He doubted Jeff was at home: he never was. He assumed Lisa was somewhere in there, probably under the influence, given it was already 9 pm, and the kids were with the nanny in the back wing. He knew his mom was out; it was Foundation night for one of her many charities. Riley wasn't sure why she did so much, unless it was for the kudos, but when it came to those good works, her energy was unflagging. He knew where his dad was; Gerald was inevitably away with his current affair du jour. He didn't hide it. Everyone knew. His mom knew, but as long as she had the name and the prestige and money that went with it, then she was clearly happy to let her husband do what he wanted.

The car stopped on the circular drive. The chauffeur opened the door and lifted out the two bags, offering a wide smile which Riley didn't return. He just nodded to dismiss him. He was unable to find the words, despite the fact that normally he would spend time to talk, to ask about the daughter who had just left for college. Tonight, well, tonight all he wanted was to move inside, into this mausoleum he called home, and shut his door on the world. He caught Jack's frown, saw him return the chauffeur's smile and gave the man a quiet, "Thanks." He could almost hear the thought, *Jeez, Riley, you're a rude entitled asshole.*

* * * *

Jack followed Riley in the side door. It led into a spacious boot room, immaculate and tidy and nothing like the boot room at the ranch. There were no jackets, no freaking boots, no dirt, nothing to show that anyone actually used the space. He said nothing, just followed in Riley's footsteps to a large hallway. Crystal chandeliers hung from high ceilings, and a marble staircase wound up from the entrance hall to the first landing. It was icy perfection, spotless.

No letters sat on the hall table, no *Quarter Horse News* magazines piled haphazardly, no newspapers. Jack sighed inwardly, missing the casual warmth of his own home compared with the stark airless hotel that this was.

Riley took the stairs three at a time, his long legs eating up the curved steps. Jack followed at a more sedate pace, passing arranged fresh-cut flowers placed just so on a middle step. Riley turned left at the top and strode down a long corridor. He opened a door, turned on the lights, and gestured Jack inside. After Jack walked in, Riley leaned back on the closed door, tired-eyes and frowning, and Jack looked around at the room.

It was larger than the entire floor he shared with his sister and mom, separated with carefully placed furniture. It looked like a designer's idea of a den. There was a small library area, a huge flat screen TV, large red sofas, and thick red drapes framing floor to ceiling windows. Jack couldn't see anything outside apart from the faint and distant glow of downtown Dallas. It was unnerving that they would be framed outside from the light in the bedroom if anyone cared to look. It was kind of sparse as a living area, white where it wasn't blood-red, empty of anything welcoming. It probably cost a fortune for some decorator to create.

"I'm guessing this is my home now?" Jack finally said, his drawl more pronounced as the last few days started to catch up with them.

Riley nodded. "Master bedroom, adjoining bathroom," he recited, waving casually at various doors. "Separate extra bathroom, second bedroom, games room, this room, and that's it." He frowned at Jack's thoughtful grunt. "What?"

"Which one is the guest room?"

"That one." Riley indicated a door to the back of the large room, but stopped Jack with a hand on his arm as he started to walk towards it. "We're both in the master," he said simply.

Jack opened his mouth to argue, noticed the stubborn set of Riley's mouth, and sighed inwardly. *Well, it was worth a try.*

"Show me," he said. Riley obediently opened a door and flicked on the light. Then he leaned on the frame, leaving barely enough space for Jack to get by.

Is the dumbass trying to be irritating, or what? Jack bit back the snide remark that wanted to be said. Maybe Riley was having second thoughts about sharing the room with a gay man? Who was also his husband, even if it was in name only. That was fine by Jack, but he didn't intend to put up with the man being a jerk. He pushed past, maybe a little too close, his thigh brushing against Riley's hard-muscled leg. Jack kept his voice low and growling as he near-whispered the words he knew Riley had to be thinking.

"How are we gonna cope with being in the same bed with no sex for a whole year?"

Chapter 12

"What?" Riley choked. "What the fuck? "

"I'm guessing you have maids 'n shit that would notice if we were sleeping separately?" Jack drawled, gazing around the spacious bedroom. The bed looked big enough to sleep half a dozen linebackers without them getting too friendly.

"Yeah," Riley replied sullenly.

Jack looked from the bed to Riley and back again and did his damnedest to make his smirk as infuriating as possible. "It's a good-sized bed," he pointed out. "No biggie."

"So the whole, 'How are we gonna manage for a year?`, what was that?" Riley demanded, his hands on his hips and his eyes narrowed. He looked very much like a disrespected parent.

Jack snorted, a reluctant laugh breaking through his resolve. There was nothing in the contract between them that said he had to play nice in private, and something told him he could get a lot of mileage out of needling his straight husband. He shrugged off his shirt and drew his T-shirt over his head. There were three doors to choose from, and two of them were probably walk-in closets. "Shower, which way?"

"There." Riley pointed in the general direction of the door off to one side. He looked dumbfounded, but verging on cross, looking everywhere but at Jack's naked chest.

Jack just had to get in one more jibe. "Tell you what though. Y'all just keep to your side of the bed, Het-boy, and I'll see if I can keep myself from being carried away with lust and maybe try'n keep it in my pants."

"I…" was all Riley managed, shaking his head vehemently. He was scarlet with embarrassment, and Jack counted it as a win.

Jack shut the bathroom door behind him before Riley could come up with a coherent answer, smirking at the look in Riley's eyes and at the horrified open-mouthed denial on his lips. Then his smile faded. There was something else in his husband's eyes, and Jack wondered if Riley wasn't quite so conventional in his sexual tastes as he'd thought. There had been heat there, right alongside the confusion.

Well hell, he thought, examining which dials he needed to turn in Riley's frankly awesome walk-in shower. *This is gonna be a long year. I may as well have some fun.* For a split second, he wondered if it would backfire on him, then shrugged it away. No. As far as he was concerned, Riley-baiting was the new national sport.

* * * *

Riley stared at the bathroom door for a good minute or so, willing his flush away. He wasn't sure what had just happened, but it left him feeling too hot in his own skin. Finally Riley gave himself a mental kick in the ass and dove into the other bathroom for a fast shower. By the time Jack finished in the en suite, Riley was in bed and under the sheet, pretending to be asleep. It was the coward's way out, he acknowledged, feeling the dip in his bed as Jack climbed in.

He wasn't sure Jack slept, and as it was, Riley guessed he himself had only had an hour at the most. He'd watched the bedside clock move from minute to minute, hour to hour, hearing Jack's even breathing in the darkness of the room. His head was spinning with images of Jack's momma, her quiet grace and her easy acceptance of what Jack had done, despite the concern in blue eyes so like her son's. Then there was Josh and the argument he'd overheard between the two brothers. He had assumed Josh would demand and rant and state exactly what Jack could or couldn't do, the same as Jeff would do to Riley. It had shocked him when Josh pulled Jack in for a hug, called him *kid*, affection falling from his lips as easy as the shouting only thirty seconds before.

He thought back to the way Beth had questioned him, all spit and fire as she stood between him and her brother, so slight a stiff wind would probably blow her over. *Are you your daddy's boy?* Her question was like a stab in the heart, because, at the end of the day, yes, he was. He was just like his dad, and one day blood would tell. He had looked into Beth's eyes and lied. Faced with this pregnant girl with such a huge battle in front of her, it made him feel lower than a snake. And if Jack ever found out that Riley had put money in place for Beth's care even before he'd said yes? Shit, he was a dead man then, as his proud husband was likely to kill him. Another secret he needed to keep, another worry niggling inside his head.

And now, as the alarm clock moved round to 6:30 am and Riley moved to slide out of the bed, he wished for more sleep to deal with what he knew he had to face. Silently he padded to the window. The day was new and fresh, the sprinklers on the manicured lawn bordered by white fencing helping to make it so. There were several vehicles parked around the circular walled fountain, among them his black SUV, the only one pointing away from the house and down the avenue approach.

"Riley?" Jack's voice was tired, thick with sleep and Texas drawl. "S'time?"

Riley turned to face his husband of less than twenty-four hours, watching him as he rolled on his back and stretched warm limbs against ruby red sheets. He was yawning and rubbing a hand along his stubble-rough jaw.

"Early," he replied, causing Jack to groan into the soft pillows as he pushed at the restricting covers and bent one leg at the knee.

"So how is today panning out?" Jack asked, the words *who do we have to fool?* unspoken.

Riley grimaced as he watched out of the window. His dad and Jeff were climbing into one of the limos close to the front door, and he followed it with his eyes as it headed down the avenue. He sighed, but then thought that actually, just maybe, breakfast would be easier without them.

"This morning, my mother and possibly Lisa, Jeff's wife. Maybe Eden, my sister. There's kind of this breakfast thing we do. Normally I'm down with

my dad and brother, but they just left."
Riley turned back to the window,
watching the dust swirling in the wake
of the limo, his fingers unconsciously
touching the glass.

* * * *

The knot of tension in Jack eased
slightly. He knew Jeff only by
reputation and from watching various
TV interviews, and would have thought
he was an arrogant asshole even if he
wasn't a Hayes. And as for the Hayes
patriarch, well, Gerald hated the name
of Campbell, had done so since way
before Jack had been born. Worse, the
man had basically treated his mom like
shit at Alan Campbell's funeral. So,
yeah, no love lost there either. Jack
couldn't understand where the whole *we
hate the Campbells* crap was coming from.
Life was too freaking hard and too
freaking short to hold on to grudges.
        "So tell me about them and where
they stand on the Campbell Hate Scale,"
Jack prompted. He frowned as Riley
momentarily slumped before pulling
himself straight and turning back to
Jack.
        "The Campbell Hate Scale?" he
asked cautiously, but Jack didn't
answer. "Well, my mother is kind of…"

He paused, looking Jack directly in the eyes. "It's not easy to describe her. I mean her family is old money, goes back generations. She has what she likes to call breeding, and what I like to term snobbery. She's difficult, and she won't like what I've done. She's had me half-married off to various Texas debutantes over the years. She doesn't ever mention your family, leaves that to my father and Jeff, who seem to spend an awful lot of time discussing you, come to think of it. And I don't totally know why. Do you?"

"Hell, no," Jack snorted. "I have no idea why your dad and brother have such a problem with the Campbells. God knows we're no competition for you guys. Shit, we're not even in the same line of business anymore, and that fucking court case was years ago."

It must have been obvious to Riley that Jack was about to start on a rant, because he quickly carried on. "Lisa and Jeff have been married about ten years, and I have a nephew and a niece, both of whom have a full-time nanny. Neither of the kids will be at breakfast," Riley added with a small hint of disappointment in his voice that Jack honed in on immediately.

"That's a shame. I'd a liked to have met them," Jack said, watching as Riley frowned, apparently surprised at his sincerity,

"Then there's Eden," Riley continued, and paused. "She's probably the only good thing my parents did. I mean, she's a complete airhead, thinks shopping defines her life, but she has a big heart. I kinda keep my eye on her when I can."

Jack nodded. He knew firsthand what it was to worry for a little sister. The openly affectionate words Riley used to describe his sister, his niece, his nephew, seemed somehow wrong. It jarred with every impression Jack had formed of the Hayes family. Still, that didn't mean Riley's heart wasn't dead inside him. What man, with a sister of his own, would use Beth's health as a bargaining chip in a fake marriage?

Riley left him to his thoughts, taking clothes into the large bathroom, and exiting fifteen minutes later. Jack came back to the here and now and gave his husband a reluctantly appreciative once-over. Riley was wearing similar clothes as he had on the flight, dark jeans and a dark shirt that pointed up his powerful frame. His blond hair was still damp and pushed off his face, emphasizing his angular cheekbones and eyes in an intriguing combination of greens and browns. He really was a ridiculously good-looking man.

"All yours," Riley offered, crossing to a large walk-in closet and pulling out a black leather belt. He was keeping his head down, avoiding Jack's eyes.

"Thanks." Jack climbed out of bed and strolled into the bathroom.

* * * *

As soon as the door closed, Riley released the breath he'd been holding. The tension across his shoulders and up the back of his neck was incredible, tight and painful. He moved his head from side to side, trying to release the pressure. This always happened whenever he brought someone to his family, be they friend or lover. This was always how he ended up, stressed and tense, and he threw a prayer to the heavens that his dad and brother would remain absent. He imagined the article on the marriage would appear today in the gossip column, alongside the best picture they had taken at the ceremony that he had anonymously sent. He had organized this marriage as a kick in the face to his dad and relished the moment his dad found out Riley had played him at his own game, but that didn't stop the actual fear he felt at his father's reaction.

The bathroom door opened, and Jack walked out, a drift of steam behind him, his back, shoulders and chest glistening with water droplets and his hips wrapped in a towel. Casting one glance at Riley, he took off the towel and dried himself, not bothering to cover his nakedness. Then he rummaged in his bags for boxers and his clean jeans. Jack's body was lean and strongly made. His defined muscles were due to hard work, Riley knew, not a gym regimen. Riley couldn't not look. It was impossible to pull his eyes away from the thick half erect dick that hung between his husband's legs. He just stared as Jack pulled on the boxers and jeans, and tried to pretend that his own flesh wasn't swelling as well. Then Jack turned to face Riley with the jeans unfastened and the dark blue cotton of his underwear clear against the open fly.

"See something you like, Het-boy?" he enquired, quirking an eyebrow and tilting his head to one side.

God help me, yes! "Fuck you" was all Riley could come up with in the moment. Balling up a sweatshirt, he threw it at Jack, who caught it with ease and unrolled it, looking down at the Dallas Cowboys logo, worn and split after many washes. "Wear that," Riley said. "It's my favorite shirt, and it will give our story more credibility." He waved his hand in a gesture of *whatever*. Jack pulled his lower lip between his teeth and held up the sweatshirt to inspect it. His expression was doubtful, but eventually he pulled it over his head.

Riley swallowed. This was getting stupid. He needed to get a handle on these stupid lust-ridden feelings that kept washing over him. Freaking Campbell and his no sex rule was going to kill him by a week from Sunday. *I am not gay, I am not gay, I am not gay. I might be a small bit bi, but I am not gay.* The sweatshirt was long on Jack and hung way over his belt. But the age of it had thinned the material to the point where it clung to Jack's form, and it didn't help that Jack used his large capable hands to smooth the material down over his flat stomach. *I am not gay—*

"Fuck's sake, Campbell, this isn't a live sex show. Let's get a move on," Riley snapped, waiting by the door, arms crossed over his chest, his foot tapping impatiently.

Jack didn't answer, just followed his new husband to the top of the stairs and then held him back by his sleeve. Irritation had Riley turning sharply, Jack catching him on the turn and pulling him close, leaning up and guiding him in for a kiss.

"For appearances," he whispered simply just as their lips met, and Jack reached up to tangle a hand in Riley's hair, holding his head still and close. Finally Jack released him, and Riley pulled back so slowly he could feel Jack's breath lingering on his skin. His mouth was tingling from the pressure of the kiss, his blood was heating up, and he knew his mouth was half-open, making him look like a bemused idiot.

Jack took his hand confidently and moved to take the first step. "C'mon, Het-boy, let's do this thing."

Chapter 13

The large breakfast room was empty save for one maid who was dishing hot cooked food into servers, and she said nothing, simply smiling softly and leaving as the two men entered. Jack dropped Riley's hand and moved straight for the bacon and sausage, his eyes widening at the mass of food available. He was used to a big breakfast. His momma was always there with pancakes and bacon, eggs and sausages. He had often been working a good solid three hours before he ate and he needed it. But this —this obscene pile of food— this was kind of odd.

"I'm guessing y'all have big appetites?" he asked wryly, picking up a plate and piling it high with fried goodness before sitting at the table and trying not to stare at the gilt-edged crockery and sparkling silver cutlery. Riley wasn't far behind him, although he'd added pancakes and also juggled two glasses of orange juice. The maid came back with fresh coffee, and Riley, who had virtually inhaled his breakfast before Jack was even halfway through his, was sitting back and sipping at the fragrant coffee with a look of bliss on his face. This was obviously relaxed Riley at his best, and Jack sought to examine this rare species more closely, watching as suddenly Riley stiffened and paled at a single word.

"Riley?"

Both men stood. Riley's mother. Perfect in dove gray and pearls, her dark hair —bottle brown Jack thought— loose about slim shoulders. Her makeup was perfect, and a cloud of Chanel announced her presence. Riley stood, as did Jack, and Riley dropped a small kiss on her smooth cheek.

"Mother."

"And Jack Campbell is here because?" Her voice was friendly in that false way that meant she wasn't at all pleased to have a Campbell at her breakfast table.

"I have something to tell you," Riley began, holding out his hand blindly. Jack caught it and moved closer to Riley. "Yesterday… I got married. Jack is my… This is my husband, Jack Campbell-Hayes."

There was silence, sudden and all encompassing. "How perfectly ridiculous, Riley" was all she said, then added, with a good healthy portion of derision. "It's far too early for this nonsense." Riley couldn't find the words, and Jack just stared. He had expected a reaction from the matriarch of the Hayes family, but dismissal hadn't been on his list of first options, having already settled on southern belle fainting or icy anger.

"Ma'am," Jack started. "No nonsense. We got married yesterday, in Vancouver."

"I don't know what is going on here." She blinked at Jack, her lips thin and pressed hard together, a small twitch in her eye the only evidence that she felt anything. "This joke is not funny, Riley." Turning on her heel, she left the room, the Chanel moving with her. All the oxygen rushed back into the space she had occupied, and both Jack and Riley breathed deeply.

"That went well," Jack said wryly.

"It's okay. She'll speak to Dad, or maybe Jeff, then she'll come back and rail at me at a later time that suits her." Riley sounded unconcerned, like the icy calm that surrounded his mother was perfectly okay. Jack thought of his mom, of the passion in her, the grace that still remained even when she smacked Jack upside his head with a spoon. She would never have just left the room. They would have argued, shouted, screamed, hugged, made up, perhaps all of that in the space of five minutes. It was what defined Jack's life and the life of his siblings, that passionate discussion that was the beginning and end of arguments, nothing lingering or festering for days.

"Riley?" Another voice. "I can't believe you took the jet! I needed it!" This must be Eden. "Annabelle and I wanted to go and shop in New York and— Well, hello, gorgeous." Her voice changed as she pulled Riley in for a hug and noticed Jack standing beside him. "Where did you come from, handsome?" Jack winced. He was being hit on by a girl only a year or two older than his sister.

"Eden, meet Jack, Jack meet Eden, my annoying brat of a sister."

"Helloooo, Jack," she drawled, sliding her hand to touch his arm, only dropping it when Jack backed up quickly, knocking into a chair. She was tall, not as tall as her brother, but at least five ten, and had hair that was long and straight about her shoulders and the color of sunshine. She was gorgeous. Even Jack could appreciate that. Gorgeous and confident and very, very young.

Riley snorted a laugh. "Eden, seriously, back off. That is my husband you're coming on to."

If Eden was surprised, she didn't let on, her eyes carefully and coolly assessing her brother and then Jack.

"That's some statement there, big brother. Wanna expand for me?"

"Coffee?" Jack asked, crossing to pour fresh coffee and folding into the chair he had just left. He wanted to hear exactly how Riley was going to explain this to his younger sibling.

* * * *

Two men read identical reports that morning. One read it on-line, his usual habit, along with his morning coffee. Said coffee splattered across the screen at the headline *Texas Oil Heir Weds in Gay Marriage*. The other read it in a newspaper, traditionally, laid out across his expanse of desk.

Jim Bailey got the first phone call from Jeff at 8:56, the second from Gerald at 9:02.

The shit had well and truly hit the fan.

By 9:20 Gerald Hayes had left for home.

By 9:40 Jeff Hayes was well on his way to his fourth shot of whisky and cursing the day his little brother had been born.

* * * *

The limo turned in a graceful arc around the fountain, and Gerald Hayes climbed out of the back, his back rigid, his face set. Riley stood at the window of his room and turned to Jack with a shrug.

"Now it starts," he said.

"*Riley Nathaniel Hayes!*" his dad bellowed from the hall.

"Show time," Jack said so quietly Riley had to strain to hear.

Chapter 14

Side by side, hand in hand, the two men descended the stairs. Gerald looked up as they moved closer, the breath catching in his chest, seeing a Campbell taking the steps one at a time, a male version of the only woman he'd ever really loved. Then finally they stopped in front of him.

"What the hell is going on here, Riley? I won't have a Campbell in my house!"

"Campbell-Hayes," the upstart dared respond.

Gerald ignored him. "What is this nonsense in the papers about marriage, boy?" He moved close, and despite being a good few inches shorter than his middle child, he loomed over them both.

"No nonsense, Dad. Jack and I are married."

"Same-sex marriage isn't legal in Texas! This is ridiculous! For this, you drag the Hayes name through the mud?"

"It is legal, Dad. I'm married as per every single proviso you added to the employment contract for shared vice president."

"Enough is enough, boy! Is this some kind of joke? That contract quite clearly stated—"

"That I should marry for at least one year," Riley interrupted. "There was not a single word that specified the sex of the person I had to marry."

"I will have this thrown out in court! This is a joke! You— married to this—" Gerald's anger reddened his face, his temper muddling his words. "This *homosexual*," he finally spat out. "That is not what the contract was about, and you know it!"

"I married—"

"I will have this lie, this abomination, thrown out!"

"You can't, Dad." To Gerald's horror and disgust, Riley tightened his hold on Campbell's hand, leaning into him for silent support. "See, I married for love."

Gerald's hands clenched into fists at his sides. He wanted to wrap his hands around his middle son's neck, the stupid, fucked up *child*.

"When a court sees you're not even gay—"

"Dad," Riley said patiently, "I'm bi, always have been. I met Jack, and I fell in love, end of story."

"This is an abomination in the eyes of the Lord!"

"So is shellfish," Campbell muttered under his breath, and Gerald saw him squeezing Riley's hand in support.

Gerald took a step closer. His fists rose at his sides, and spittle formed on his lips. "I won't have this under my roof, boy, you hear?"

"Sir—" Jack began as Riley hesitated, clearly blindsided by the near violence in Gerald's voice.

"Don't even think to talk to me, Campbell," Gerald spat out, not looking at him. He stared into Riley's eyes, the betrayal cutting deep inside. How could this boy do this to him? Hadn't Gerald given him everything?

The door opened and closed behind them. Gerald turned on his heel to look at the new arrival. Jeff, his son and heir, stood with his back to the door, just listening. His plans for his eldest son, for Hayes Oil, started to crumble around him and sudden grief —a feeling he thought he'd buried a long time ago— clutched his insides. Turning back, he found himself looking directly into the sea blue of Donna Campbell's eyes reflected in her son. At once he was assailed by memories of summers so long ago, and it sent steel to his spine.

"I will get this thrown out. You hear me, boy? You think you're clever? You don't know the half of it. I will not have a bastard Campbell under my roof, infecting my family with their sexual deviancy and their working class filth. End of story," he finished, deliberately echoing Riley.

"Don't talk about my husband that way, Dad," he said quietly, markedly calm against the fury and temper thrown at him. "I love Jack, we married, and we are living together in my apartment."

"Know this, Riley," Gerald said. "I will get this stopped. This changes nothing."

"Do your worst, Dad. I wouldn't expect anything less."

Gerald spun on his heel, walking with purpose down the hall to his home office, the door slamming hard behind him.

Chapter 15

Jeff started to clap his hands, slowly, rhythmically. "Well played, little brother. Well played."

Jack let out the breath he didn't even realize he'd been holding. Only certain words stayed in his head, not the abuse or the hate that dripped from Gerald's mouth, but the words Riley had used. One sentence that kind of summed up exactly why Riley was doing what he was doing, or what he believed he was doing it for.

Jack dropped the hold he had on Riley's hand and turned to climb the stairs. "We need to talk," he said softly, waiting for Riley to snap out of his staring match with Jeff and get him back up to the apartment. Riley blinked up at him, and then cast one last look at Jeff before climbing the stairs at a slower pace, finally closing the apartment door behind them. Riley leaned back against it, worrying his lower lip with his teeth, showing more in that single action than he'd done since they had made this bargain.

"You wanna tell me what you meant about the vice president thing?" Jack asked, crossing to the leather sofa and sitting on the edge, hands twined together on his knees. He wasn't going to move until he had the story, the entire background of how they'd ended up here in this room. "Are there reasons for this charade other than just pissing off your father?"

* * * *

Riley sighed and shrugged, knocking his head back against the wood and closing his eyes, he didn't want to show Jack this disillusioned side, this knocked down by the family side. He wanted to be confident, in control of himself. It just wasn't happening, and he couldn't for the life of him understand why. He still had so much to process: the high of confrontation, the success of what he'd done edged with the complete disappointment in his family. Well, his family apart from Eden, who despite trying to hit on the gay married guy, at least seemed to accept the marriage. His mother had yet to give her considered opinion, which he knew would be delivered wrapped in the same ice that ran through her veins. His father had almost popped a vein in temper, no acceptance of what Riley had done, just anger and vitriolic hate. And as for his brother, those few words, the sarcasm, the sardonic, mocking, scornful words…

Well, it was no different from what he was used to.

And now Jack wanted to know the details. How could Riley begin to tell this confident man in front of him just how much temper, anger and rage he held inside himself? His only hope was to tell him enough for it to make sense. He needed to start now.

"So it began with my father saying he was retiring. Maybe not retiring as such, but certainly standing back, and calling Jeff and I in to portion out control of Hayes Oil. I deserve my share. Long story short, I didn't get my share." Riley sat on the other sofa, aware he probably sounded like a spoiled child.

"You sound like a spoiled child," Jack pointed out.

Great. "There are reasons why I should, why I want to have some control. I need to stop them from…" There were far too many secrets and needs that Riley had spent so many years hiding. Wording it right was not easy.

Jack leaned forward, his face carefully blank. "Need to stop them from what?" Riley stared into blue eyes, the light making them translucent, and freckles sprinkled over the far too pretty face of his new husband. *Pretty.* And he really wanted to unload, to Jack, to anyone. Only Steve knew the real Riley, the Riley that still survived the shit piled on to him, survived the secrets and the knowledge he had. He didn't know Jack from the next man. He had only ever heard the detailed, impassioned stories about how the Campbells tried to cheat the Hayeses out of money and land.

About how Alan Campbell had dragged the name of Hayes through the courts, accused Gerald of falsifying land records and forging contracts. How could Riley trust the son of the man who tried to destroy his family? Dysfunctional though it may be, it was still his family, his name.

He stiffened his spine, angry at almost letting his barriers fall at the soft voice and the serious expression on his husband's face. At the questions from his cowboy, he pushed the man who wanted to share back inside and pulled stubborn, willful Riley to the foreground.

"All you need to know is that you're mine for a year, and we need to try a damn sight harder if we have a hope in hell of convincing my father he has no chance of fighting this marriage. , and as it stands, I have fulfilled his contract stipulations."

"Okay," Jack said patiently, "tell me about the contract."

"Simply, my father handed over majority rule to Jeff, being as he is A. married, B. has children, and C. is apparently, therefore, not gay. Which then means he is the best person for Hayes Oil. However, the middle child, apparently, being unmarried, childless, and possibly therefore gay can't be considered as an equal partner in what is a family company." Riley tried to keep any trace of bitterness from his voice, but it wasn't easy to do, and he saw Jack wince in reaction.

He stopped. Familiar anger was climbing his spine, pushing into muscles that tensed and clenched, the pain in his neck pushing up into his headache. Unconsciously, he massaged the back of his neck and tilted his head, stretching the muscles, wincing at the pain.

"As a proviso, he added that should I marry for love and stay married for exactly one year, he would reassign the percentages. I would have the same percentage of Hayes Oil as my brother."

"Married, for a year, for love." Jack repeated. "Can I just point out that, given you have probably worked your way through half the Dallas women under the age of twenty five, finding a suitable wife in amongst them would be fairly easy?"

Riley stood suddenly, a fire in him that Jack could pick so easily on the same thing that Jim and Steve had.

"No," he spat out, turning away from Jack to face the window, trying to calm his emotions before he turned back. Jack just sat and stared up at him. "See, that would play straight into his hands. I would be stuck in a marriage based on a lie. Should we have a child, I couldn't leave that child, that woman. He knows that. He wants me tied down, finished."

"You seem to assign an awful lot of slyness to a man you call your father," Jack pointed out simply. "What makes you think he'd—"

"You don't know him. He might be my father, but he's used to manipulating me. This time he isn't getting away with it."

"You need to show me this contract, this agreement that your father pulled together so I know my role. Maybe Josh should have a look?" Riley was instantly horrified. To have an outsider see the proof of his father's disregard of him was too much. No. He couldn't do that. As usual, words failed him, and he fell back onto his usual method of communication. Superiority.

"All you need to know, Campbell, is that you keep your head down, keep to your side of the bargain, and in turn, I will keep to mine." In a flurry of movement, Riley moved to the door, wrenching it open. "I need to get out of here."

* * * *

Jack blinked, watching him leave. Stress and violence surrounded his new husband like a suffocating blanket. "Campbell-Hayes," he said to the empty room, and sighing, he followed Riley down the stairs and out of the front door.

The Riley he'd seen, a flash of in the man who'd leaned exhausted against the door, had vanished in the blink of an eye. He recognized barriers when he saw them, because he used the same tools to hide his own worries. It was self-preservation that made him not push as hard as he had wanted, sensing Riley was jonesing for a fight.

Riley wasn't aware of it, but his face showed so many expressions from anger to sadness that Jack had a hard time distinguishing the separate emotions.

Chapter 16

The whisky was the oldest, finest, most expensive that Gerald could find, and he had drunk enough to still be on a short fuse when Jeff knocked and entered the office, a smirk on his face.

"Did you really think he was going to take this lying down?" Jeff pointed out, arms crossed on his chest. He seemed composed and in control though Gerald couldn't see why.

In contrast he was furious, almost apoplectic, and he could feel the red in his face. He was pacing the not altogether small space behind his antique desk. "Enough," he spat, finally stopping the pacing. "He is simply being stupid. It will pass."

"He is far from stupid. In fact, I think you underestimate him."

"I am quite aware of how I have underestimated your mother's son," Gerald said fast and instantly, anger at the core of the heated words. "And don't think of talking *at* me, Jeff. You should be thinking of how we can get around this."

"How we get round this?"

"If he finds the papers, if he realizes—"

"It won't happen. We go to source," Jeff said. "Leave Riley alone as the easily maneuvered child that he is and instead focus on Campbell. Turn him against his new…" He hesitated with a look of distaste on his face. "*Husband*."

Gerald raised his eyebrows, admiring the cunning that was twisting in his son.

"His horses," Jeff said. "I hear he's doing more than well with his horses, so we go there first."

"I want that Campbell away from this family."

"Consider it done," Jeff said confidently.

"The day your bastard brother gets any kind of control over my company is the day that hell freezes over," Gerald added, hearing the hate in his own voice.

"He won't. Believe me, I won't let it happen." Jeff matched the venom with the vindictiveness that controlled his every move. "I am not giving up my birthright and certainly not to anyone polluted by association with a Campbell."

* * * *

Jack caught up with Riley as he stood by one of the 4x4s in the drive. His new husband was just staring at him, expectation etched into his features. It sent a skitter of wariness down his spine as the tension permeating the house followed him outside.

"Keys?" he asked. Riley threw them over the roof, and Jack snatched them out of the air and threw them up, thoughtful and suddenly feeling the need for open space. "Where to?"

Riley shrugged. "Beer," was all he said.

"Get in. We're going to the D."

Riley climbed in without argument, but stared resolutely out of the window as they left for the Campbell family home. His phone rang twice. The first time he just cut off the call, but the second time he answered it, with resignation in his voice and words that just fell off of his tongue with practiced ease. Jack only got Riley's side of the conversation, but whoever he was talking to obviously peeved Riley, judging by what he was saying. His frustration and exasperation were obvious, despite turning away from Jack.

"No, we're not. I can't understand why you— Jeez, the kids need their momma. You need to listen to me, Lisa. *No*, I've heard that before. Okay, okay, yes, it's true. Yes, I will." He shot a quick look at Jack. "Yes we'll be there—

Whatever good that does." He closed the cell, settling back to face the front and glaring out of the windshield.

"And?" Jack finally said, curiosity pushing at him to question when Riley didn't immediately answer.

"Lisa, Jeff's wife, wanted to check if we would be back for dinner tonight, that's all. She's aware of what's happened and she's…"

As his voice tailed off, irritation sparked in Jack. What the fuck was up with all the half sentences? It was driving him freakin' mad.

"She's what? Pissed? Sad? Devastated she lost you? What?" Jack snapped, taking the next bend maybe a little too sharply and causing Riley to slide against the door with a loud exhalation of breath.

"Scared, she says she's scared," Riley bit out, rubbing at his shoulder and frowning.

Jack said nothing. He added another question to the long list of questions he was writing in his head, a list he would damn sure pull out later.

When he drove through the main gates with the two D's entwined in an intricate twist of metal, he felt every ounce of stress falling away. He was at home, pulling himself visibly taller, a smile on his face, pride in every pore, whilst next to him, Riley seemed to sink lower into his seat. He drew to a stop outside the main house at right angles to the red-sided barn, turned off the engine and leaned against the steering wheel. He had something to say, something that was eating away inside him. Riley had to know, needed to know, what Jack had inside his heart.

"Okay, Het—" he started with his usual lack of reverence, then pushed that down. This was not a joke. "Riley, this is gonna be one hell of a long year, and before we do anything else, before we take one step outside of this truck, I wanna get something off my chest."

Riley paused with his hand on the door. "Okay?"

"I want you to know that I hate you— what you did— that you used Beth against me. I hate that you knew before me and that I had no choice in this." He realized he sounded confused at what he was trying to say, but Riley wouldn't look him in the eyes.

* * * *

Riley said nothing. He just opened the door and climbed out, his feet heavy on the hard packed ground below them and then he stood, looking at the barns and the house as he had done that first day, wondering at how quickly the week had gone. He knew in his heart, where guilt and anger both battled for dominance, just what it was that Jack was explaining.

Suddenly it was just as important for Riley to say what was inside him. "Are you gonna make my life miserable now?" he started. "Are you gonna get your revenge for what I did?"

Jack climbed down from the seat and came round to stand next to Riley, leaning in so he could speak low and firm. "I don't have the capacity for the kind of hate the Hayes family seems to have, Riley. Beth is ill and has been for a long time. She's pregnant and could die. I have two mares about to foal that could make the D the best horse ranch in the state, and now I have the money to help me with both."

He stopped, sighing, then reaching up to grasp Riley at the back of his neck. His hold firm, he pulled Riley's head down. "I don't have anything left inside to deal with you and your petty squabbles. For now, I need to play my part, keep my end of the bargain, and that starts with fairly obvious public displays of affection."

Riley didn't argue as Jack placed warm lips against his, his hands twisting harder in Riley's hair, holding him in place. Jack ran the tip of his tongue over Riley's lower lip, pushing for him to let him in. Pulling back briefly, all he said was, "Fuck's sake, make it a good one for the audience, Het-boy," and then he was drawing the very breath from Riley's body as he slanted his mouth and began the hottest open-mouth kiss Riley had ever been on the receiving end of. It wasn't hard to go with the flow. His hands rested on Jack's hips, one moving to settle at the dip in his spine and one, resting on the belt of his jeans. Whispers of wanting more drifted in his subconscious.

This wasn't a woman, a soft gentle woman, bending back in his arms and letting him lead. This was a battle to take control. A small groan started in his throat as he felt himself hardening against Jack's leg and the flush of arousal burning in the tight restricting denim. Jack said nothing, just twisted slightly, pushing Riley back against the car, his own arousal hard and insistent against Riley. Finally Jack pulled back, Riley chasing the kiss and whining at the loss before he realized where he was and exactly why they were kissing.

"I signed the damn contract, Riley," Jack whispered against damp kiss-marked lips, "and I will be the husband you need. Doesn't mean we have to like each other." Without another word, he turned on his heel, walking halfway to the house and stopping. "Coming?"

Riley was stunned and verging on embarrassed. For a good few minutes, he didn't know what he felt, apart from freakin' turned on. He willed his hard-on to go away as Donna stood on the steps calling down to them both. Riley pasted a smile on his face, a genuine *I'm pleased to see you* smile and joined Jack, who was damn well holding out a hand to grasp, like they were a real couple. Taking a deep breath, he climbed the stairs for the third time in one week.

"The vet is here, Jack," Donna said quickly. "Nothing awful; Solo-Col was just restless." Jack looked back at the first barn, clearly torn between what he wanted to do —visit with family— and what he needed to do— visit with his horses.

"Riley, I just need to go check on her. I'll be back in a bit," he finally said.

"Er— you want me to come with you?" Riley offered, also weighing up pros and cons, though it was more along the lines of death-by-horse versus death-by-Campbell family.

"I'll be ten minutes," Jack said, releasing Riley's hand and jogging towards the barn.

Riley sighed and climbed the last few steps. Jack's mom quickly and efficiently pulled him into a tight hug and guided him into the warm kitchen. It smelled the same. Something was cooking, and Riley guessed it was some kind of stew in the large pot on the stove. The smell of bread permeated the rooms. He sniffed the air appreciatively and was treated to the incredibly awesome sight of fresh cookies and coffee on the table.

Donna glanced out of the kitchen window towards the barn. "You know what Jack can be like." She chuckled. "You realize he'll be at least an hour, if not more." She pushed a fresh coffee his way and indicated he should help himself to cookies, which he did, with a polite "Thank you, ma'am."

Beth came in sometime between the first and second cookie, sitting down diagonally across from Riley. She didn't look at him, just sat quietly sipping on some foul-smelling herbal tea and nibbling on a cookie of her own. Where was the brave girl who'd stood between him and her brother, the one who questioned his motives? She wasn't here in this quiet child-woman who didn't say a word.

"So," began Riley, just for something to say, deciding to stay off the subject of pregnancy in case Donna wasn't in the loop yet. "I've seen you hanging around sometimes with my friend, Steve."

Beth actually smiled and then blushed. "I met him in the hospital when I was fourteen, I guess. He had been through all the same stuff as me and come out the other end, living and well, and he looked after me in the ward. He was only there when my family couldn't be, but it was the lonely times. Three in the morning, the dead hours." She paused, her thoughts obviously lost in memories.

"He's a good guy," Riley offered, wanting to tell her about the Steve that he knew, the Steve who supported him and laughed with him, the man who gave him space away from his family, and put up with all his shit. But he found he couldn't stumble on the words to talk to the girl he'd betrayed to her brother.

Jack wasn't as long as Donna had suggested he might be but was definitely away longer than ten minutes. When he walked back into the kitchen, he had a look of uncertainty etched into his features.

"Wanna see the horses?" he offered.

It seemed like an impulse question, but Riley took him up on it. He found himself in the dim interior of the main barn, his hands gently stroking the softness that was Solo-Col. He listened as attentively as he could as Jack explained her bloodline, her potential, the one point four million her foal could bring if it all went well, and how this foal could be the making of the D.

Riley followed Jack to the fence that formed one end of the corral, leaning against it and looking thoughtfully at the horses in the fields beyond. Quietly Jack leaned in for another kiss, quick and fast, whispering, "We're being watched" against Riley's warm face.

As Riley listened to Jack, listened to the pride and love for bloodlines and the family ranch, he could feel the tension across his neck start to release, as if this was maybe somewhere he could just listen to Jack ramble on and relax.

* * * *

Donna watched them from the kitchen, thoughtful, knowing her son, loving her son, wanting him to be happy. It was easier to lose herself in times when she was happier, before

Alan had gone too far, lost his dignity and her love, before resentment took him from her. The pride of the D was in her son, in every inch of him, and she just wondered what deal he'd made with the devil to keep his family safe.

Beth started to leave the table, and Donna couldn't keep things inside any longer. She turned to pull her youngest into a close hug.

"Sweetheart," she began, trying her best not to cry, not to scream, to be the best mother she could. "I think there's something you maybe want to tell me?"

Chapter 17

The knock on the door was loud in the quiet apartment. It had been a long, hard, tiring week, and a virus had laid Steve low. His usual sunny outlook on life was somewhat dented. He had received final word from the lawyers on his trust fund and discovered he couldn't get access to it before his thirtieth birthday, whatever the reason. But that wasn't even all of it.

He'd been sitting in silence ever since he had received the phone call, and now he was waiting for Beth, worried to death. Seven simple words— "Are you alone? Can I come over?" — but she had sounded half defeated, quietly sad, and it sent shivers down his spine. He knew what it was like to deal with the threat of death. He had pulled through, and he thought she had too, and it was all over.

He hesitated before opening the door, twisting his hands in his hair, his heart heavy. This wasn't the first time, nor would it be the last, that Elizabeth had called or visited just to talk. But with the whole pregnancy thing, his levels of support and love for Elizabeth and her unborn child threatened to break him in half. Last time they'd met had been the worst. On his knees, with a diamond solitaire in his hand, he had proposed the best solution— "Marry me Beth." He had asked out of love, but all she saw was the age difference, seven long years that had made him a man, and the fear of why he was proposing.

She wouldn't tell him who the father was, but he had his suspicions. He'd even considered confronting the person he thought responsible for creating life with the girl he loved, but he didn't. Not when she cried and begged him to leave it, telling him that one day he would know. "You can't protect me, not from him," she'd sobbed, and then just stopped, like every word she said would be a clue for Steve's fertile imagination to build on.

Taking a deep breath and pasting on the *best friend* smile he had practiced to perfection, he opened the door. Beth was standing there on the threshold, looking like the world had been pulled out from under her. Without words, she fell into his embrace, standing still and silent, her head on his chest, her breathing shallow, and he pushed the door shut.

"Hey, princess," he began softly, "what's wrong?" He felt her full body sigh as she gripped into the soft cotton of his shirt.

"Momma knows," she said simply and quietly, so soft he had to strain to hear. Donna knew?

"Oh baby girl." He didn't know what to say to that one. "It was gonna happen sooner rather than later." Beth nodded against his chest. "How did she… What did she say?" A sob hitched in her throat, and if it was possible, she was burying herself deeper into his embrace. Had Donna not understood? Had she been angry? That wasn't the Donna he knew. "Tell me, Beth, what did she say?"

She only cried harder, and desperate to just see into her eyes, he swept her up into his arms, wincing at the slight weight of her and crossing to the sofa, slumping into the corner and holding her close. With his free hand, he tilted her head back, her beautiful blue eyes wide and full of tears, and he buried that same hand in her long dark brown hair. "Beth?"

"She was good. We talked and… She said she was worried, but she knew having children… She said it completed her. It made me feel…" She stopped, her voice choked. "I'm just so sorry…" Those simple words shattered him.

"Sorry? What for?"

"For letting her down, for letting you down, for Jack, for Josh… I've failed every one of you."

Steve tightened his grip. He couldn't reconcile her thought processes here.

"What?" He wished he could form a better sentence.

"I've done this. This is my fault. I'm a burden on my family, and I've been so stupid."

"No, never, I love you Elizabeth Campbell. Your family loves you, and you saying you have failed us is just plain stupid." His voice cracked with emotion, and her eyes filled with more tears as she half-nodded.

"I want to make it all go away, Steve."

He held her as she cried, talking and muttering, until finally, she grew quiet in his arms, her breathing steady as she slept against his chest. He reached for his cell, scrolling to find Donna's number and quickly letting her know Beth was there with him.

It was only much later that night that he remembered one single sentence Beth had added as they talked quietly.

Jack was broken when he told me he knew.

What did she mean? Had he guessed? How had her brother known about the baby? Had he guessed? He'd thought she wasn't telling him yet.

* * * *

Jack sat back on the sofa in Riley's apartment, waiting for Riley to get out of the shower, as relaxed as he could be. In less than half an hour, he'd be facing the entire Hayes clan at dinner. Riley had given him as much of a heads up as he could about each member, but none of that explained why a clearly inebriated blonde was leaning against the inside of *their* door, a glass of red wine in her hand and a thin smile on her face. Clearly this was Lisa. Jeff's wife.

Dressed in little more than what he imagined qualified for underwear, a thin silk wrap falling off delicate shoulders, she glanced towards the shower and began to walk that way. Jack stood and blocked the movement with a polite, "Ma'am?"

Carefully she leaned into him, her eyes a little unfocused. "Jus' have some business to take care of with the stud there," she all but purred, syllables lengthened and sultry as she pouted up at Jack and gestured towards the closed bathroom door.

"I'm sure it can wait," Jack offered politely, wincing as scarlet-tipped nails rested on his fresh white shirt, and her pout grew bigger.

"When I got the invite, I'm sure it didn't mention a threesome, handsome." She slurred her words, tossing back long blonde hair and tilting her hips to his. Carefully he placed hands on her arms and pushed her back, wine sloshing in the glass, her heels making her unsteady. *Jeez, talk about cliché, underwear, a little silk robe and heels. Not so much for the classy then.*

"I'll be sure an' tell Riley you visited," Jack said firmly, guiding her to the door. A sudden look of clarity sparked into otherwise dead eyes, and she narrowed them.

"You're that Campbell boy, John, Justin—"

"Jack."

"Jack. Jack Campbell, what you doing here in the Hayes prison?" she finally asked, sipping at the wine and leaning into his hold, the only thing keeping her vertical.

"Campbell-Hayes actually," Jack returned. "Riley and I are married." Her eyes dropped to the platinum ring on his ring finger, and then back up to his face. In a smooth movement that belied her apparent drunken state, she thrust the wine at him. He took it out of pure reaction, releasing one of his hands and causing her to stumble.

She pulled herself tall. "You're so gonna need that, big guy," she said simply. Tottering on her heels, she let herself out of the room, leaving Jack wondering what had just happened, with a glass of wine in his hands. He was still standing there when Riley emerged fully dressed from the bathroom, his eyebrow raised in question at the wine in Jack's hand.

Jack just shook his head, silently saying, *don't ask*. "Have you been there, Het-boy?"

"Where?" Riley was clearly confused.

"Lisa."

"My brother's wife?" Was Riley being deliberately obtuse about this? After all, he had allegedly invited Lisa up here for some inter-family sex.

"Your brother's wife. Yes."

"Erm— no— you don't fuck with family." Riley was hesitant but firm, and Jack believed him. Riley may have the morals of a tom-cat, but about this, Jack really did believe him. "Ready?" Riley finally said as Jack just stared at him.

"As I'll ever be," Jack replied, placing the wine glass on the table and straightening to see a nervous-looking Riley by the door.

Riley paused, turning back to face Jack. "Just so you know, we are gonna need some definite PDAs tonight. Think you can handle that?" There was irritation in Riley's voice, a subtle change, a certain stress. Jack imagined it was a manifestation of fear, and it made him feel better to think that. In answer Jack moved carefully past Riley, sliding a hand over the younger man's black silk shirt, his fingers brushing Riley's left nipple. He heard a hiss of indrawn breath as his hard thigh touched Riley briefly.

"I can handle anything you need, Het-boy," he said, his voice low and growled. "Just follow my cues." Riley followed him to the top of the stairs, and Jack held out his hand. "Husband?" he smirked.

Riley took his hand, and they started down the sweeping staircase. "Fuck you, asshole," Riley forced out behind a covering smile.

"Not if I fuck you first," Jack said, fast and clear, smirking again as Riley stumbled on the next step. "Careful, baby," he added for any audience below. "You wouldn't wanna fall and break your neck, would you?"

"Riley, you made it."

Eden's voice. Jack looked over the side of the stairs to see Riley's younger sibling, casual in jeans and a tee, a grin on her face.

"And you, little sister, are running late."

They reached the bottom of the stairs, and Eden leaned up to hug her brother in close.

"Meh, they're used to me by now," she pointed out laughing, and with a smack on Jack's backside, she scampered up the stairs, turning right at the top to her own private area. Riley had a fond smile showing. It was a new expression, one Jack hadn't seen before, and it intrigued him. In this dysfunctional shit-fest of a family, this brother and sister actually seemed to be close. Very interesting.

Riley's mom was sitting, waiting. Riley's dad, however, was notably absent, as were Jeff and Lisa's kids. Riley slid into an empty chair, and Jack pulled out the one next to him, laying a large and very warm hand on his husband's thigh.

"Evenin', y'all," he drawled in his best cowboy tone, relaxing back in his chair. Riley's mother glanced his way and then back to her discussion with Jeff, not even giving Jack the time of day. Jack just inwardly smiled, squeezing Riley's leg and causing the poor unsuspecting man to shoot suddenly upwards in his chair. The blonde, Lisa, arrived, thankfully in more clothes than before, and she sashayed to sit opposite Riley.

"Are you okay, Riley?" she simpered, her eyes like flint over the rim of her glass, half smiling and pushing her hair back with her free hand. In response Jack just leaned into Riley, pushing his long bangs to one side and dropping a small kiss on his exposed sun-burnished skin, glancing back at Lisa with a look on his face that closely resembled, *Yeah right, bitch, in your dreams*. She nodded at the win, sipping her wine carefully, then looking back at her mother-in-law and pretending to listen. Score one to Campbell-Hayes for marking his territory.

A maid hovered at the door, and she was dismissed with a curt, "Does it look like we are all here?" from Jeff. It was only when Hayes Senior, in all his dark-suited arrogance, deigned to join them that they actually began to eat. Jack didn't remember much of what he ate, but thankfully, Eden placed herself diagonally across from him, and at least he could carry out a conversation with her. A conversation beyond the usual crap centering on the Texas Oil industry and who was knifing whom in the back. It was only when he felt Riley tense beneath his hand, which had remained for the most part on his husband's strong thigh, that Jack snapped back to the conversation down at the other end. Someone had mentioned a familiar name, something had been said that caused Riley to stop eating. His knife and fork clattered onto the plate.

"Oh, I'm sorry, Riley, that Steve boy is a friend of yours, I believe?" This from Lisa, who was leaning into the conversation, a look of barely restrained glee on her face, spoiling for a fight. Riley said nothing.

"I hear your friend is seeing that Campbell girl, Madeline or something." Sandra was sipping her own wine, speaking to her husband and Jeff, deliberately facing away from Riley and Jack. "She must be so pleased to be mixing with a good family like the Murrays." This time she looked directly at Jack, who simply raised an eyebrow in response, not willing to rise to the deliberate provocation he could see was being spun.

"Seems like a family trait, Campbell kids deliberately marrying into money, but I guess that's one way to get yourselves out of debt." This from Jeff, who exchanged nods with Gerald.

"How is she to know any different?" Gerald said scornfully. "She has the good example in her brother after all. He's just married one of the richest men in the state. Poor girl probably doesn't know any better than to whore herself out to get the same."

Jack's temper went from gently simmering to boiling in seconds, but he waited for Riley to jump in and defend him, wanting just one word, like a husband would, even one that wasn't real. But he said nothing, not one single thing. Jack stood abruptly.

"Ladies," he said simply, nodding to Eden who sat with incredible stillness in her chair, her eyes wide. Then he added a single word: not a question, more a command. "Riley."

Riley looked up at him, then over at his father, who sat with a challenging look on his face, daring his son to leave. With no more hesitation, Riley stood and followed Jack out of the door. Words of disdain followed them in soft voices.

Jack virtually dragged him up the stairs, his temper still high, so many thoughts pushing through and fighting for priority: his inherent worry for Beth, the vicious words at the table, the fact that Riley had just sat there, the whole Lisa flirtation. It was all too much.

They actually made it to the room and had closed the door before Jack completely lost it, pushing hard at Riley's chest, catching him off guard and causing him to stumble back against the wall. Jack was on him before Riley could catch his balance, one hand flat on his chest, the other by his head against the door.

"Know this, *husband*, you fuckin' back down on me like that again, and I will make sure you live to regret it."

"Jack—"

"Fuck you, Riley. Fuck you and your family. You'd better make sure they leave my sister out of this!"

"Alright." Riley raised a hand, pushing against Jack's chest. "I'm sorry, okay? I'm sorry."

"My sister!" Jack kept his voice low, threatening, and Riley got the message.

"Off limits, I'll make sure of it."

"Do that, Het-boy, do that."

In a blaze of anger, Jack turned away, pulling off the wool sweater, and shucking the dark pants, grabbing at jeans and his tee. He pulled them on and dragged an old denim jacket over his shoulders.

"Where are you going?" Riley asked softly, and he winced as Jack reached past him to open the door.

"Getting out of here. I'll be in the car. If you wanna come with me, Het-boy, then you get your rich ass downstairs. I'm leaving in ten."

Chapter 18

It didn't take long for Riley to decide. He knew in his heart he owed Jack an apology, and it wasn't just the threat of physical violence that made him see it. For too many years, he'd just switched himself off from all the shit at the dinner table and family events and cut himself off from anything to do with them. Tonight was different. It was apathy that stopped him from saying anything, not a lack of courage on his part. Riley deserved every word that had been thrown at him. He glanced down at what he was wearing, black pants and the silk shirt, and wondered where they were going that meant Jack chose to wear jeans. Quickly he changed into his normal dark jeans and the same worn Cowboys sweatshirt he had made Jack wear earlier that same day at breakfast.

In five minutes he was at the door of the truck, climbing into the passenger side and saying nothing as Jack started off down the drive with barely restrained anger in every sharp movement of his hands. The truck had tinted windows, which was good considering the paparazzi starting to gather at the main gates to the Hayes mansion. It hadn't taken long, just short hours since the announcement in the *Times*, and already the vultures circled, zoom and wide-angle lenses at the ready, waiting to get a view of Riley Hayes and his new husband. Riley saw the flashes, thumbed his cell and sent a quick text to Eden to at least give her a heads up. She normally thrived on all the publicity, but still, her supposedly heterosexual brother married to a *guy* was going to turn the Hayes estate into a three ring circus without a safety net. Riley didn't give a shit about the rest of the family, but Eden and his niece and nephew didn't deserve the stress. Eden would know what to do. Maybe she'd pull Lisa to one side, warn her somehow, and try to push through the alcoholic haze their sister-in-law was permanently in. Maybe she'd even get the nanny involved.

"Where are we going?" Riley finally asked, looking at Jack expectantly. All Jack did was turn up the stereo, the strains of some heavy rock anthem filling the empty space. Riley just turned to look out of the window at the flat Texas land disappearing beside the truck, the steady thrum of tire on blacktop drowned out by the heavy rock vocals.

* * * *

Jack drove with purpose and, inch by inch, the tension inside of him drained away; next to his horses, driving was the one of the only things that relaxed him. But where they were going now was the ultimate antidote to life. It was the same place he'd been going since he was old enough to pass for drinking age, sometimes on his own, sometimes with Josh. He always left with lightness in his heart that belied the financial problems and the worries he held inside for Beth and his mom. Shooters was little more than a roadhouse on a back road, kept alive by locals with knowledge and bikers who had it pinned on some kind of word of mouth biker's map. It was old and worn and felt anonymous and safe to anyone who strayed that way. When they stopped outside, Jack turned off the stereo, crossed his arms on the steering wheel and leaned forward.

"Okay, one question before we go in," he started carefully, not sure how to word this one. He wasn't worrying about Riley's reaction to being asked. He was more worried about his own temper if Riley gave him the wrong answer or Jack saw he was lying.

"Is this what you do?" Riley turned to him, snapping. He seemed tired.

"Wait 'til you get men in your truck and then refuse to let them leave until they answer questions?" Jack assumed he was referring to this morning at the D and half smirked.

"This is *your* truck," Jack pointed out and watched as Riley actually huffed his irritation.

"What then?" Riley snapped back. "What else have I done?"

"All I wanna know —jeez— I know what you said, but seriously did you really not invite Lisa up for sex today?" Jack just blurted it out, and then held his breath, the sudden stillness in the car unnerving.

Riley blinked at him, his mouth falling open, and denial so obvious in his face. "Fuck no," he said, frowning, "and if she said I did, then she's just screwing with ya."

"Okay."

"Okay?"

"Right."

Riley snorted. "Me and Lisa—"

"Whatever."

* * * *

Before Riley could phrase a comeback on Jack's less than witty response, Jack himself was outside the car, keys in his hand and a look of impatience on his face. Riley climbed down more sedately, idly looking at the other occupants of the parking lot. It held mainly bikes, with a few beat-up trucks, and his brand new SUV stood out like a sore thumb, not being helped at all by the R1LEY personalized plates. He cast a final worried glance around him before following Jack to the door, hearing the reassuring click of the central locking as it secured the car.

The door opened to controlled chaos: noise, talking, music on a jukebox in the corner, a small stage, people of all types standing in groups, couples, or singly, drinking beer. This was what Riley could make out in the half-gloom. The room smelled of smoke, beer and aged wood and had a decidedly Spartan interior that disappeared into the murky obscurity of half-hidden corners where conversations, to Riley's untrained eyes, looked decidedly shady. He unconsciously moved closer to Jack, decided that for all his own six foot four of muscle, experience definitely outweighed brawn on this occasion.

* * * *

They reached the bar, Jack scouting the clientele with a quick glance and ordering beers with a casual

flick of his hand and a smile dripping
with charm.

With beers in hand, they settled in
one of the dark corners, Jack wanting to
slide lower in his chair, and do what he
did best— people watch. Tonight,
however, he had a man sitting opposite
him, his partner. Riley looked a little
shell-shocked and more than a little
uncomfortable, squirming slightly in the
wooden seat, nursing the beer and every
so often leaning his head back to
swallow the cold liquid.

Jack sighed inwardly, wishing he
could just relax and enjoy, but all he
could do was watch Riley's freaking
throat as he swallowed the beer, watch
the cold liquid clinging to Riley's lips,
watch Riley's tongue as it chased the
stray drops— just watch. He shifted in
his seat, uncomfortably hardening in his
pants as he watched long graceful
fingers that had never known manual
labor gently slide up and down the
bottle, circling the lip and dropping to
rest on the table. This was ridiculous.
Riley freaking Campbell-Hayes and his
stupid freaking hands and his stupid
freaking neck. It was enough to break
the no sex rule here and now. Not to
mention what was under that
sweatshirt, a strong chest, tight muscles
that flexed and bunched under the silk

shirt he'd worn for dinner, and the tightest —yes, really— the tightest ass he'd seen outside of a rodeo.

"So," he began, shifting again to relieve some of the pressure, "two days down, three hundred sixty-three to go."

"Uh huh," Riley offered in reply, which was kind of weak given the opening Jack had thrown out there.

Jack didn't respond, just slid to a more comfortable position and shut himself off from the crap that was his life at the moment, watching a few casual hook-ups, seeing couples disappearing into the shadows. He wondered why he'd thought it was a good idea to bring his *husband* to the place which only three weeks back was *the* place he'd last had anything resembling sex. He didn't see the guy in here tonight, but that wasn't unusual. Visitors came and went, transient travelers who crossed the country for business or pleasure, so Jack didn't expect to see him. He was, however, very aware of the guy at the bar who was staring at Riley. He was tall, dressed in denim, a Stetson low on his head, beer in his hand, and he was definitely staring. Definitely. Staring.

Jack guessed he should have been prepared for this, but it didn't stop the unexpected stab of anger that this man was calculating the chance of success quite so blatantly. Shuffling his chair, he moved closer to Riley, whose expression resembled that of a startled jackrabbit caught in headlights.

* * * *

Unsettled by Jack's glare, Riley glanced behind him, expecting to spot his dad or his brother and seeing no one he recognized. Relief swept through him. At the same time, tension knotted in his gut, and he had an intuition that maybe it was time for one of Jack's PDAs. Conflicting emotions were fighting inside him. A healthy dose of lust, which he couldn't get a handle on, tangled up with embarrassment and shame.

Well, he imagined if he thought about it, he could blame Steve for the lust part. Steve and his stories of hot, sweaty, hard sex with partners in the past, long before his friend had fallen so damn hard for Beth. Stories of being held, of being dominated and pushed by someone of equal size, of explosive orgasms just by being told what to do. Riley had always been intrigued by that, listened intently, even asked questions. He was so used to being careful, to being so huge, so big compared to the many girls he'd slept with or, as he should label it, fucked. They all got off on it, his size, his strength, and his ability to hold them with one hand and take them over the edge. Sometimes though, in some of his kinkier hook-ups outside of the debutante market, some of which involved the exchange of monies, he enjoyed being the one to be pushed around.

And now, here he sat, with Jack moving closer, his eyes focusing on something behind Riley's head, and there was anticipation curling in his groin. His heart was quickening, and his blood racing in his arteries and veins. Jack deliberately placed his beer on the table and leaned in to talk, low and intimate, but Riley beat him to it.

"There isn't anyone here who matters for a show," he protested, even as Jack's hand slid up under the hem of his sweatshirt and touched his skin. Riley couldn't stop a full body shudder, pushing back in his chair.

Jack smiled, his lips close, damn close. "Every husband needs to mark his territory."

Thoroughly bemused, Riley spluttered when Jack bit gently on his lower lip before soothing the pressure with a touch of his tongue. Noise receded, worry receded, thoughts just vanished, and the beer bottle in his hand slid through damp fingers and clattered to the table. All that was left in his world was Jack and the fire in his blood. Far too soon he pulled away, leaving Riley anchorless.

* * * *

Jack watched out of the corner of his eye as the man at the bar turned his back. He smiled inwardly, relaxing back in his chair. He could make a career of these PDAs, especially considering how Riley freaked.

Chapter 19

"Beth, wake up, babe. Beth."

They'd fallen asleep on the sofa, Beth curled into him like a cat and his arms curved round her protectively. As the sun pushed its way through the half turned blinds, Steve knew he had to move them to somewhere more comfortable, if only to save her back, which he knew had to be aching. Half asleep, she stretched against him, leaning up to entwine her hands around his neck, pushing against his warmth and sighing.

"M'up," she murmured, wincing and stretching again. Steve wondered how much more he could take of this stretching half-purring kitten in his lap, wanting nothing more than to scoop her up and carry her to his bed. He wanted to kiss her, from her dark hair to the freckles on her face to the gentle roundness of her belly where her child was growing. He wanted so much. He just didn't know how to begin to ask.

They stumble-hugged into the kitchen, settling at the table for breakfast.

"I hope I can keep this breakfast down," Beth said miserably as she poked at the cereal Steve had placed in front of her. She'd said morning sickness hadn't been so bad, and at twenty weeks, it was in the past now, but the anxiety from last night was probably still churning inside her. He worried.

"Can I ask you a question Beth?"

"Uh huh."

"You said last night Jack knew. Did he guess? Was he cool with it?"

Beth closed her eyes and rubbed at them with small fists.

"He was devastated, Steve. He cried. He sat next to me, and he cried." Steve grasped at one of the fists, pulling it away from her face. "It was awful. I hurt him so much."

"Maybe we should have told him? You shouldn't have had to tell him alone."

"I didn't have to tell him; he knew. Somehow he knew. I didn't ask him how. I probably should."

They sat in silence, eating cereal and lost in thoughts. Finally Steve stood, rinsing bowls and idly skimming through yesterday's mail and the newspaper. In among the papers and the envelopes, one article on the inside pages of yesterday's paper caught his eye, and the world fell from beneath his feet.

Son of a bitch.

* * * *

Jeff hated these clandestine meetings. He cursed his little brother for forcing him into this position.

"Just the Campbell family. No one hurts my brother. Well, not much anyway."

* * * *

"Mr Murray is here," his secretary announced even as Steve pushed into Riley's office. His face was carefully blank, and his eyes full of something Riley couldn't define. He scrambled to stand, then he rounded the desk. A pissed Steve was something that worried him. It took a lot to get his friend upset, and in the far reaches of his mind, Riley knew why Steve was here.

"Steve—" he began, holding his hands up to placate his only real friend, wanting to say "I'm sorry" but unable to speak the words before Steve's clenched fist connected with his cheekbone and sent him staggering back against his desk. He ducked, but the next punch connected with his temple, and he felt a sudden dizziness as his head snapped back. Steve was looming over him, pushing him back on the desk, his hands wrapped in Riley's shirt as he shook him.

"What the fuck have you done, Riley?"

"Steve—" Another blow connected with his chin, and Riley had nowhere else to go. Summoning every bit of strength, he pushed back at Steve. It was like trying to move a brick wall. Finally he managed to get a handle on it, moving away from Steve, blood dripping from a cut on his forehead, and his hands out in front of him again.

Steve was breathing hard, a hand unconsciously over his heart, and Riley winced at the sight. He'd never meant for this to happen.

"What did you do, Riley?" Steve repeated, his voice controlled now. "I told you about Elizabeth Campbell in confidence, as my best friend. You know what she means to me. And you do what? You use it to get Campbell into bed with you? What the fuck?"

"Steve, I'm sorry. It's not what you think." *No, not just into bed. Not at all. Just to get what is rightfully mine…*

"Not what I think? Are you telling me you didn't somehow use what I told you about Beth against her own brother?"

What could Riley say? It was exactly what he *had* done. He was standing in front of his best friend, the only one who looked through the Hayes name and saw a man capable of more. Now, that man was destroying the friendship as easily as snapping a pencil. No. He had destroyed it himself. Final. Sudden.

Steve began backing from the room, his hand blindly finding the handle behind him. *Are those tears in his eyes?* "You bastard!"

"Steve. Wait. Talk to me," Riley was pleading. "Let me explain."

"No," Steve said simply, and he slipped from the room, leaving Riley bleeding and guilt-ridden in the map room.

How could they ever get back from this?

Chapter 20

They slipped into a routine as Mr and Mr Campbell-Hayes. Riley spent his days at Hayes Oil, and Jack spent his at the D. Early mornings and late evenings, they came together at the Hayes Mansion, having breakfasts and dinners in the simmering cauldron of bitterness that was the Hayes family.

Jack had simply nodded when Riley explained the bruised face. Well, not explained exactly, but waved it away. He mumbled something about Steve and a fight, and Jack didn't pry. Riley took to pulling his hair across the cut to hide it from curious eyes, and luckily none of the paparazzi shots showed anything other than Riley relaxed and at ease with his smiling husband.

Articles came and went, and within a week, the story had been mostly forgotten. It didn't seem to matter how rich Riley was, or how much of a ladies' man he had been before. Somehow it seemed like the marriage was controversial, but acceptable. Money obviously did buy a lot of things in Jack's opinion, including the influence to stop printing stories, the responsibility for which he laid squarely at Gerald's door. Gerald, who refused to look at him let alone talk to him, which was really very okay with him.

Twice they revisited Shooters, and twice, Jack felt public PDAs were necessary. Twice he almost lost it by dragging Riley in for more. It was becoming increasingly difficult for Jack to remember he hated the man. They held hands in the house, kissed in the house, always the show, always when an audience was close, but when the doors shut on the world outside, that was the end of it.

* * * *

Down time meant Jack lost on his laptop, calculating feed and finances, planning visits for breeders and riders keen on Solo-Col's foal, and Riley idly doodling in his journal.

If Jack saw what Riley doodled, what his husband's brain was thinking up, then he may well have wondered what exactly Riley was doing with this whole fair-percentage, arranged marriage thing. Riley's plans were complex, a company of his own —an ethical land exploration company— away from Hayes Oil. Each night the journal was locked away in the safe in the apartment, testament to Riley's reluctance to share his thoughts with the world just yet.

* * * *

The Saturday of the party had been and gone. It was an event Jack listed as yet another facet to his husband's complex, and sometimes bizarre, personality. Riley had relaxed, easy given the only Hayeses in attendance besides him, were Riley's nephew, Luke, as spoiled as any seven-year-old could be, his sister Annabelle, Lisa, and Eden. Add in twenty or so other children, ice cream, and a bouncy castle, and it was hyper Riley at his best.

And then there was tonight.

The first real function they were attending as a married couple, some annual fundraiser for a charity Jack had never heard of. Still, he had agreed to all of this in the contract. So, donning black tie, he was pacing the apartment waiting on Riley who, yet again, was getting changed in the bathroom. Jack laughed to himself. If Riley knew Jack watched him when he slept, he would probably freak, given that, when he was awake he covered everything. Jack spent many lust-filled minutes staring at exposed skin when Riley's sleep T-shirt pulled up. Last night he'd even contemplated leaning forward and tasting the younger man, and that was something that would certainly worry Riley.

"Come on, man." Jack really hated being late; it was a pet peeve of his, and he could feel his irritation rising, only to completely disappear when Riley came out of the bathroom. Every molecule of oxygen was sucked from Jack in a flash. *Jeez, holy hell on a stick.* Six-four of Riley, with his hair brushed back, his face smooth of stubble, the tux. *Jeez, the tux.* It molded every muscle and every inch of his broad shoulders and was enough to tempt a saint. Riley paused outside the bathroom, the intensity of Jack's gaze obviously unsettling him, causing him to glance back over his shoulder to check if there was someone behind him.

"Erm—" Riley began, a blush rising on his cheeks, his hand going to his hair to pull it forward over his face. Jack was there in an instant, catching the hand midway.

"Leave the hair, Het-boy," he managed to force out. "Let's go."

* * * *

The journey was made in an uncomfortable silence, Riley driving, and both men lost in their own thoughts as they headed straight to the center of

Dallas. The skyline was closer, the buildings taller, and the apprehension in both men darker and persistent.

When they reached the venue, they left the car with the valet, and the next five minutes was a blur of holding hands, exchanging small demonstrative kisses and accepting congratulations from TV and tabloid journalists alike.

It was a sit-down four course dinner, but there was a lot of standing around time, which meant guests could mingle as much as they wanted. This ended up with Riley mingling, and Jack doing the whole hanging 'round the drinks area shuffle.

When dinner was finally served, Riley was seated next to his husband, watching as he picked at the plate before him.

"Jack," he whispered, leaning in close, "aren't you hungry?"

"Yeah, but I'll wait until the meat arrives," Jack replied, just as softly.

"Jack, the salad *is* the main course. Look, it's huge. Seriously, there's no meat coming." There was a shot of amusement in his words.

"You've got to be fucking kidding me. You're joking, right?" Jack looked horrified, which only added to Riley's amusement levels.

"Hardly. You don't need meat at every meal," Riley offered, forking another bite of salad into his mouth and inwardly agreeing with Jack that it was certainly lacking something.

Jack was quiet for all of ten seconds, and then he couldn't hold in his opinion one second more. "Are you really a Texan? I mean, really? Riley, if I have a headache, I'd put bacon around an aspirin before I take it."

Riley just smirked and shook his head, distracted by a conversation to the left. This left Jack to pick morosely through the salad leaves and unidentifiable chunks of vegetable swimming in some kind of oil. Riley was almost sure he heard a muttered; "We better stop at McDonalds on the way back to the apartment."

* * * *

Dinner finally over, they separated. Jack back to the drinks, nursing his second whisky that evening, and watching Riley making the rounds as was expected of him. Watching and growing more and more irritated at the simpering women falling all over *his* husband, touching *his* husband's body, his hair, like he was some sort of prime rib at a barbecue. Not only that, but the bastard seemed to be enjoying it if his open smile was anything to go by, and he wasn't exactly pushing them away. The itch of irritation grew and twisted until finally enough was enough. The final straw was seeing Rachel Adams, an ex of Riley's, drape herself around him, signaling in no uncertain terms that she was clearly interested in some kind of reunion. Eyes narrowed, Jack watched her brush against *his property*, her hands low on Riley's crotch.

That was it. In a few quick strides, he was at Riley's side, cutting in between Rachel, vacuous blonde number four, and simpering brunette number three. Smoothly separating Riley from their clutches with a polite "Excuse me", he guided his husband out of the main room and into the darkened corridor before Riley could protest.

* * * *

Jack paced, and Riley stood. Jack fumed, and Riley waited.

Finally Riley said what he thought Jack probably needed to hear, some kind of defense of what he'd allowed to happen. "I was just—"

He didn't get to finish. Jack crowded him against the wall, and *shit*, Riley was getting tired of being pushed around like this. Jack made him feel like some kind of naughty kid, and damn if it wasn't riling him to the point of losing it here and now. Then Jack's hand went south as quick as he could say *Holy shit*, and everything changed.

* * * *

Unerringly locating Riley's dick in his loose dress pants, Jack grabbed it forcefully and leaned close to Riley's ear, hearing the quick indrawn breath from his husband. A spark of lust flashed through his own body as he contemplated what to do next. Finally he decided. He was tired of all the pussy-footing around, and the darkness of the hallway invited sin. He moved his hand on Riley's hard dick, listening to the groan in Riley's throat.

"Riley, you know who this belongs to? This belongs to me." He gentled the touch, twisting his hand. "I saw you flirting and sharing with those girls out there, and I'm telling you now, I don't share. No one else gets to see this. No one else gets to touch it. No one else gets to taste it. Just me. It's mine for one *whole* year, and I have the contract to prove it."

Riley tried to form a reply as Jack moved his hand again. It was good to see the other man speechless for once.

"Don't worry though, *husband.* I'm gonna treat it so good. I've decided that I'm gonna make it, *and you,* feel so damn good you'll never look at another woman again. You only have to say the word, and I'll show you what you signed up for." His voice fell into a heated whisper, the words low and drawled. "Now do we need to get out of here? I'm thinking I might need to take you home and show you who you belong to." Riley's eyes widened, his dick fully hard, iron in Jack's clever hands. "I can make you scream. You wouldn't even know your name when I finished with you."

"Jack—please." Riley's voice was broken. Everything Jack wanted to hear.

"Please?"

Riley blinked, unconsciously pushing his groin into Jack's hold. Jack knew what followed next was certainly not a decision Riley made with his upstairs brain. "Fuck, Jack. Let's get the hell out of here."

They took the back door and were in the car within the space of minutes, neither saying anything. Jack was so fucking hard, knowing Riley was just as hot for this.

They only made it halfway home. Riley pulled off the road into an empty parking area. The engine was silent for mere seconds before Jack was there, pulling Riley away from the wheel and pushing him down as fast as he could. His lips were stealing kisses. The taste of his husband was intoxicating, and he bit into soft flesh. The touches were uncoordinated, desperate, like nothing Jack had ever experienced before. Jack's hands were at Riley's dress slacks, ripping at the zipper and button, encouraging Riley to lift his hips.

It was messy, and it was fast and clumsy. Hands were replaced with his mouth, and in the quickest movement Jack had ever made on a lover, he closed his mouth over the tip of Riley's hard dick, swirling his tongue and then impatiently swallowing him deeper. He used his work-roughened hands, alternating between jacking him off in the space between his mouth and the curls at the base of Riley's sex, and moving to cup his balls, gently, then more firmly. Jack was almost coming himself, just at the intense needy noises leaving Riley's mouth, his hands flailing to catch hold of something, anything, before gripping Jack's short hair.

Two weeks of lust that had built inside them, two weeks of teasing and unrestrained touching were enough to have orgasm curling at the base of Jack's spine. His fingers brushed Riley, at the tight ring of muscle, and it was all too much for his husband. Fisting his hands tighter in Jack's hair, Riley arched and was coming fast and uncontrolled. Jack swallowed and tasted, releasing the tight suction of his mouth with little finesse. He tugged his own slacks open, wet slick hands jacking himself off and his shadowed form curling into Riley as ropes of cum decorated his hand and Riley's jacket.

Jack brought his cum-covered hand up to Riley's mouth, pushing the spider web of white inside on shaking fingers and leaning for an open kiss. The taste and texture of his cum was mixed with the taste of Riley's skin. It was lust, it was need, and it was heaven. Breathing heavily, Jack heaved himself up and away, leaning against the opposite side of the car. Riley was lying immobile, his face stony in shock.

Fuck, Jack thought, *so much for no sex for a year*.

Chapter 21

Jack didn't know what to say. He really had no idea that his teasing and prodding and then the whole grabbing his husband's dick would end with possibly the hottest, most intense, sexual experience of his life. He blinked steadily at Riley, who was way over on the other side of the car, pressed against the door, silent and still, shock carved onto his features. The tension in the space was palpable, and Jack imagined Riley's heart was beating the same frantic rhythm as his. He watched in fascination as Riley wiped the back of his hand across his mouth, looking down at it as if he could see evidence of what Jack had just done, of what *they* had just done.

"You're not gay," Jack said, quite proud of his achievement in stringing together those three words. Riley said nothing at first, just blinked steadily.

Finally Riley simply said, "I pulled the car over." Like that explanation was enough to explain why he wasn't running for the hills, screaming.

"Then your dick was more than a little interested in a little man-on-man action," Jack pointed out, wincing as he spoke and at the frown growing on Riley's face.

"I've been with other men before," Riley frowned.

"Yeah, just not with ones you blackmailed into marriage."

"This is serious," Riley snapped. "It's clear I'm obviously having some sort of no sex rule breakdown."

"After two weeks?" Jack snorted, despite the fact that he'd been feeling the effect as well.

"More like three," Riley replied thoughtfully. Jack looked over at a half dressed Riley, his shirt pulled high, laid out in front of him, and he cursed that he wanted to lean over and taste more. He was the instigator here, his damn pride demanding he determine if Riley was okay with this.

"So let me get this straight," he said. "You've gone without sex for three whole weeks, and it has, all of a sudden, overnight, turned you gay for me?"

As he spoke he straightened his clothes and moved to his knees to loom over the man, trapping him against the door. He could smell Riley, the smell of his cologne, the smell of arousal, the smell of sex, and he leaned in until his lips were mere fractions of an inch from sun darkened skin stretched across high cheekbones, his breath hot against that skin. He didn't say anything, just hovered, waiting— hesitating.

Outside, the dry storm that had been threatening all day, broke with startling brilliance. A shaft of lightning tore the air in two outside the SUV, illuminating hazel eyes and showing a flash of desire previously hidden in their depths. The lightning startled both men, and Riley moved subtly so that Jack's lips touched skin.

He could feel Riley's whole body shudder and hear the neediness in the small unconscious noise that originated in Riley's throat, and Jack couldn't help himself. Slowly, he traced small open-mouthed kisses on Riley's face, across the cheekbones, feathering across eyelids that closed against the touch, and down to soft lips that parted on a sigh. Jack slanted his mouth, the touch of tongues sliding, teeth nipping and tugging at full lips, his dick hard and ready for round two. He wanted so much of this man, and it didn't seem to matter to his sexual self that part of it still felt wrong. Gently he eased back, needing to say something.

The lightning flashed around the car and lit up the uncertainty in Riley's eyes. Jack sighed, resting his forehead against Riley's. This was a man who had blackmailed him, made him believe he had no option but to marry him, for reasons that, to Jack, made no sense.

How was it that the feelings inside him were all about lust and need when they should have been about hate and revenge?

"We need to talk," Jack said. "We can work this out. You're not gay. We'll get a second bed and look after the apartment ourselves. We can chalk this up to a bad night. I can keep my hands off you. This was you and alcohol, nothing more."

"I didn't drink anything," Riley replied quietly. Was that disappointment in those gentle words? It certainly sounded like it.

"But *I* did, and I clearly took advantage of you." Jack started to move back, but Riley grabbed at his arm to stop him.

* * * *

Riley looked down at himself, at two hundred twenty pound of muscle and more than average height and then over to Jack, who despite being solid as a rock and only five inches shorter, was probably an even physical match to Riley.

"I'm not some fainting virgin, not some tiny girl that you have *forced* yourself on. Believe me, cowboy, if I hadn't wanted it, then you wouldn't have gotten it." Riley finished the sentence with steel determination in his voice.

"Riley," Jack sighed again, "I haven't felt enough lust to touch and take like that since I was a horny sixteen-year-old and tryin' to get into Mike Hollister's pants."

"And your point is?" Riley was trying to stay calm even as he released Jack's arm and let the man slide back down into his seat.

"Like I said, we need to talk."

"Let's go home then— to talk." Riley added the last bit on the end, thinking *friends with benefits* in his head, his dick hard in the twisted material of his pants and his breathing shallow. Pulling the material together, he fastened the fly and turned back to the wheel, sliding on his belt and starting the engine. He looked back over his shoulder at the road behind them, ready to pull out.

"Riley, the storm," Jack said suddenly. "I really need to check on the horses. Can we maybe talk at the D?"

Riley's heart twisted at that, the suddenness with which he thought that was a good idea overwhelming him. Just to stand in the scarred kitchen, watching Donna bake, watching Beth tease her brother was like some kind of 1950's sitcom, surreal and warm.

"Yeah," Riley agreed, and U-turned away from the Hayes mausoleum and towards the D. It felt good to just be driving, his skin prickling from the electricity in the air, his head full to bursting with what had just happened. That he'd let Jack do that —take him to the edge and over it— surprised him. The loss of control was bewildering and new.

Jack was clearly as lost in thought as he was, and neither said a word. Anticipation thrummed in Riley's veins as they neared the D, and he was so deep in thought considering what had happened, that he only just managed to swerve to avoid a dark SUV barreling down the center of the road. He cursed viciously, slandering the parentage of the out-of-towners, and caught sight of the smile that curved Jack's mouth.

* * * *

They turned onto the D, the same pride washing over Jack as they passed under the curved D's and began the mile trek to the main house, the plush SUV cushioning them from most of the potholes. Jack stretched each muscle, thinking on the horses in the barns and how they might be reacting to the electrical disturbance of the intense storm. Solo-Cal was only a week away from foaling, just one run of seven days, and he knew his baby was restless in storms. He hoped Riley would understand if he suggested he had to sleep in there with them tonight.

The flicker on the horizon as the dark buildings loomed in front of them was nothing more than a reflection of lightning. Jack was sure of it, until it grew stronger, orange, steadier against the dark sky, and suddenly dread stabbed him like a knife.

Before Riley had even stopped the car, Jack was out, screaming against the wind and the heat, "Call 911 and get Mom and Beth out of the house!"

The main horse barn was on fire.

The blaze was a living, breathing thing, climbing wood, destroying feed, and devouring everything in its path. Jack didn't hesitate. Even though it would fuel the flames, he threw the big doors wide and raced from stall to stall, releasing the horses so they could stampede to safety. The fire had started two-thirds of the way inside the barn and was already spreading up into the hayloft. It was also blocking his way to the last two horses. His precious brood-mares. Jack dove through the conflagration. Solo-Cal and Taylor-Wood were rearing in their stalls, fear in their whinnies, fire reflecting in their wide staring eyes.

He needed to get his babies out. Dodging debris that hissed and spat, he pulled off his shirt and wrapped it around Taylor's head, blindfolding her. The mare's panic eased a little, enough for him to loop a rope over her neck and lead her out of the stall. Then Riley was skidding to a halt next to him, gauging the situation and pulling off his own shirt, covering Solo's eyes as best he could.

The only way out was through the main doors no more than forty feet away, but that meant through the barrier of flames and smoke. Crooning to the shaking mare, Jack coaxed her into a trot and ran with her, holding his breath as they passed through the blaze. He could hear Riley and Solo behind him, the mare squealing as wisps of burning straw landed on her. They were almost there. So very close. Part of the upper floor cracked and split and tumbled behind them, and they were out.

With a final effort, Jack managed to guide Taylor well away from the fire and to the far fence, turning back to see Riley leading Solo out after them. He shared a grin of success with his husband, who raised a hand in salute. The shirt slipped from Solo's eyes, and the horse bucked in fear, twisting in terror of the flames. Unable to shout over the noise of the fire and the storm, Jack knew he would never reach Riley in time. All he could do was watch as Solo spun on her heels, forcing Riley to leap back. Beth was there as well, reaching up to snag a rope about the mare's neck. Solo lashed out, her hooves narrowly missing Beth.

Riley pushed between the horse and the girl, thrusting Beth aside as Solo's hooves plunged towards them again. Beth fell and rolled to safety under the bottom rail, but Riley was crushed brutally against the white fence before Solo lunged away to join the other horses milling in the drive.

Distantly aware that Beth and his mom were herding the horses into the paddock farthest from the blaze, Jack dashed to Riley's side. He was unconscious, blood frothing at his mouth. A lung was surely pierced.

Thunder exploded over their heads, and the rain fell in a blinding sheet. It was chaos, the fire department arriving as the last flames were flickering and dying in the rain, the paramedics lifting Riley into the ambulance, and the lights flashing randomly in the inky blackness of the night.

The fire department waited, damping down what was left of the barn. The lightning damage had been so instant, so complete, so devastating, that there was only a twisting shell of black wood standing as testament to the stables Jack's grandfather had built. They muttered that the storm had been a blessing as well as a curse. It may have started the fire, but even as the flames had reached destructive arms for the main house, the rain had extinguished them.

Chapter 22

The hospital was quiet. The Emergency Department was temporarily empty apart from a few traffic accident casualties and Riley.

Beth stood in the hospital lounge, a protective hand across her belly, her daughter a gentle movement under her palm, and gave thanks. The rain may have saved the house, but Riley had saved her and her child. And he'd saved Jack as well, because she knew he would have tried to rescue both horses and would still have been in the barn when the roof fell if Riley hadn't gone in to help him.

Riley's cell was still in her other hand. She'd scrolled down the numbers to find the one she needed and held her breath until it was answered, only letting out a sigh of relief when the cheerful voice identified itself as Eden Hayes.

"Eden, it's Beth Campbell, Jack's sister. It's your brother. There's been an accident."

* * * *

Eden sat in disbelief at her brother's side, the pain in her heart overwhelmed only by the pain in her head.

Your brother has internal bleeding
He needs blood.

His blood type is A negative—
accident on the highway— used our
reserves— we have some flying in— need to
operate soon— can you donate?

* * * *

Sandra Hayes had only done what every rich trophy wife did in defense of their social position. She wasn't going to lose her status or her money, and the promise she'd made twenty-seven years ago when she held her new baby in her arms would not be broken now.

She listened as Eden explained. "So we need blood, Mom. You need to come to the hospital, and you need to get tested for a match." She didn't know what to say; she simply passed the phone to Gerald, who was looming over her with a questioning expression.

* * * *

"Eden?" he asked.

"It's Riley, Daddy. He's in the hospital, and he's been badly hurt. He needs blood. Daddy, please help."

Gerald looked at his wife, at the stretched skin on her face, at the diamonds in her ears, and the vacant expression in her eyes. Hate built inside him. They had promised and made a deal: her silence in exchange for his support of the bastard son, the result of many one-night stands and affairs from his *untrained* wife.

Now he had her leashed and she'd been so since the day he'd agreed to pass Riley off as his son. He wasn't about to run to save Riley. Actually it solved quite a few problems for him if Riley were to die. It was certainly a solution to dividing out the business, the problem that had been plaguing him for some time. It was such a shame that the brains of Hayes Oil, the one son of his that had the instinct for oil, wasn't even his own damn blood. Fury and frustration flooded him as he listened to Eden begging for him to come save her beloved brother, talking about rare blood types and antigens. There had to be a way he could turn this to his advantage.

How could he delay going? What excuse could he use? He knew damn well he wouldn't be a match for Riley even if he did go. He wanted to say, "Well, good luck finding a match, Eden. I hope your mom is a match, because he sure as hell doesn't share my blood." But he didn't. He said nothing; he simply handed the phone back to Sandra, who assured Eden they would try and get there as soon as possible if they could, maybe…

Sandra looked at her husband, the only sign of her anxiety a faint trembling in her right hand, and he stared right back.

"They'll find out," she said, her voice low and tremulous.

"Not if he dies, they won't," Gerald said, dryly, turning back to his book and sipping his expensive whisky. "Let's face it, you should have terminated him when you found out you were pregnant but didn't know which one of your many men could have been the father."

"Gerald—"

"Enough, Sandra, enough."

* * * *

She slipped, like the ghost she was, up to their rooms. Her heart, what was left of it, was in pieces. Her son. The one good thing that had come out of her plan to escape so many years before, and now he was dying. She wished she was able to show her love for Riley. But she'd acted the part of Dallas high society wife for so long, it had become very close to reality. She had never been a real mother to her boy. So many times when she heard the hate in her own voice, looked at him as he grew tall and strong, she regretted the act she needed to keep up. She regretted it and sought some kind of atonement, throwing herself into charity works that helped the abandoned children, the homeless single mothers. She regretted it until the best champagne numbed her senses, until her money gave her prestige, until the Hayes name gave her safety. Then there was no regret.

But there was one thing she could do to give her son a fighting chance. If he needed the rare blood, then Riley's father needed to know. Contrary to what Gerald believed, there had only been one man that fall of 1981, one man who had loved her, a young intern in Hayes Oil who had worshipped the very ground she walked on and shown her what love should be.

She dialed the number she knew by heart, and he answered on the third ring.

"It's me. Can you come to the hospital? There's been an accident and —Riley— he needs you."

* * * *

It had been nearly five hours since the fire when Jack half-ran into the emergency room, sliding to a halt next to Eden. She was hunched uncomfortably on the hard plastic chairs in the lounge, Beth perched beside her.

"I had ta get the horses safe. Fuck, I'm sorry. Is he okay? What's happening, Eden?"

Eden lifted tear-filled eyes to his, seeing cuts and abrasions on her new brother-in-law's face and blood on his shirt. She could hardly string the words together, fear twisting inside her. "I don't know. He's in the operating room. They… needed blood… his blood type." She shook her head, confused, exhausted, in shock, assuming her mom and dad were somewhere in the hospital, because Riley had received the blood he needed. "We won't know for a while."

Jack pulled her in for a quick hug, his clothes reeking of smoke and horses. Then he strode to the desk, asking questions, demanding answers. Beth moved closer to Eden, and Eden felt a hand curling around her shoulders. Eden could only cry for what had happened to the brother she adored.

Jack went back to stand with them. "They don't know more than you do. Do you know much blood he lost?"

"I don't know. He has internal bleeding. Mom and Dad donated." Jack nodded. Eden knew it was at times like this that a real family pulled together. It was good to see that, despite their obvious problems, at the end of the day the Hayeses knew that family was family. A sob left Eden, and she hunched forward in her seat, murmuring just one word, *Riley*.

"I know he saved my life," Beth said softly. Eden leaned into the embrace.

"Can you tell me what happened?" Eden asked.

So Beth started to explain how Riley had pushed her away, taking the brunt of the bucking horse.

* * * *

"No one will know it wasn't the storm," Jeff said simply.

"So we can guarantee the end of the whole horse business for the Campbells then? Do you really think this will be enough?" Gerald was curious as to how this plan of Jeff's was going to work.

"It's simple; the barn will be gone, along with Jack's dreams and his two brood mares. Given that I'm assuming the pre-nup gives him no money inside of the marriage or after divorce, he'll crumble. We'll slip in, work that vulnerability, and offer him money to help."

"Then he'll agree to our terms," Gerald said. "We can arrange an annulment, and it's the end of the problem."

Jeff nodded eagerly. "Riley doesn't fulfill the terms of the contract you drew up, as divorce or annulment cancels the contract. I get to keep my controlling percentage, and my younger brother learns his place."

"Yes, that he does."

* * * *

"Can I ask how my son is doing?" he asked gruffly, his voice still thick with unshed tears and a grief cutting deep into his heart.

"He is still in surgery, sir. Would you like to go up with the rest of the family? I can take you."

He stood silently for a while, looking down at the papers he had signed, and then back at the understanding face of the blood bank nurse. He coughed. He couldn't handle sympathy or understanding at the moment, knowing it might push him over the edge.

"No. It wouldn't be…" He searched for the right word. "Appropriate," he finally offered. "I'll wait here for news." He had known. In his heart, he had known all this time that Riley was his. It was the only reason why he stayed at Hayes Oil, so he could watch his son grow into the man he was so proud of. Jim Bailey had known.

Chapter 23

Eden didn't know what to say to Steve, even as she looked for his number with shaking fingers. She knew for some reason Steve and Riley had argued, but over what she didn't know. Hell, he needed to know his best friend was hurt, and jeez, Beth looked dead on her feet. She needed her friend here, even if he didn't want to see Riley.

"You can go if you want," Eden had said to the slim woman who stood at her side. "I'll be okay."

"You're family. I stay," Beth had replied simply, warmth in her eyes.

It made Eden blink back tears, to hear those simple words. So much time had passed since the family she knew had done anything except fight and scheme and destroy. Even Riley had lost it along the way. She wasn't stupid. She could see him changing every day that Hayes Oil had him in their clutches; he'd been becoming harder and more determined to win at all costs. To have Beth next to her, showing her own brand of unconditional support, it was so easy to drift into a place where people actually appeared to give a damn about her and Riley.

She thumbed through the contacts to find Steve's number, his familiar "Yo,

Eden" a jolt to her heart. She always wondered why he put up with the shit the Hayes family dumped on him. The meals where comments were made on his lifestyle, where his heart condition was laid out for discussion in cold hard facts, the times Riley just dragged him upstairs to avoid the vitriol. Still he stayed. He visited for Riley. He was Riley's only real friend, and the only one who saw through the crap. Eden always thought that Gerald Hayes liked Riley friendless. It kept controlling his middle child that much easier.

"Eden?" Steve's voice sounded puzzled. Eden wasn't usually this silent, and given it was four in the morning, it would be obvious something wasn't right, "Eden, you're scaring me, babe. Where are you?"

"It's Riley. There's been an accident. He— I need you, and Beth needs you. Can you come, Steve?"

There was no hesitation in Steve's voice. "Are you at Mercy?"

"Yes."

"I'll be there in ten."

The phone went silent in her ear, and she pulled it away as the call ended message flashed on the screen, meeting Beth's eyes full of compassion and understanding, and suddenly she couldn't take any more. They had said it would be another hour at least, that it could be many more than that, and she needed air, needed to breathe.

"I'll get coffee," she said abruptly, and before Beth could touch her, or say a thing, she fled the lounge.

"He's all she has," Jack offered quietly, encouraging his sister to come sit with him, offering her his arm to lean on. "At the house, there is no one for Eden except for Riley, and the same for Riley. He only has Eden."

"That's really sad," Beth said softly, her hand on her belly, reassuring herself that everything was okay. "To have no one left."

The door swung open to reveal a disheveled Josh standing in the doorway, his eyes frantic to find Jack, and the relief was blatantly obvious as he found him. Jack stood to greet his brother, pulling Beth with them until the three stood in a close embrace.

* * * *

Donna waited in the doorway, seeing her children there for each other, together. There was sadness inside her that Alan had never taken the time to see this love in the family. He'd never seen that she'd chosen *him* over Hayes, that her love for him was enough for her. She didn't need money and prestige and a name that mattered in the pages of the *Dallas Morning News*. For all their issues, it was times like these when she missed her husband and his wide smile. She missed the start of their relationship when they had love and affection and had run away to marry, conceiving Josh in a small no-tell motel outside the Vegas main strip. Her eyes went to Beth. It wasn't right that Josh was the only one of them that didn't know his sister was expecting. He needed to know. They were a family.

"Beth?" The siblings pulled apart, Beth's face wet with tears and the boys visibly shaken, but stronger for having each other. "It seems like maybe we should share your news with Josh."

* * * *

Eden rounded the corner, hot coffee in her insulated vending cup, heading for the blood bank. Her parents might be useless, and her family might be dysfunctional, but one of them, either her ice-cold mom or her scarlet-tempered dad, had donated the blood that Riley needed. There had to be some kind of redemption there. What she found in the blood bank was not what she expected, but it pleased her to see the man she called uncle standing with a similar cup of coffee in his hand.

"Hi, Uncle J," she said, her spirits lifting.

He glanced over, blinking steadily. It was confusing not to see his usual smile of welcome, but instead a look of shock on his face.

"Eden," he said so softly she had to strain to hear, and then he held out his arms. She cuddled in to the familiarity of the man who let her color pictures in his office and who'd been her show and tell project at school on three occasions. He was the man who had taught her to ride a bike, build a tree swing, and how to handle boys, and she loved him totally.

"Are you here with Dad?" she asked into his soft T-shirt. Her nose was tickling at the splitting logo on the front, something to do with his beloved football she assumed. She leaned back in his arms to look past his salt and pepper beard to his lips, pressed together in a harsh line, his eyes full of something. Something that almost looked like fear.

"No, Eden, your father isn't here."

"Mom then?"

"No."

"So they left?" Eden was bewildered. Surely they would have at least spoken to someone about Riley?

Stayed to see he was okay? Eden felt the sigh run through Jim and the rise and fall of his chest under her hands, and she dropped them to rest on his arms, touching something that felt like… a bandage.

Eyes widening, she looked up at him in shock and sudden, instant, realization.

"They're not here, Eden."

"Why? Were they here? Did they go? Is something wrong?" Eden's voice was broken, and her eyes searched his, looking for some kind of denial or answer to her unspoken question.

"I think we should sit down, Eden," Jim said simply, guiding her to sit and half turning towards her. "I've wanted to tell Riley for so long."

"Tell him what?"

"Riley is my son." Eden stared back at him, a myriad of emotions on her face.

"Are you *my* father?" There was hope in the question.

Jim cupped her face in strong capable hands. "Oh, baby, you don't know how much I wish I was your father as well as Riley's."

Eden held out her hand, determination in her words. "You need to come with me, to be with the family."

Jim tugged back. "I can't, Eden. You don't understand. Your mom and I—"

"Just come with me Uncle J. Trust me. Riley will want to thank his daddy."

"I want to, Eden." He stopped, finally tugging his hand away. "But I won't. Riley doesn't have much from his family, apart from you, but at least he has his name, and that's important to him. I won't destroy that."

* * * *

Josh sat back on his seat, his mouth open in an O of surprise. "Expectin'?" he parroted what she had just said, paling as she nodded. "Your heart, Beth." He was only saying what everyone else had said to her.

"I've seen a specialist. It can be okay," she offered helplessly, knowing what he needed to hear, that his little sister was going to be fine, but it just couldn't be said.

"Can be okay?" Josh stood and stared into her eyes for a moment. "Who did this to you?" he finally demanded, startled as Jack made to stand between them, ever the pacifier in their sibling rows.

"She won't say, Josh, and we shouldn't push it." There was fire in

Jack's eyes. Fire and determination for the matter to be laid to rest. Josh simply nodded, and she knew what he thought— there'd be time for details later, when paternity tests could be carried out with no room for error. Jack took a step back, obviously trusting their older brother to do the right thing, and in one smooth movement, Josh had pulled Beth into him for a hug, and was saying the things she needed to hear.

Releasing her, he pulled Jack into a bear hug and then stood back. "It's about time we get to share being an uncle!"

Beth smiled up at her brothers. It was good that they both knew. Very good.

Chapter 24

Jack closed the cell, a smile on his face that belied the worry he was feeling about his husband. One piece of good news— momma and baby doing well. The veterinarian gave the usual provisos. Solo's foal was strong but premature, and she'd need care, but Solo's injuries were minimal as well.

"Mr Campbell-Hayes?" The nurse stood at the door, looking expectantly from Josh to Jack.

"Me," Jack replied, standing abruptly. "Is Riley okay?"

"If you come with me, the surgeon would like to talk to you." Glancing back at his family, strengthened by their unspoken support, he followed her to the side room where a man stood, hardly older than him. Everything he said was a blur.

"Everything went well— nicked an artery— blood transfusions from his father—unconscious— sleeping—"

"Can I see him?" *Can I just touch him and maybe check that he's still alive?*

"The nurse will take you through as soon as he's situated in ICU. Do you have any further questions?" Jack tried to follow what he was saying. He had hundreds of questions… *What happened? Why did Riley push Beth out of the way?*

Why did he run right into the fire? He just had none that he had to ask to surgeon. So thanking him and shaking his hand, he turned to follow the nurse who babbled on about having someone famous in the OR and the last time that had happened it had been some bit actor off of *Dynasty*, way, way back. Jack half listened, apprehension rising in him, wondering if he should go back and get Josh, or his mom, just to… to what? Hold his hand? Hell, he was an adult, not a kid. He could handle one unconscious husband.

The door opened, and he listened carefully as she said not to look too closely, that each tube and wire was there for a reason.

"He's out of any danger; everything went well."

He thanked her, delaying looking at Riley until the very last minute. Until, *finally*, he was there, next to his husband's bed, looking down at the tall man, impossibly pale against the white sheets. He didn't look hurt. Every sign of the injury he'd received was hidden under hospital issue sheets and bandages. He simply looked peaceful, his hair pushed back from his face, his eyelids shut, and his lips separated by a tube disappearing into his mouth. Sighing Jack traced a finger from his forehead to throat, gently touching each mole, each inch of skin. Fear gripped him. How was he going to talk to this man when he finally opened his eyes? How could he possibly thank him for what he'd done for Beth?

Scooting a chair closer, he slumped into it. He obviously now had time to think, and he was here for the long haul.

* * * *

Steve took the stairs, too impatient to wait for the elevator, bursting into the family room in a flurry of early morning air and panic. He sought Beth, found her, pulling her close in a frenzied hug. He then leaned back, looked at her pale face and tamped down the need to push her into a bed to sleep.

"Talk to me," he ordered swiftly, half turning to Josh, looking for answers.

"There was a fire at the D," Beth started.

"Are you okay, Beth? Is the baby okay?" Steve looked down at her belly and back up at her beautiful eyes, drowning in the depths of tear-bright blue.

Beth smiled softly, nodding. "I'm fine."

"So how bad is Riley?" Eden asked. "Is he out of surgery yet?"

"They took Jack out to talk," Josh said. "I think it's gonna be okay. The nurse was smiling." He stood to one side and looked from Steve to Beth and back again.

"Are you really okay?" Steve pulled Beth close.

"Riley put himself between me and the horse. He protected me from injury and probably saved the baby's life. He went in and helped Jack bring the horses out. If he hadn't, Jack would have been in there when it collapsed. Please, Steve, whatever made the two of you fall out, can you not forget, just for today?"

"He—" Steve stopped the words on his lips, words that would damn Riley in front of his husband's family. He couldn't say them, couldn't even begin to string them together. "Okay, okay, shall we get you home, eh?" He looked at Josh, who nodded his approval. "I'll take her back to my apartment," he confirmed, kissing away the dissent in Beth's voice and clutching her hand. "Will you let us know?"

* * * *

Josh waited until his sister and Steve had left, crossing to close the door behind them and turning back to his mom. She was sitting quietly to one side, observing everything that was happening with a careful eye.

"Is Steve the dad?" Josh asked his mom, wanting the truth.

"She's saying nothing, but in my heart, I don't think it is Steve. I'm not sure how their relationship has evolved, but no, it isn't Steve."

Josh subsided back into silence, crossing his legs and pulling at a magazine, covering a yawn behind his hands. So, if not Steve, then who?

Chapter 25

Riley woke to a new day, the light bright. Jack's face was the first he saw. His husband was slouched in the chair, breathing deeply, stubble lining his face and his hands crossed across his stomach.

"Jack," he croaked, his throat raw. He watched as Jack blinked sleep away and sat upright.

"Hey," Jack said softly, standing and pressing the button for the nurse, who arrived quickly, relieving the minute or so of uncomfortable and embarrassed silence.

She bustled around Riley, lifting the head of his bed and maneuvering him into a more upright position. He was grateful the pain in his chest was currently numbed with meds. She finally left, leaving only Jack in the room with him. Memories and emotions swirled unchecked around them, waiting to be dealt with.

"So," Jack started, "thank you. For coming in to help me, but mostly for stopping Solo from hurting Beth."

Riley nodded and half smiled. "Better squashing a six-four muscle man than an itty bitty girl, eh?" he joked, glancing down at his bandages, a flush of embarrassment climbing his face. Jack sighed and moved closer to sit on the side of the bed.

"Don't do that. Don't discount what you did like that. It was taking too long to get Taylor out on my own. She was terrified. I wouldn't have had time to go back for Solo. But when you came in—"

"I think I freakin' fainted," Riley interrupted crossly, and Jack snorted.

"Nah, I think it was more likely you passed out due to the internal bleeding from the nicked artery," Jack pointed out pragmatically.

"That sounds a damn sight more manly than fainting," Riley finally said, his voice getting scratchier and his eyelids starting to droop.

"Hang on," Jack said, sliding off the bed and disappearing out of the door.

He came back with people in tow, Eden, Beth, and Josh and a very pale Donna. It was Eden who climbed up to curl up next to her brother, but it was Donna the Campbells let through first as they crowded around his bed.

"Riley," she said, leaning over and kissing him on the forehead. "For Beth and Jack, thank you."

* * * *

Jack made his excuses, needing to meet the veterinarian back at the Double D, and one by one the others made their excuses to go. Riley assumed they felt he needed time on his own with Eden, who remained curled close to her big brother, clinging to his hospital gown, her knuckles white with the pressure. Riley held her close, not remembering the last time his confident sassy sister had come to him for comfort.

"I think I'm going to be friends with Beth," she whispered into his chest. "She's pregnant, and so sick. Did Jack tell you that?" Riley's closed his eyes with shame. That his sister sat here, her heart in her voice, and to know what he'd done to Jack and his sister was too much.

"That's good, Eden. She needs friends," he offered instead, his fingers digging into his sister's long hair as if to anchor himself to his sister's world of innocence where there were no secrets and no lies.

"Riley, I have something I need to talk to you about," she said quietly, and he shifted slightly, leaning closer, his head spinning a little from the meds. "It's about the transfusion. When they brought you in, you needed blood. A lot of blood. They didn't have your type match, and mom and I weren't matches."

Riley waited for her to say more, to explain the point, then suddenly put two and two together. "Did Dad donate the blood?" Eden uncurled herself from his side, placing her feet flat on the floor.

"Your father donated the blood you needed, only it wasn't Daddy. It would never be Daddy, 'cause, Riley," tears choked her voice, "he isn't your dad."

"What do you mean?" A frown creased his forehead.

"Jim. Riley, he's your father."

* * * *

Jim Bailey was not one to mope or sulk. Life threw what it wanted at him, and he dealt with it. From falling in love at eighteen with the boss's wife, to dealing with the devil by not claiming his son as his. Now, though, he stood outside Riley's door, trying to get up the courage to open it. When Jack came up next to him with a coffee and a smile, the simple words "Have you been in to see Riley?" were enough to make him turn tail and run.

"No, no, I haven't." he stuttered in reply, still staring at the door. Jack frowned and pushed the door opened

"Come on in then. He'll be pleased for the company," Jack said simply and walked in.

Eden was curled up again with Riley, her eyes wide and tear-filled. Riley was stiff and unyielding, and fury was carved into his face. "What's wrong?" he asked quickly, hurriedly placing his coffee on the table by the door and crossing to Riley. "What's happened?"

"Me," Jim said as he closed the door. "Me," he repeated. "I happened."

Jack rounded on him. "What the fuck did you do? Did Hayes send you? What have you done?"

"Jack, wait," Riley interrupted. He drew in a breath, looking at Jim, but Jim couldn't look him in the eyes.

"Riley—" Jim began, but Riley waved a hand in a gesture of no.

"I just can't believe what Eden told me," Riley started, turning his head away from them all for a moment. When he turned back, his eyes were wet with tears, and the spark of something else. Something real. "All along I thought it was me, you know. I thought that I wasn't good enough. Not strong enough or smart enough. *That* was the reason Gerald Hayes hated me. But I was wrong. The problem wasn't me. It was him, because I'm guessing he knew. He knew he wasn't my father." He stopped.

"We loved each other, Riley, your mom and I," Jim said quietly. "We were going to leave. She used to have a good heart, loved music, art and books. I loved her, and when she told me she was pregnant, I was the happiest man alive. You have to believe me."

Riley dropped the smile, a mask of seriousness falling over his face. "I do believe you. I want you to know one thing."

He paused, long enough for Jim to insert an encouraging, "What?"

"Jim, I couldn't be happier."

* * * *

Jack helped Riley from the car. Grumpy Riley had long since been replaced by thank-fuck-I'm-out-of-the-hospital Riley. It was with smiles that he climbed the steps to the Campbell home, Jack refusing to take him to the Hayes mansion this side of hell freezing over. He took the younger man to the back rooms, Jack's rooms, all the while listening to Riley muttering about how he could damn well walk himself.

The next day, grumpy Riley came back with a vengeance.

"I am having a freakin' shower."

"Stand up by yourself for more than thirty seconds and the shower is all yours."

"Fuck you, Campbell," Riley spat out, trying to stand and failing miserably.

"Campbell-Hayes," Jack reminded him with a grin, kind of enjoying the whole poor-Riley thing.

"And I say again, fuck you."

Jack took pity on him, locking the bedroom door, crossing to the bathroom and coming back with a basin, soap, a cloth and a towel. "Sponge bath," he said with a smirk.

"No freakin' way," Riley shouted, loud enough to be heard through the house, pulling his covers up around his neck and, for all the world, looking like a five year old.

"Bed bath and blow job or nothing."

Riley slit his eyes. "Blow job?" he asked carefully.

"No shower. You let *me* clean you up, you get a hand job or a blow job. Depends how clean I get ya. I mean I'm cleaning you anyway, no biggie." Jack shrugged.

"Jeez, Campbell. Hayes," he added the other name quickly as Jack opened his mouth to correct his husband.

Smirking again —*enough with the smirking*— Jack pulled off his jeans and half climbed on the bed to straddle Riley, lifting off his shirt and exposing acres of hospital-pale skin.

"Ready?" he asked softly.

"Shouldn't I be the one gettin' naked?" Riley pointed out.

"It's more fun this way, and I tell you what, don't hurt yourself but where I touch you… you touch me back." He ghosted a finger over Riley's T-shirt-covered chest, scratching at the material across his nipple, and pulling his hand back. "Now it's your turn, Het-boy."

Carefully he placed Riley's hand against his bare chest, directly over his heart, and waited. Riley had a frown of concentration on his face that would rival a pre-schooler in a spelling bee. But he moved his fingers slowly, across heated skin and away from Jack's steady heartbeat, to focus on the left nipple, skimming it gently before applying pressure. Jack pushed into just the simple touch of the fingers to his nipple, and he swore. Riley smirked. He moved his fingers to touch the other nipple, the look of concentration replaced by one of uncovered lust.

With the damp cloth, Jack touched shoulders, arm muscles, fingers to fingers, eyes, cheekbones, and each time Riley repeated every motion. The heat pooling in Jack's groin at just exchanging these touches was so hot it was burning him. He pulled back the covers, pushing and pulling at material until finally Riley lay completely naked beneath him, his long limbs stretched out on pristine white sheets, his dick hard and weeping.

"Stop staring," Riley breathed, moving his hips as Jack settled himself between his legs.

"Freak," Jack pointed out, leaning down and gently blowing onto damp skin, watching as the hairs stood tall and the shiver ran through his lover's body. "You are gorgeous," he said, his voice little more than a growl. "Beautiful. I just want to stare."

Riley groaned at the words, then Jack bent and licked a broad strip from root to tip of Riley's sex, looking up directly into Riley's eyes. He dipped his head, touching the tip of his tongue to the collecting pre-cum, taking Riley in as far as he could before pulling back and off.

"What?" Riley forced out, arching up in a silent plea.

"Last time we could chalk it up to drink, timing, the storm, stress. This time, Riley, it should be because we choose it. There's a big difference."

"Jeez, you have your mouth on my dick!"

"Your choice, Het-boy."

Riley managed to tell Jack everything he wanted by simply curling his fingers in Jack's hair and pulling him back down on his dick. "Keep going, cowboy."

Jack smiled even as he concentrated on laving at the pearls of pre-cum collected at the tip.

* * * *

Jack spent ages just kissing, licking, and biting on his inner thigh, before Riley's whines became more forceful, his hands guiding and pushing Jack down and then up, until Jack got with the freaking plan.

His chest hurt, and the bandages pulled as he twisted his head, but he swallowed the pain, the heat inside him pushing at his spine. He was so close. He wanted Jack to touch him like he had before.

"Touch me," he ordered, his voice broken in the demands of lust.

He felt Jack chuckle, felt the vibrations in his dick, keening as Jack moved his fingers, just circling, not pushing, just applying pressure, until every single inch of Riley was on fire. The pleasure-pain was too much, and he couldn't stop himself even if he tried, trying to tell Jack in amongst the whimpers of pain to warn he was about to—

He opened his mouth in a silent scream as orgasm hit him, and he pumped into Jack's mouth, helpless in his needs. Jack was swallowing and sucking, catching him as he fell to earth, still chuckling as he pulled his mouth off and climbed his lover to exchange a heated kiss.

"Your turn," Jack whispered quietly, taking Riley's hand and placing it on his dick.

Riley's eyes widened, even in the afterglow, as he closed his hand firmly and started to move it like he would on his own dick, just this side of rough, his thumb trailing through pre-cum every other stroke, twisting and touching and feeling. He watched Jack try to form words for this experience —Riley's first time with him— but he didn't last long, obviously close after taking Riley to the edge. With his free hand, Riley reached out to twist Jack's hair, pulling his face

down for kisses. Sealing his mouth to
Jack, he tongue-fucked his mouth,
exchanging heated breaths and feeling
Jack still as he came over Riley's hand.

Breathing hard, Jack slumped
down next to Riley. Talking could wait.

* * * *

It was the first time Gerald had
ever raised a hand to her, a slap that
sent her reeling against the wall and to
the floor.

"You told him. And told him to go
the hospital. You stupid bitch. We could
have let Riley die naturally, and we
could have stopped having to worry
about Riley if you'd just kept quiet."

He walked away, leaving her dry-
eyed and shocked on the floor. She
hated herself for the deal she'd made,
and he clearly hated that for a short time
she'd found comfort in another man's
arms, but their relationship had always
been civil at least. A mutually beneficial
marriage, her old money, his new
money, how could it go wrong?

Still, she was a mother, with a
mother's instincts. Deeply hidden
maybe, but still there. Inside
somewhere, she had love for her son.
How could she not save his life? For
Sandra Hayes, this was the point at

which she finally died inside, because no part of the old Sandra remained. Nothing. The last piece of that civility in her marriage wrenched away from her heart, leaving her empty.

The pills were easy to find. The doctor had been happy to prescribe sleeping pills over the last few years. They sat in her bathroom, steady and welcoming, and the warnings on the bottle were always very clear. Don't mix with alcohol.

The whisky, gin and brandy… Well, they were also *very* easy to find.

Sandra stared for a long time at the amber liquid in the glass, at the high sun filtering through the crystal and casting rainbows of design on the marble top of her dressing table. The pills lay in her hand. She had counted them, and there were twenty-nine of them sitting in a small pile, the chalkiness of them strange against her soft skin. She looked at them carefully and then lifted her eyes to look at her face in the mirror. Nearly unlined, with full makeup, her hair just so, diamonds sparking at her ears, a necklace flat against her graceful neck. None of it was real. Cosmetics and a surgeon's knife had held back the years, just so she could be what others expected, what she had wanted to be, what she tried so hard to be.

She had never had Gerald's love, not really, nor that of her eldest son. She had driven away Riley and had failed Eden. Still, this wasn't the way to deal with these mistakes or with her despair. She was a strong woman, and generations of women in her family had been in worse situations than this. Carefully, she placed the tablets back in the bottle and replaced the stopper on the decanter, a stronger determination in her shaking hands. She had things to do. Gerald needed to know some things. Lisa needed help. Her daughter needed saving. And, as for her middle child, her beautiful strong man who held so much weight on his shoulders, well, he needed to know the whole truth. She needed to place another call to Jim. It was long overdue.

She wasn't ready to die today.

Chapter 26

Jeff sat in the car for a long time, considering every word he was going to say, looking at the shell of the burned barn and cursing his idiot brother and that fag Campbell for what they'd managed to do. With the horses surviving, with Campbell able to carry on with his half-bitten excuse for a farm, Jeff was left with weaker leverage. Still, he had what Jack needed, money, and he intended to just go on in and ask. It was Campbell himself who climbed down the steps from the front door, meeting Jeff as he got out of the car.

"Hayes."

"I came to visit my brother," Jeff replied. *Enough with the pleasantries.*

"He's sleeping at the moment; if you wanna wait in the house then you're welcome."

"Well, I have a small piece of business that we could maybe discuss while I'm waiting on him." Jack's eyes narrowed, and the cowboy folded his arms and planted his feet in his Texas dirt, his face carefully blank. Obviously the cowboy wasn't going to let this be taken into the house.

"Go on," he prompted.

Jeff tried to call the bluff, moving towards the house and then stopping when Jack didn't move a muscle. Well, Jeff decided inwardly, that was a good thing really, wouldn't want his little brother to find out just yet.

"I have an offer for you," he started, pulling himself tall as he attempted to loom over Jack, who merely blinked at him in return. "I heard about your unfortunate… incident… with the barn and your horses. Damn shame, heard they were good horses an' all."

"They're still good horses. One has foaled, and momma and baby are doing fine," Jack pointed out.

* * * *

Jack thought back to the telephone conversation he'd just had with the fire investigator, who had categorically stated the fire was arson and not the fault of a lightning strike. Jeff seemed mighty nervous for all his blustering dominance, and something somewhere in Jack's mind started to connect.

"As I said, I am very pleased y'all are okay."

Jack narrowed his eyes. Was it just his imagination or were the man's words slurring with his Texas accent, pushing through the clipped vowels of his expensive education? A sure sign

Jeff was struggling with the wording of what he was saying. Jack knew it because Riley did that too.

"I wanted to thank you for what you've done for my little brother, helping him the way you did with the whole arranged marriage business, and I want you to know that the Hayeses always make good on favors. I want to make you an offer on both horses in exchange for something that won't be a hardship."

"My horses?" Jack chose to ignore the reference to arranged marriage. He was so not going to rise to subtle innuendo and devious guesswork.

"Ten million dollars for the foals, outright, passing them to me immediately, in exchange for the money. It's more than enough I imagine to breed again. All I want from you is proof of annulment."

Jack considered every word Jeff had just thrown at him, then sighed, exaggerating the movement, his fists clenching and unclenching as his anger pushed to the fore. "An annulment? Do they even do those anymore?" he finally asked, pasting an innocent and curious look on his face.

Jeff obviously didn't register the change in Jack's demeanor, or hear the sarcasm in his voice because he just pushed on. "I know you can't have consummated the *marriage*." This he spat out like a nasty taste in his mouth. "And I understand why you did it. You probably only entered into the marriage for money for the ranch. I'm more than willing to match and double whatever Riley agreed to pay you if ten million isn't enough. It won't be any loss to you. You sign the papers that I'll get written up, and there it is. End of the marriage. Then you can leave my little brother to me. He won't be your problem anymore."

"Well, I'm kinda enjoying having him around," Jack responded, trying his best to appear calm. "You may have to offer more'n ten to buy me out of this one."

Jeff nodded eagerly. "I can do that; I can push it to fifteen if it's a done deal by the end of the week."

Jack sensed Jeff's hidden glee that he almost had a deal, the billion-dollar oil company would easily swallow fifteen million in a day.

"Tell you what, then." Jack moved one step closer, not at all intimidated by the tall hard-nosed businessman standing in front of him with the smirk on his face. "I have a one-time only offer for you." Jeff leaned in, expectation on his features. "You take your millions and get the hell off my land, and I don't shoot you in the ass."

Jeff's eyes widened. "Campbell, what the—"

"Campbell-Hayes," Jack snapped back, some of his control slipping. "Campbell-freakin'-Hayes, and I'll thank you to remember that from now on." He took a small step closer, and in an unconscious movement, Jeff stepped backward. And so it went until he had his back against the car, and Jack stood toe-to-toe with him.

Jeff blustered, "He's not even gay! He's not a fucking fag, and it's not real." More words tumbled out of Jeff's mouth in a sudden torrent of anger. "I'll take this to court. You won't get away with it. It's a lie, and I'll prove it."

Jack leaned even farther towards the tall man, trying damn hard not to hit him. His voice was a low contained growl, heavy with intention to make his point.

"If you do, then I will bring photographic evidence of me and your brother making love on every single surface at the Hayes Mansion, including the bed in your apartment." Jeff pushed him away, open disgust and disbelief on his face, and climbed into the car. "Fuck you, Campbell," were his parting words before he gunned the engine and drove off with a squeal of tires and a cloud of dust and debris.

Jack stood for a while, watching the cloud of dust dissipate. *Campbell-Hayes.* He sighed.

* * * *

Riley was standing at the side window, a spectator to the end of the confrontation. Jack didn't realize he was being watched, and Riley wished he could have helped except he was too doped up to do anything except lean weakly against the sink. The glass of water he had come for was cold in his hand.

Riley moved away as Jack looked back at the window. He stumbled to the table and sat, waiting for Jack to come back in, his heart in his throat. He had heard part of it, just some of the conversation near the house before Jack crowded his brother towards the car and out of earshot. It was the kind of stunt he expected his brother to pull, to try and buy Jack's support, but it still cut him to the core. They'd never really been close; there had always been an edge to Jeff that Riley felt uncomfortable with. He'd seen a few too many deals fall into Hayes Oil's lap against all odds, and he wasn't a stupid man; Jeff or

Gerald was clearly paying off parties to obtain contracts. To offer Jack that much money though? It was more than he would make staying with Riley. Jack may well have thrown Jeff off of the Double D, but once he had thought Jeff's offer over he would see it was more financially viable than keeping Riley around. His throat was tight with emotion, and he searched for reasons why Jack should stay with him.

He looked up as Jack entered the kitchen, and he waited for the storm.

"Fifteen million," Riley stated finally as Jack grabbed a beer and slid in the chair opposite. No other reasons for Jack to stay had presented themselves, and he didn't want to have to resort to upping his own monetary offer because he didn't want to sink any further than he already had. "You should take the money." Jack shook his head.

"I don't want the money, and I won't pull out now. A deal is a deal, and you stand to lose a lot of money if you don't get your percentage."

Riley sighed quietly. "Jack, do you have any idea how much I'm worth? Even with just the percentage I have?"

"How far past obscene are we talking?" Jack asked with a laugh. "I'm guessin' maybe I should've asked you for more for the D?"

Riley just nodded, deadly serious. "I can give you more, if you agree to stay married." He was anxious to hear Jack's response, his stomach churning. He didn't even know what he was saying. He wasn't sure he even wanted more of Hayes Oil any longer. How could so much have changed in such a short time, with so many new doubts circling in his head? Was he actually considering buying the rest of the year with Jack, just to keep him in his life? Jesus. How sad did that make him?

"I'm gonna forget you said that," Jack replied, tipping back to swallow down half the beer in one go.

Chapter 27

Beth slid further into Steve's hug as they talked softly, his left hand over hers, feeling her daughter kick back at the touch. His right hand was curled into her long hair, stroking and soothing gently.

"Beth, can I ask you something?"

"Mmm hmm."

"And you promise me not to get angry in return?" Steve felt a full body sigh go through Beth as she burrowed into his shirt with a soft murmur of agreement. "The father of your baby... Do you love him?"

Beth stilled, lifting her head, blue eyes wide with shock. "No, I hate him."

Steve closed his eyes, dropping a small kiss on the top of her head, inhaling the smell of apple and feeling every muscle in his body relax.

"Can I ask you something else?"

"You're pushing it, Murray," she said softly, a smile on her face, a smile that gave him strength.

"Elizabeth, you know I love you, and I hope, in my heart, that one day you could come to love me too. Or at least... Jeez... Beth, will you marry me?" He waited, and the seconds grew to a minute, but he didn't push it. He just waited, imagining the reasons, each slightly wilder than the last, that Beth would give for saying no.

"Yes."

* * * *

It had been three days since the sponge bath-blow job incident, something that Jack hadn't instigated a repeat of since, much to Riley's confusion. It had been good, hadn't it? Riley had certainly enjoyed it, but maybe Jack hadn't. After all, Riley's experience in the whole gay scx thing was limited to anonymous one offs. He was so confused. Was this *thing* they had a real marriage now? Had they really taken that step that meant, for the rest of the year of the marriage, they would be with each other in more than name? Every time Jack was with him, talking to him, helping him to shower, never taking it further than just helping, the anticipation was enough to kill Riley.

He'd actually managed a full dinner tonight. He'd sat at the scarred table in the kitchen with Donna and Jim and Beth, just listening to the teasing between Jack and his sister, and desperately missing Eden. Jim had become somewhat of a fixture at the D, and Riley was learning a lot about his real dad, about the pressure the eighteen-year-old had been under to just walk away from the woman he loved. They spoke of the threats to Sandra that Gerald had loved to make— that she would be cut out of his life, he'd take their sons, and publicly disown her. Jim told Riley of the last day, the single day that would live with Jim forever, the day Sandra said she didn't love him, could never love him. The day she'd chosen Gerald.

Riley had gone into one of his daydreams. He seemed to be doing that a lot lately. His brain was processing all the things he was hearing, and all the things he was feeling. Still, this evening he could concentrate on nothing but Jack. The thoughts that twisted in his mind, wondering what it would be like to have sex with a man. Not just any man, but making love with the gorgeous sexy cowboy he'd married. It just made his head spin. Sense memory of the feel of him, hard and soft, muscled and strong under his hand, was making him hard in his jeans, a constant problem around his husband.

"You with us, Riley?" Jack asked, startling Riley out of his thoughts, causing him to glance round the table with a blush climbing his cheeks. He wondered if Jack could read his thoughts. "Tired? Sore?" Jack added softly, subtle concern crossing his face.

Riley blinked steadily, not sure what Jack wanted to hear, too used to giving answers that people expected, and having to really think how he *did* feel.

"No, not so tired," he started. "Feeling good, actually." He saw Jack's eyes widen, and the older man sat more upright in his seat. "Just missing Eden, I guess," Riley finished.

Jack moved abruptly to stand, clearing the table, scraping plates and loading the dishwasher, all the while humming under his breath. Every so often, he glanced back at Riley who looked back steadily at him while listening to Jack's mom and sister talk babies.

* * * *

Jack wondered if Riley felt anything for Beth, wondered if his husband's heart had thawed enough for regret over what he'd used against Jack to get him to agree. He'd sensed a change in Riley since the fire, a softening in him, an understanding, as the spell of the Campbell family was cast about him. He couldn't say he had anything other than healthy lust for the tall man who sat at the kitchen table, but respect was at least starting to build alongside the desire to bury himself in that—

"Jack, did you hear me?" Donna asked, laughing, pulling Jack out of his daydreams of fucking Riley.

"No, Momma," he replied, smiling ruefully at her, knowing that tone, knowing he was on the teasing end of her tongue.

"So then," Beth piped up, "he just plain jumped off the roof, straight into the pile of manure." She collapsed in giggles at the grimace on Jack's face. Thing was, Riley was smiling as well, and also kind of smirking, and Jack groaned inwardly. Great, now he had ammunition from the great raft of embarrassing things Jack did as a child. Making the decision, he reached out to Riley.

"Time to bring the torture to an end. Bed for the invalid, I think," he said simply, daring Riley to say differently.

There was a slight pause, Riley's eyes widening slightly. The smile that had been on his face fell into a look of discomfort, and he began the whole worrying his lower lip with his teeth thing. It was probably only seconds, but it seemed like minutes, as the question hung in the air between them. Finally

Riley stood, taking Jack's hand and curling his fingers through Jack's. Beth startled to giggle again, Jim looked strangely proud of the open affection, and Donna just looked on fondly as the two men left the kitchen.

* * * *

Riley followed Jack along the long corridor to the back of the house where Jack had his own rooms. Just two, one the bedroom with the large queen-size bed —the sick room— where Riley had slept for so long, and the other set up as an office full of paperwork and schedules, photos and posters for seasonal schedules. Jack had spent some time in the bedroom earlier, after he'd sat Riley at the kitchen table to chat to Donna as she prepared dinner. The window was slightly open to the warm Texas evening, the filmy curtain material moving subtly, and the lights were low. He'd put fresh sheets on the bed, and the whole room smelled less like illness and more like… more like Jack. Riley frowned, tugging his hand free of Jack's, sighing and crossing to sit on the bed. He guessed from the way he'd been pulled into the room that he had done or said something wrong at the dinner table, and he waited to be told.

It startled him when Jack crouched down between his knees, looking up at him, his hands solid against Riley's thighs.

"You gotta promise me," Jack started with a smirk, "that you tell no one the stories you heard at dinner, on pain of death."

Riley wasn't sure what to say. It didn't sound like Jack was angry with him or disappointed in his family for sharing all those stories of Jack's childhood.

"I won't," Riley finally offered, ducking his head again, suddenly unaccountably and stupidly shy.

With a sudden surge, Jack stood and encouraged Riley to scoot back on the bed, only hesitating when Riley winced at the pull on his chest.

"You may fancy yourself all fixed, Het-boy, but you're still hurting, aren't you?"

"A bit, nothing major." Riley lay back on the soft pillows.

"Jeff's visit today got me thinking, Mr Campbell-Hayes, that there's no sense in us both going without for the rest of the year."

* * * *

"Sex, you mean?" Riley offered quietly, and Jack felt like smacking him for sounding so miserable. He chose to ignore what Riley had said.

"Tonight we could maybe make this marriage a real one, consummate it, become lovers in every sense of the word. Then your brother will have no more ammunition left." He kneeled on the bed and then leaned in to drop a gentle kiss to the skin on Riley's long neck, opening his mouth and kiss-biting into the warmth of the pulse below his lips. Tenderly he traced more kisses up his husband's chin and settled his mouth onto Riley's, his tongue encouraging Riley to open his mouth for a kiss.

He sensed Riley pull back against the pillow in the half-light. "I haven't… I've never had sex with a man, bottomed, topped, nothing. I don't know if I can do this."

"For tonight, just let me do all the work, eh?" Jack paused to steal a heated kiss, kissing away any words Riley wanted to throw into the conversation. He lifted his head. "Okay, here is how we play it. I want you to fuck me. I'll show you, open myself up. You can help, and then you can just lay back, and I'll show you what it can be like."

Riley whimpered and breathed a sound somewhere between a groan to stop and a plea for more, arching unconsciously into Jack's weight across his groin.

"You wanna do this, Het-boy?" Jack noticed the nickname didn't drip its normal sarcasm; it was affectionate and intimate, and Jack couldn't fight the feeling of wanting more, of wanting Riley inside him.

"Do you… is that what you normally do?" Riley seemed spooked, and Jack chased a trail of kisses from his throat to lips.

"I'm flexible," he finally said, dipping to taste Riley's sinful mouth with a heated exchange of tongues.

Riley finally got with the plan, pushing with his hand to move slightly down the bed and lay flat. Jack could taste Riley for hours, just kiss and suck and tongue-fuck his mouth until neither of them could breathe anymore; it was so damn natural it was scary. Riley responded with equal ferocity, and Jack was being ultra-careful not to lean on his husband's chest where the bandages still lay, raising to his knees and arching over his new lover. He began talking, over and over as he would to a spooked horse, repeating words to still Riley's fears. "Beautiful… Needy… Mine. I'll look after you…" a narrative of kissed words over his body. He slipped Riley's clothes from him as they kissed until finally Riley lay naked under him, pliant and warm.

Pushing his own jeans and boxers off and lifting his T-shirt over his head, Jack lowered himself to one side, reaching into the bedside cabinet. He pulled out what he needed.

"Okay? Last chance."

Riley didn't seem to want hesitation or the time to think, demanding kisses and touches, grabbing Jack's arms and just holding on. It blew Jack's mind the way this man arched up under him, stealing breath with every touch. He couldn't remember a connection this instant, this intense, with any partner before. He knew he should stop, give them time, not race after this so fast. But if he'd taken the time to stop and think about this, he might never have touched Riley in the first place. It was like playing with fire. He sat up, Riley chasing the kisses, his head lifting from the pillow. Jack hushed him with a single finger on his kiss-bitten lips as his lover tried to ask why Jack had stopped.

"Don't ask me if I want to stop now. I don't want to stop," Riley whispered urgently.

As if to emphasize the point, he pushed himself against Jack's thigh and, at the same time, letting out that God-damned half-whimper that curled lust and want into the base of Jack's spine. It was an invitation to sin, Riley spread out on the bed against the white cotton, his limbs languid and stretched, the dips and lines of muscles so simple to trace with tongue and teeth. Jack leaned back on his haunches, smoothing slick over his fingers, capturing Riley's hand and mixing the smooth oil over his hand as well.

"Remember the game, Riley. Copy what I do," Jack whispered, and Riley nodded, watching intently as Jack pushed a finger inside himself and studying as he pressed in a second. He pulled at Riley's hand covered with the slick and encouraged him to explore with one finger alongside Jack's own fingers. The feelings were intense, strange, both the heat and the touch. Jack keened and leaned over, pushing back on their joined fingers. It was too much, and he could feel his orgasm starting to build.

He wanted to say, *"I need to slow down; it's too fast"*, but all that came out was a muffled half groan as Riley arched up under him. His husband was seeking any kind of friction for his neglected dick, and Jack pulled his fingers and Riley's out just to slow things down a bit, exploring his husband's long lithe body instead with taste and touch, focusing on bruised lips that demanded to be kissed. Leaning up and away, he pulled a condom from the small pile and held it in front of him. They were both clean, the contract had demanded tests, and he really didn't want to use the extra barrier. Riley seemed to understand, reaching for the condom and throwing it to the floor. From then on, it was pure sensation, awkward, uncomfortable, embarrassing, and ultimately, the most intense sensations Jack had ever felt.

Primal need and the chase for ecstasy made Jack move into position ,and he breathed deep as Riley's dick pushed past the strong muscle. He was nearly there, and the look of astonished fear in Riley's face would have made him laugh, but he knew the almost religious joy that Riley was feeling. When Riley stopped, finally seated, joined completely, Jack could barely breathe. They moved together, Jack positioned just so, Riley pushing up in counter rhythm at the right angle, and soon, there was nothing except a need to come *right the fuck now.*

"I can't, Jack… I can't…" Riley moaned, pulling Jack's head down by his hair, his damp hands tangled in the strands, insistent that Jack should be kissing him.

Jack was so near, and Riley's eyes were closed, his muscles tense. Jack could see it would be seconds before Riley lost it inside him. Jack just needed… needed…

"Touch me." he half ordered, half begged, and Riley was there, wrapping a huge hand around Jack's dick and moving and twisting to push Jack over the edge.

It was Jack who lost it first, by seconds, hot and hard and clenching around Riley so tight it must have helped to push the younger man over the edge after his husband. It was intense, and it was perfect, Jack half falling as he moved into the ripples of orgasm that chased along his spine. Riley had tears in the corners of his eyes. Jack kissed them away with murmured praise and thanks until he finally stilled his movement and, careful of Riley's chest, sank in for kisses that he needed more than air.

They stayed locked in the intimate embrace until Jack rolled off and to the side, sleep pulling him to cuddle into Riley's side.

"Know what, Jack?" Riley said tiredly, pulling Jack in closer.

"Wha'?" Jack replied, on the very edges of sleep.

"You, cowboy, are worth *every* dollar I paid."

Chapter 28

Jack pulled from post-coital bliss to temper, quicker than you could snap a finger.

"What the fuck, Riley?" he bit out angrily, pushing away from the furnace of his husband and sitting upright. Riley just blinked up at him, a blank look on his face, a blank look that quickly turned to stunned shame. He too scrambled to sit up, the bandages pulling and the sheets tangling round his legs.

Jack jumped off the bed, pulling on the discarded jeans and T, all the time ignoring Riley and his pleading words. "I didn't mean it that way, Jack, please. It was a joke."

Jack silenced him with a sweep of his hand. "Way to make your husband feel like a whore," he bit out, leaving and slamming the door behind him.

Stunned, it took Riley a few seconds to get his head around what he'd just done. It had been a joke, and as usual, his nerves and his stupid dry sense of humor had backfired on him. Scrambling to his feet, swaying at the rush of blood to his head, he picked up the jeans and tee he'd been wearing, and sat on the edge of the bed trying to pull the damn denim over his uncooperative legs. His stomach was still sticky with cum, and he wiped at it with furious sweeps of cotton bedding, then pulled on his tee and rushed to the door, dragging it open and calling after his escaping husband.

Donna walked out of the kitchen, a mug of coffee in her hand, a curious Jim standing beside her.

"Riley? What's wrong? Jack went out of here like he was lit on fire."

"It's me. I fucked up," Riley said on his way to the front door. He opened it to see the truck was still there. That meant Jack hadn't left the D. He slipped on his sneakers.

"Riley, sweetheart…" Donna's voice was quiet and Riley looked back at her with determination on his face.

He couldn't stop to talk or exchange pleasantries. "Donna, I need to—"

"The barn, the old one at the back. He'll be with his babies," she explained simply, and Riley had the grace to blush at his rudeness. "Riley, one last thing. I don't know what's wrong, but if the two of you need to talk about something, make sure you listen to the stuff he doesn't say." Riley nodded, shuffling down the steps, his heart pounding in his chest and his breathing more than a little labored. He needed to slow down, or by the time he reached the barn, he wasn't going to have the power of rational speech, let alone be conscious.

He picked his way past the debris of the first barn, his eyes drawn to the charcoal blackness of the charred wood. His head filled with images from that night, of Jack worried and scared for him. The images mixed with the feeling Riley had building inside him, want, need, desire— love. He couldn't love a man. He wasn't gay, had never been gay, and he didn't know what to think.

He rounded the corner, the side of the older red barn looming in the diminishing light of evening. He saw no sign of Jack yet. He wanted to call out, but then he didn't want Jack to have time to run, because damn it, Jack *needed* to hear what Riley had to say this time. When he saw his husband, it almost drove him to his knees in self-disgust. This strong, proud man sat in the hay, the foal's head in his lap, crooning nonsense words to her. It was all Riley could do not to drop to his knees beside Jack and just beg for forgiveness, when what he needed to do was get Jack to understand why he'd said what he said.

"Jack," he finally said into the dim interior. Jack refused to look up and meet his eyes. "Look, I'm sorry. I know I upset you but—"

"I'm not a girl. I don't need touchy-feely crap, Riley, so quit with the explanation. Let's just chalk it up to experience. I know where I stand. I won't forget again."

Riley was stunned, completely and totally speechless. Is that what Jack thought? Carefully he lowered himself to sit next to Jack, curling a hand in the foal's soft mane and scratching idly.

"At the beginning, Jack," he started softly, "maybe a few weeks ago, I could have accepted that crap from you. When this all started, hell, I owned you. I bought you, paid for you. In my mind you were just another pawn in the Hayes game to get what I wanted." Frustrated he bent his head, wiping a hand across his face. How the hell was he going to get Jack to understand how he'd changed? "You meant nothing to me. As for Beth…" He paused, knowing he needed to be totally honest about this before Jack would believe anything else he said. "Beth meant nothing to me. When Steve told me what had happened to her, it was just another mark in the column for screwing with my family and choosing you to do it with." He stopped again. Honesty was hard when it meant opening himself up like this.

"I don't think I'll ever totally forgive you for that," Jack half-whispered, and Riley felt his stomach twist and his heart fall.

"That isn't me though, Jack, not the real me. I don't mean to hurt people. I'm not the man who buys people. I'm not like *them*. But— I don't expect you to accept that at face value." He pulled his legs up to his chest, wrapping his arms around them and dropping his chin to rest on his knees. This was one of the hardest conversations he'd ever had. "If the only way to beat them is to play their own game then, hell, I knew I could do that. So way back, when I first approached you, it wasn't to give Beth support or to fall in love with you. You were just a commodity, something I could use as leverage."

Jack looked sideways at him, clearly picking up on a couple of things Riley had said. "You betrayed Steve's trust. He was your friend."

"My only real friend, apart from Eden," Riley said sadly. "And yeah, he was just another pawn. One day he might forgive me, although I'm not holding my breath. He didn't come to the hospital to see me. I know he was only there because Beth needed him."

"Doesn't it hurt that this only friend of yours hates you for what you did?"

Riley looked up sharply. What did Jack want from him? "You want me to sit and cry to show you I hurt? 'Cause I could do that for you if it would convince you. At the drop of a hat, I could show you how this is screwing with me, but I can't let myself do it. If I start to let it out, I feel like it's gonna destroy me."

Jack nodded. "So that's how it started," he prompted carefully, leaving a silence that Riley had to fill.

"Then it changed. I don't know when or how. I wish I could go back and touch that moment, and hold it, that very minute that the real Riley started to dig for the surface. It could have been when I saw Beth so obviously pregnant, so pale, or when Steve knocked me to the floor and told me he hated me. Maybe it was just now when I hurt you so bad because I wasn't thinking. I don't know. I just know what I have with you, however you label it and however long you want it to last, it's real." Riley's voice hitched, twenty-seven years of Hayes pressure pushing down on his shoulders, forcing emotions back into his heart. "I don't know how else to say it. I don't see you as a pawn, or an asset.

I see you as a person, my husband, my lover. I don't own you, and I don't want to own you. I want to take the pre-nup and tear it into pieces, I want to take that damn contract and burn it to ashes. Money shouldn't define your life, and it shouldn't define mine or what we have." He stopped, suddenly aware that he was still talking and of how silent and still Jack was. Maybe he had really fucked this up. Jack hadn't given any indication he wanted this thing to go past the year, had never said a word, and always joked about counting down the days until his freedom from *Het-boy*. "Jack?"

"I get that, Riley. All of that. Thing is *I know*. I see you changing, see that you're different. Maybe I just put too much on to you, expecting you to know what I needed, what I wanted."

"What do you want? Tell me, and if I can give it to you—"

"I want to see Beth healthy, my niece born, and Beth safe. I want a husband who's also my lover. I want Riley Campbell-Hayes in my life. I can't see past the year with him, but I know what I want now."

Riley held out his free hand, and Jack curled his fingers into it, linking them. His eyes remained steady on Riley's.

"Okay," Riley finally said. "Okay."

Chapter 29

Donna didn't seem surprised at the visitor on her doorstep. Sandra guessed she'd been expecting her arrival for a few days. "Sandra," she said politely.

"Donna," she started carefully, "I wonder if I might speak to Riley?"

"He's in the barn with Jack. They should be back soon," she said, widening the door and indicating Sandra should come in, which she did, but not before hesitating on the threshold.

Sandra followed Donna to the kitchen, her eyes widening at the sight of Jim sitting at the wooden trestle table. He immediately stood, spilling coffee over the side of his mug, an instant blush climbing his cheeks. They had seen each other on a few occasions at Hayes Oil, but never in a situation where they needed to talk. Both of them just stared, years of history separating them.

"Iced tea, Sandra, or perhaps coffee?"

"Tea would be lovely, thank you," Sandra replied, her southern politeness her armor. With that she could cope with anything.

"I want to thank you," Jim started, and Sandra blinked nervously. *Please don't say anything that is going to break me.* "For telling me that Riley needed me."

"You're very welcome. He did need you," she said carefully, and slid into the seat diagonally across from Jim, thanking Donna for the iced tea and sipping on it slowly.

No one spoke. It wasn't uncomfortable silence, not really. It was thoughtful and only broken when the front door opened and laughter spilled into the house. Riley and Jack appeared, holding hands and smiling at each other. Jack saw her first. He stopped in his tracks, tightened his grip on Riley's hand, and moved closer to him, protective.

"Mom," Riley said simply, waiting for Jack to release his grip and then closing the distance to draw her into a patented Riley hug "S'good to see you. We were gonna come to the house tomorrow when I got the all clear." Sandra stiffened in her son's embrace, still unnerved by his exuberant shows of affection. Then she pulled back.

"I came to talk," she said. "Is there somewhere we can go that is a bit more… private?"

"Y'all can use the good room," Donna offered. "It's the one room we keep tidy, and there's no horse smell."

Sandra nodded her thanks, and Riley offered his arm, chatting about something to do with foals that went straight over her head. He shut the door behind them and she sat on one of the brown leather sofas, opening her purse and pulling out a brown envelope.

"I want to say something first," she began. Riley settled to sit opposite, his face an open book of worry.

"Uh huh."

"First, I want to say that I'm sorry, no, more than sorry, about the way the family has treated you over the past years, Riley. You were not a child from my marriage, but I want you to know you were a child born from love, and I never regretted the deals I made to keep you, not for one day."

"Momma?"

"I regret losing Jim. I regret what it did to him to have you taken away, and I regret that Gerald hated you every day since you were born." She stopped, her voice not quite so steady, nor forged of iron. "I want to try and make it up to you one day. I don't know how I can do that, or how I begin to win back your love and affection, but I want to try."

* * * *

Riley couldn't bear to hear any more. He rose and crossed to sit next to her, capturing her hands in his, the skin smooth under his touch. "You're my momma. I may not understand you sometimes, but I'll always love you, and you don't have to try." Sandra lifted wet eyes to his, the same hazel green as his, a look of hope in them. What else could he say? He would just sit there, take what she had to say to him, and then just go and find Jack and maybe have some more, frankly awesome, sex.

Finally Sandra lifted her hand to lay it flat on his cheek.

"I couldn't be prouder of you," she said. "Despite *us,* you grew up into a fine young man."

"Thank you, Momma," Riley said simply, pressing his cheek against her hand. There was hope here, and then it all came crashing down.

"The Campbells own half of what we have."

His world turned on its axis as certainly as if she'd called the Campbells in and told them to their faces. He couldn't make sense of her words.

"I don't understand," Riley said carefully as his mom handed him the folder.

"I mean it, Riley. In there is every shred of evidence. Hayes Oil should have been split fifty-fifty with Alan Campbell. It isn't all ours, half of it belongs to Donna and her family."

"Okay," he started carefully. "Then we give it to them and help them to get what is rightfully theirs." What they should do seemed simple to Riley, absolutely black and white.

"Riley, listen to me. I want that too, but I also wanted to give you the chance to bury this, to put an end to all the drama and the worry. If you show this to them, you stand to lose everything. They can wipe Hayes Oil out with one clever lawyer. You could lose it all, your money, the land, the offices, your cars—"

"Momma." Riley stood, pulling Sandra with him. "You don't understand. I don't want any of that." He placed a hand over his own heart. "I think I have everything I want or need in here."

* * * *

Donna thought it looked like a council of war. Beth had called Steve, reasoning that her fiancé should be there for it, and he now sat with Beth. She and Sandra were sitting opposite them, and Jack and Riley leaned back against the sink. Josh had arrived not long before.

Anna, his wife, had settled their kids in the TV room with game controllers and snacks and was now half sitting on Josh's lap. Jim was poring over the papers, flicking from one to another, from one statement of intent to another contract, to bank statements aged with time. Finally he lifted his head to look at Sandra, his eyes sad, resigned. It was Donna he spoke to though, Donna who had supported and loved Alan Campbell in his hours of despair.

"It's true, all of it," he said warily, wondering what the Campbells were going to say now.

"How long have you known about this?" Donna asked Sandra, willing her to be honest. Sandra looked down at the table.

"I copied papers from the very start, hid them in a safety deposit box. I wanted my own leverage if he ever went back on our deal with Jim and Riley. I never really looked at them. But I know I always suspected it of him. I was just too scared to do anything about it." She looked over at Riley, who smiled encouragingly, and then back at Donna, waiting for Donna to make her decision.

"I don't want it," Donna finally stated. Jim knew the hate and betrayal had destroyed her marriage. They had spoken of it in detail over the last few days. It had driven her husband to an early death. She had already told him she wanted no part of any battle for money.

"Mom," Josh said, exchanging a loaded look with his wife before nodding carefully. "We don't want it either." Anna smiled a soft smile at her husband. "I have what I want, a business that supports my family, a wife I love, kids I couldn't be more proud of, and a family that I'm close to. I don't want any part of Hayes Oil or the money."

"Elizabeth?" Donna prompted gently.

"I want to live to see my daughter," Beth said softly. "That's all I want."

Steve wrapped an arm around her, pulling her in close. "Fighting a war isn't going to help that," he said to everyone in the room.

"It's just you, Jack. What's your decision, son?"

Chapter 30

So many emotions flooded Jack — anger, distrust, shock— he didn't know where to start putting them in order. He turned to Riley, because what he needed to say needed to be said to his face.

"I'm right that we would be turning down fifty percent of the billions that Hayes Oil turns over, the millions in the bank, the land, the control? Not only that, but with legal moves, we could maybe have it all?"

Riley nodded. "Hayes Oil as it stands would cease to exist, I guess."

"With secrets this big hanging over your dad, surely he must have known it was really just a matter of time?"

Riley shrugged. "He probably never realized Mom had the papers. Jack, you should do this. You should fight for what is rightfully yours. If you do, then I'll back you." Riley's eyes sparked with fire and utter determination. Jack stopped him, raising a hand and laying it over the rhythm of his husband's heart, feeling the bandage that covered his upper body.

"You just told me in the barn that money shouldn't define your life, that it shouldn't define mine," Jack said gently, seeing the denial rise in Riley and then fall away just as quickly. Jack's whole world had tilted on its axis. He didn't know how to explain it to Riley except in five simple words. "I don't want it, Riley."

"Jack—"

"No. I don't want it." Jack wanted to say other things, important things, but couldn't seem to string a sentence together. He couldn't even begin to explain why he had the absolute certainty that was his decision. He just knew in his heart it was right. Instead he pulled at Riley and cradled him in a hug that was protective, gentling, safe.

Silence followed, until Beth's words took them by surprise.—

"Is now a good time for me to say Steve has asked me to marry him?" Beth looked at each member of her family in turn. "I said, yes," she added, leaning into Steve and exchanging a soft smile. No one said a word, waiting for Donna to speak first.

Donna just smiled and held out a hand to her youngest. "Oh, baby, I'm so happy for you both." Then the dam opened, and Beth was swept up in hugs from her brothers, Jim, and Anna. They all talked at the same time, asking about plans and dates, and the room was filled with happy smiles. Sandra chose that moment to make her excuses and leave.

Jack released Riley's hand so that Riley could walk his mom to her car, and he saw him pulling her in for a hug.

* * * *

Riley, for his part, didn't feel right. It was all wrong. The Campbell family should benefit from Hayes Oil. It should have been Jack with the privilege and the money, and he shouldn't have to scrape to survive. It should have been Josh at an expensive law school, and Beth with the surgeries she needed without fear of bankrupting her family. He left the room, because it was all too much for him to process. He made his farewells to his momma then he found himself in their bedroom —his and Jack's room— the windows open again and the smell of impending rain heavy in the air. Dejected, worried, upset, he slumped to the bed.

He had wanted to hug Steve to congratulate his best friend. It was what Steve had talked about for so many evenings, those evenings that Riley hadn't lost to drink and women anyway. He'd met Elizabeth Campbell at the hospital, and for Steve, befriending the young patient had quickly turned into love. He'd worried over the age difference, he'd worried over his being ill, and he'd talked and talked and talked. The only thing was, Riley hadn't really listened, not like a real friend would. He'd just learned what was useful to him and turned on his best friend. And tonight, Steve couldn't even look at him, and Riley couldn't blame Steve one little bit.

The door to the room opened, and Riley didn't look around, assuming it was Jack. "Sorry," he began. "I'm just…" He couldn't form a word of what he wanted to say past the bitter irritation at feeling so damn useless.

"Just what?" Riley twisted. Steve and Josh were in the room. Josh closed the door behind him and leaned on the door. *What the hell?*

"Just—" The words still wouldn't come, still wouldn't push through the self-pity he was heaping on himself.

It was Josh who started the conversation, pushing himself away from the door, and standing feet firmly apart and fists buried deep in his jean pockets. "Did you use Beth's pregnancy to get Jack to marry you? Just so you could get what you felt you were owed from Hayes Oil? All so you could fuck with your father?"

Riley looked at Steve and then Josh, and then back again. He sighed inwardly, the guilt spiraling out of control inside him, and he knew he just wanted a clean slate. He needed for everyone to know what he was, so that he could maybe make himself a better person.

"Yes." Riley flinched as he said it, waiting for Steve to hold him whilst Josh whaled on him, knowing he wouldn't put up a fight, knowing he deserved it. Josh closed his eyes, hunching his shoulders. Riley thought he could see grief in Josh's face, read sadness as he opened his eyes again. "I'm sorry. I wasn't the person then that I am now. How can I…?" *How can I get my friend back? How can I say sorry to Beth? Should I tell Beth?*

"You and Jack seem kind of friendly, despite the start," Steve commented drily.

Riley felt himself blush at that. What could he say? Steve was asking him to be honest, demanding honesty where none had been before. Josh tilted his head, patiently waiting for Riley to speak.

"I think I love him," Riley said quietly. It was simple in the end. So very simple.

Josh nodded, seeming to come to some sort of big brother decision in his head, and held out his hand towards

Riley, which Riley took pathetically quickly.

"Okay," was all Josh said, and then turning on his heel, he left the room and pulled the door shut again.

"Steve—"

"Like Josh said," Steve interrupted swiftly. "You did what you did, for reasons I will never understand, because of a father I will never understand. It's come right in the end, and I won't hold a grudge against my best friend."

"I haven't been a very good friend," Riley offered sadly, an apology in quiet words.

"You only ever see the bad stuff in yourself, Riley. Without your encouragement, I would have given up on Beth a long time ago." Riley felt his throat tighten with emotion. It was overwhelming that Steve saw this good in him, that Steve wasn't focusing on the bad stuff that had happened. "So, we're cool?"

Riley nodded and crossed to pull Steve into a manly back-slapping hug. "We will be."

"Kitchen. Beer." Steve moved back and opened the door, waiting for Riley to follow, that stupid, inane, mischievous Steve-smile on his face, the smile that Riley had missed. Without hesitation Riley went into the kitchen after his friend, catching the tail end of an embarrassing story about Josh and a pair of red silk panties. Jack took his hand, pulled him in for a hug. He glanced at Josh and Steve and then up at his husband.

"Okay?" he asked quietly.

"Okay," Riley replied, leaning down to kiss full lips gently, pulling back and smiling. "Okay."

The conversation turned to celebrating, with Beth demanding a dinner out. Riley instantly offered to take everyone to the best restaurant in Dallas on him, and Beth quietly refusing.

"I just want to go The Rusty Nail. It's a bit of a dive but has the best steaks in town. I just want simple, just us, no fuss. I wanna call Eden, so she can meet us there."

They went in two trucks, Steve the designated driver in one with Beth curled next to him, and Josh with Anna on his lap in the back. Donna drove the second with Jim. Riley and Jack squeezed in the back, talking about what had been happening. Between them, Josh's kids chattered excitedly about what they were going to do at the babysitters.

It was just what everyone needed— air, escape, normalcy, beer.

No one spoke about the decisions they'd made, just focusing on the proposal. The bar's restaurant was busy. Friday seemed to be a popular night for everyone, from couples to groups. Music was drifting from strategically placed speakers and the smell of steak and potatoes permeated the air. Josh ordered various beers, whisky chasers and wine with a softly spoken and sarcastic, "Your round, Richie Rich" in Riley's ear. He smirked, and Riley half smiled back, kind of uneasily, given he didn't know Josh all that well yet, despite their discussion earlier.

It was a mere half an hour before it started to go horribly wrong. Beth and Eden disappeared into the bathroom, Beth unable to hold the water she was sipping any longer than ten minutes.

"You slumming it, Hayes?"

Everyone looked up at the clearly inebriated guy leaning on the back of Beth's empty chair, his face twisted in a rare kind of anger.

"I'm sorry?" Riley answered, clearly confused. "Do I know you?"

The man snorted a bitter laugh. "When you paid me shit to work for your company you knew me. When you fired me with no grounds, you even knew my name! Where do you get off coming into my bar and—"

"We're just having a quiet meal here, son." Jim interrupted the flow of venom with a firm touch on the man's arm, trying to guide him away from the table. The man wrenched his arm free.

"You here with your fag husband, huh?"

Jack stood abruptly. "Why don't you just go back over to your table and shut your goddamn mouth?"

"You must be Hayes's cocksucking faggot of a husband." The man lurched forward, and Jim tried to pull him back as Jack drew himself up to his full height.

"That the best you got, Bubba? My Momma's called me worse things than that," he said clearly, turning to Donna and wincing as his mom started to protest.

"Jackson Robert Campbell, I have never—"

Eden and Beth arrived back at the table, both puzzled to see this man toe-to-toe with Jack, Jim on one side, and Riley and Josh both standing now. "Jack?"

"I see the little Hayes whore is here too. How are tricks, Princess Eden?" Eden looked at Riley blankly. She had no more idea who this man was than Riley had.

That was enough to encourage Riley forward. "That's my sister you're talking about, asshole. I don't tolerate anyone speaking to Eden that way. You really need to apologize to her and to my husband before I kick your ass." Riley then swallowed. Had he actually just said that, in a strange bar, in the middle of nowhere, with a group of buddies circling the guy looking for the fight? *Shit.* Steve moved next to him, a hand on his lower back, and Riley had never felt so relieved.

"Fuck you. I ain't doing no apologizing to no damn Hayes!" The man and his friends crowded closer. In the background, tables were being moved, people obviously used to bar brawls. Riley could see the bartender was moving bottles from the counter, taking side bets on who was gonna come out on top and dialing the cops at the same time.

Jack turned to the table. "Momma, you need to get Beth and Eden out of here. Josh, you need to stay out of this, 'cause I sure as hell am gonna need you to bail me out of jail tonight." Josh refused, standing close to his brother.

"I know good lawyers," Josh pointed out.

"Beth…" Eden sounded scared, and Beth pulled her hand as they moved away from the brothers and Riley.

"This isn't the first time they've brawled, and it won't be the last," she said clearly.

Riley looked at Steve who looked shell-shocked at the vitriol this guy was throwing at him. The man's friends stepped up to join him, which was the girls' cue to move to the door. Jack stepped forward, away from the others, talking to the first man who had the problem.

"Dude, I'm gonna let you have the first punch for free, but I want you to remember the name of the man who's gonna beat your ass— Campbell-Hayes."

The man reacted almost immediately, punching Jack in the jaw. Jack's head snapped back, and Riley moved to intervene, only stopping when Jack placed a hand in front of him, serenely righting himself, jerking his head to the side to loosen his neck, then calmly cracking his knuckles.

"It's on."

Jack's punch was a lot more accurate, and within seconds, the entire bar had erupted into a fight— Riley and Jack side by side, Steve at Riley's back, Josh well into the depths of the crowd and Jim providing left side support. It was evenly matched; every punch and hit returned with equal force, the other side mostly fuelled by liquor and anger, which gave Riley the edge he desperately needed in this new and hostile environment.

Chapter 31

Jack saw Riley pull a guy off him by literally lifting him over the bar, muscles bunching, and a knife of desire started to carve into his body. Riley had waded in with his six-four advantage, despite what had to be his incredibly sore chest. Jack tried to move to stand in front of him to shield him but was being dragged away by grabbing hands.

Riley managed one or two more swings before it became obvious the pain in his chest had started to get worse and he was faltering. Jack was never more pleased to see Steve, who had previously been behind Riley, jump into the fray. The whirling dervish of a blond took out three of Riley's opponents before they even realized he was there. Jack tried to thank him, but he was distracted by another punch, and then it was over as quickly as it had started, with the 911 call answered and the cops in the house. Donna, Beth, Eden and Anna hovered nervously as their guys limped and laughed their way to them, exchanging war stories and generally high on adrenalin and victory.

Jack looked at his suave, dignified husband in a very different way, seeing his button-down's ripped off buttons, dark sweat staining the material, and a huge grin across his face. He leaned towards him, but it was hard to string words together. He could taste the metallic tang of his own blood where his lip was split.

"You are so fucking hot," he murmured, his hand tracing the sweat path past hard nipples, the dips and highs of Riley's chest and lower to his crotch. Jack went from exuberant and horny to *holy shit* hard in less than a second as he felt his husband hard in his jeans, and he moaned low in his throat. Riley had blood on his face, his hair was flattened to his head with sweat, his jeans were torn, and his shirt hung loose about him with a tear running from neck to arm. The testosterone was swirling in them, the anger, the fear, the fight instinct pushing and shoving at politeness as Riley pushed back, his dick hard against Jack's hip.

Jesus. Jack wanted him now, his hand clutching at torn material, his eyes drawn to Riley's lips, imagining them wrapped around his dick, imagining him on his knees on the floor, sucking Jack down and— *Shit.*

"If you agree to pay for the damage, Riley, we are free to go. Turns out no one wants to arrest a Hayes." Josh's voice broke through Jack's fantasy, but he didn't move, his hands gripping harder, only blinking as Josh leaned in and half whispered, "Take it home, guys. Me an' Jim will sort the girls out."

The drive home was too long, neither man speaking, the tension in the car so thick Jack could feel it wrapping around them, the night inviting all sorts of fantasies and wants. They made it to the room in seconds, pulling the door closed and locking it. Jack ripped at the remains of Riley's shirt, dropping clothing on the floor, and Riley bit kisses into Jack's throat and moaned his appreciation.

"I want you to fuck me," Jack growled in his best porn voice, "'til I don't remember my name." He swallowed any protest in a biting, hurting kiss, pushing and pulling until he was on all fours on the bed naked, thrusting slick into Riley's hands and demanding Riley start now.

* * * *

Riley swallowed. How could he even think of turning Jack down, naked, waiting for him, begging for it? He squeezed too much slick on his fingers. He knew it was too much but didn't care. He just slipped a finger into Jack, his lover arching and keening at the pressure inside. It was quickly joined by a second, then a third, scissoring, locating his prostate and gently smoothing his fingers over it on every other pass.

"Riley, now, for God's sake," Jack pleaded. "Get inside me, Riley, now!" Riley lined up, and began to slowly push into Jack, but Jack wasn't having any of it. He drove himself back on Riley's dick.

"Jack, slow down. Fuck, I'm not gonna—"

Jack slowed for a minute, looking back over his shoulder at Riley, his eyes bright with lust, his lips parted, his breathing ragged. "Riley, hard."

Riley swallowed nervously, his instinct not to hurt being decimated by his need to just bury himself in Jack, harder and harder. Drawing on every reserve, listening to the wanton noises of the man beneath him, he set a fast, deep pace, sweat soon dripping off him onto Jack's back as he lost himself in Jack's heat.

Jack whined, demanding more. He said it wasn't enough, and he pushed back harder, a gasp of pain escaping his mouth.

"All of you, Riley, harder, all of you. Fuck!"

With a growl, Riley pulled out, forcing Jack onto his back, the muscles in his arms bunching with the exertion. He wanted to see Jack's face. "Are you sure?"

"Riley!" was Jack's only reply, and taking a deep breath, trying to center himself, trying not to lose it there and then, Riley pushed back in. He had always wondered what this would be like, to have a lover he could let go with, to not have to hold back his strength. It was overwhelming, and looking down at his sexy lover, it seemed Jack was into it the same as Riley was. Jack's eyes were dark and wide, his gaze never leaving Riley, his fingers gripping the sheets so tightly they almost ripped the material. He was repeating words over and over again, "More— more— harder— I love you," and it made Riley feel ten feet tall.

He was close, so close, trying to hold back, but he needed Jack's mouth, needed Jack's tongue in his mouth. As they kissed, Jack started to whimper in pleasure, his arms going around Riley's broad shoulders. Riley could feel Jack tightening up, and he groaned as Jack pulled Riley's head down to his shoulder and began to focus on the juncture of neck and throat, sucking and biting hard on warm skin, tasting salt, tasting blood.

Jack lost it, coming so hard, clenching around him and only a few thrusts later, Riley shouted his own release, lost in sensation and rocking into the orgasm. They kissed, the taste of the blood there again, a small moan of contentment exchanged with heavy breaths and lazy tongues.

Slowly Riley eased out, Jack almost whimpering as Riley pulled free, both feeling weak as newborn kittens as Riley used the sheet to wipe them clean. Finally they just lay there, exhausted, happy, sated.

"So fucking sexy, Riley. When I looked up and saw you fighting right next to me, it was the hottest thing I'd ever seen. *You* were the sexiest man I'd ever seen." Jack's voice was thick with emotion and exhaustion, and he was asleep before Riley could even answer. His last conscious thought as he drifted off to sleep himself was, *If that's what got Jack this turned on, we are so gonna have to get into fights more often…*

Chapter 32

It started almost as soon as she shut her eyes. The same dream. The same nightmare, pushing her to cuddle deeper into her covers, a whimper on her lips.

Sense memories from that night, the evening light soft and subtle, the steps she was taking into adulthood that night meant so much to her. Twenty, and the world was hers, her first real event after the surgery. Jack dropped her at the party with his usual words of warning, and she had rolled her eyes at the whole big brother thing. He was so damn protective, he and Josh both. It had been an evening that demanded a little black dress and Beth felt like a princess, a sexy adult princess.

By eleven, she'd been getting tired, but she had made the effort to push through the constant exhaustion that plagued her, determined to be normal. By twelve, she'd lost her friends in the house somewhere, and by twelve fifteen, she was stuck in a room with the last person on earth her brother would want her to be with. By twelve thirty-five, she lay sobbing, her innocence gone. At one, Jack picked her up, concerned to see her so tired, but she had cleaned herself up real good. He would never know.

Her nightmares were filled with running and not getting away, of fear and hopelessness, of feeling so small, so hurt—

It sent her upright in her bed, her breathing ragged, and she saw that dawn washed the room with pale ethereal light. It was okay; she was here, home, at the D, grounded, safe. But the nightmare remained in her memories, and she knew where she would go now, where her nightmares always sent her now—

They sent her to find Jack.

* * * *

Jack had been up since five, his head buzzing with post beer and fight aches and pains, his ass just this side of sore, and his world a hell of a lot more complicated than a few weeks ago. He'd left Riley curled on the bed, the man not stirring when Jack's internal alarm clock had pushed him out of bed to see to the horses. It was his quiet time, leaning against the fence with coffee, looking over Campbell land, pride in his every pore at what his family had achieved. He smiled, remembering the sleeping giant in his bed rolling into his space as soon as he moved, cuddling into pillows and murmuring something in his sleep. It was all he could do not to climb back in bed just to hold his husband, kiss away the bruises around his left eye, and the cuts to one of his hands, but his babies needed him.

"Hey, big brother." Jack smiled at hearing the voice behind him. Beth had taken to standing with him at this ungodly hour, watching dawn paint pastels across the wide-open sky, claiming Miss Campbell Junior was tap-dancing on her bladder. Unbidden, she curled into his side, and he pulled her close, enjoying the touch.

"Hey, little sister," he said softly. "How's my niece doin' in there?"

"Moving it on up to level two," she replied, rubbing a hand on her belly and smiling ruefully.

"How did it go yesterday at the hospital? With all that happened we never—"

"Everything is good; the heartbeats are strong, hers and mine."

"I wanna come to the next one, talk to the doctor, maybe—"

"Jack, quit with your worrying; I'm doing well, and I have Steve with me. Speaking of whom…" Beth deliberately stopped there, waiting for the inevitable big brother response.

"What about Steve?" There it was— big brother worry, large as life.

"He makes me happy, Jack. I love him, and I know you and Josh worry." Jack stiffened imperceptibly, and then inch by careful inch, he relaxed.

"Not only is he years older than you, which I guess I'm kind of over now, but he's bi, Beth. I just worry. To settle on one…" He wasn't sure how to word it, but Josh had expressed the same concern last night.

"To settle on a woman like me when he could have all those men out there?" Beth offered wryly, causing Jack to blush.

"No, Beth, I didn't mean it like that. I like Steve, and he's a good friend to Riley. I like that he looks after you. Is that what you wanted to hear?"

"More than. So we have your blessing, then?" Jack hugged her tighter; reluctant to let her go, but knowing he needed to.

"Of course you do, baby girl, of course you do."

"Thank you, Jack. He makes me happy, makes me feel safe."

"Anyway," Jack continued, tongue firmly in cheek, "me 'n' Josh can always take him out by the barns and have a *quiet* word if he fucks it up."

"Ass."

* * * *

Lisa settled back in her chair, the book balanced on one knee, the glass of wine in the other. It was her favorite time of day, no Jeff shouting at her, and her son curled on her lap reading from the fairy tales in the big gilded book, the only real thing she'd brought to this marriage. It was quiet time, post school and pre-Jeff coming home. He had just called and left a message. He wouldn't be home until 10 pm, and that made her stretch her toes deliciously. Six whole hours of peace.

She winced at the pull of old bruises on her spine and cursed the need to lean forward. Carrying these marks may have become second nature now, but that sure as hell didn't make it any easier physically.

The nanny arrived to take the children to tea, and as usual, she kissed them both, feeling a little lost as they disappeared for their nutritionally appropriate meals. As the door began to shut behind them, a hand stopped it, and a soft voice came into the room.

"Lisa, may we talk?"

Lisa smiled. She had affection for Sandra Hayes, not love exactly but affection nonetheless.

"Of course." She patted the seat next to her, but Sandra just hovered. What was she waiting for? She looked pale, a little nervous, her eyes bracketed with tiredness. Finally it was as if she reached a decision and handed Lisa a wallet, filled with photos, some in color, some in black and white, some taken from a distance, some distressingly close up.

"Jeff's women." Sandra said gently, sitting down next to her, allowing Lisa the time to look at them closer.

Lisa checked each photo, although it killed her to do so. Some of these women were just a little older than her daughter, than Jeff's daughter, and in each one, there were marks and bruises. Blood and cuts and, in the closer photos, she could see eyes full of pain. She twisted her hands together, tears rolling down her face. She'd always known he had a streak of hate in him, but as long as he kept his temper somewhat under control and his twisted demands away from her, she'd been able to blank the rest out. Yes, she'd felt his hands on her, and every time he took her he had to hurt, had to force. For the children she stayed. She lowered her head as shame flooded her. It wasn't just the children; it was the money, and the safety. Now she had the evidence of Jeff's indiscretions in glossy eight by tens on the chair next to her. She had known he strayed, but these pictures were horrific, bruised women, hookers with scars, cuts and black eyes.

"What do I do with these?" she finally asked. "I need to take them to the police or—"

"You need to do what's right for you and the children."

"I have to help these women—"

"There's nothing you can do for them now, but *you* need to get away from this family before this happens to you, or god forbid, one of the kids," Sandra said simply. Lisa just shook her head. She had no way out of this. She was trapped here in this prison of luxury. She had no independence, nothing. She stumbled to her feet, her arms wrapped around her chest.

"I can't. I have nothing. Everything I have is in Jeff's name. I only have what he allows me."

"Child, everything Gerald has is in *my* name. If you check, most of Jeff's assets will be in your name, less tax that way. You need to get what you can, now. Transfer it, take the kids and just go before he destroys my grandchildren, like Gerald destroyed my children."

Lisa sobbed some more, while Sandra just sat and watched, until finally Lisa lifted her gaze, steel in her spine. She dropped her arms and lifted her shirt, turning her back to Sandra, listening to the gasp, knowing what the older woman saw.

"He hurts me," she half whispered, facing Sandra and allowing her shirt to fall back in place.

"I didn't know…" Sandra sounded confused, shocked. "Please… tell me… the children—"

"I swear he never touched the children."

"How long until he does?"

Lisa felt sick with dread. Her children. She struggled with the decision. For the kids, she had stayed. Being with Jeff meant that her kids had everything they wanted, everything they could ever need. She had never told a living soul, but Jeff had taken to using his hands on her without love or respect, smacking her, pushing her around like she was some ten dollar whore. She had become a shell of the woman she had once been, and the children were changing as well. Disinterested in life, spoiled, greedy, stubborn, taking cues from their father about how they should approach life. For the kids, she knew she had to leave. They would hate it at first, but they would grow to see that she was right.

With determination, she dragged a suitcase from her closet and dumped it on her bed. "Can you help me?" she asked.

Sandra walked to her side, closed the case and left the photos on the sofa.

"You need nothing from here. Let's just get the children and go."

* * * *

"What are you doing in here?" Jeff sounded stressed, exhausted.

"Waiting for you, son," Sandra said simply.

"Where's Lisa?"

"She's gone, Jeff. I helped her leave." Sandra was staying remarkably calm, not sure how Jeff was going to react, and then instantly knowing he was going to react with the same anger and violence he approached the rest of his life. She knew even as she said what she'd done that he'd hit her. Even as his hand connected with her face, the same as Gerald's had, she knew she deserved every smack, every punch, that she was being made to feel. Finally he stopped —the haze of red lifting— and Sandra on the floor in front of him.

"No one leaves a Hayes," he spat.

Chapter 33

Riley was poring over figures, his brow furrowed in concentration, his coffee mug close by. The Campbells may not want the Hayes money, but he wanted to stop the way the company was being run.

"So, if we are to make this happen and get installed at Hayes Oil, we need to look at figures," he started carefully. "Eden has twenty-two percent, me the same, Jeff has the forty-eight percent, and I think we can track down who holds the remaining eight. From what I've managed to find out today, it seems an offshore holdings company has a total of six and the rest is kind of spread around."

Jack leaned back in his chair, thoughtful, not seeing exactly where this was going.

"I think you should be looking to your momma to fill in the gaps," Jim said, emptying Riley's cold coffee and replacing it with a new mug of hot fragrant brew.

"My mom?" Riley looked confused, and Jim slid the papers over to him, leaning back to swallow coffee in one smooth move. Jack just stared at the paperwork in front of his husband, waiting for him to look and frowning as

Riley pushed the whole lot towards him, seemingly unable to even look at what may be more damning evidence against his family. Jack lifted it and opened to the first sheet— certificates, in the name of Sheriton holdings, a total of just short of six percent, the offshore holding company they knew about. Jack dug further, linking the wording in each sheet, following the same path that Jim had. Blinking he looked up, meeting Riley's confused gaze, knowing his husband was scared of what was in the folder, because it would hold more truths about his family, more shovels to dig the grave.

"Sandra Hayes owns Sheriton holdings; she has the six percent." Jack was suddenly excited, remembering Sandra's visit to the D yesterday and her wish to help her son. "And if we can persuade her to side with Riley and Eden, just to give a simple majority, we can push forward with replacing the management team with a new one, namely your team."

"Jack, wait." Jim leaned forward. "Y'all came to me with this *idea,*" he waved his hand dramatically, "to force control of Hayes Oil over to a new management team, and on paper, it all works, the equations balance and we could do this. But…"

"But what?" Riley inquired at the pause.

"It's simple. I don't understand why you want to hand over control of the company, and unless I do understand, then I won't be signing anything." Jack and Riley exchanged glances, which didn't go unnoticed by Jim. He narrowed his eyes.

"A way back," Riley finally started, "I took over the land exploration side of Hayes Oil, the R&D arm. It was my baby, and it did well. I rode the wave of success, and I never questioned when the exploration turned to acquisition. That was Jeff's forte, his role. I was naive." He stopped, his hands twisting on the table in front of him, and Jack placed a steadying hand on top to still the nervous movements. There was vulnerability about Riley when he talked about Hayes Oil that inevitably made Jack switch to protective mode. "I mean, I'm not stupid. Hayes Oil is huge, competitive, a corporation that wields its power with finality. Some of the decisions that were made were out of my control, but they didn't sit well with me, on ethical or emotional grounds.

I always knew I was wrong at Hayes Oil, like it wasn't me working there, but some stranger reading from a script. It just felt wrong." He shrugged.

"I wish I could explain how unhappy I was. I started to plan my own company away from Hayes Oil, from the ground up, ethical exploration, ethical land acquisition, that kind of thing. I researched other petroleum companies, and there were other business models that I admired. I liked where they were taking their business, and I wanted to do the same to Hayes Oil. I couldn't, I lost it and any control I might have, and I don't think it was ever going to be given to me. Dad gave a larger holding to Jeff, never gave enough to Eden and me that would allow us to make a difference. He came up with this contract proposal, gave temporary holdings to Jeff, citing the crap that I had a year to get married for love, stay married for love, and then he would re-allocate the holdings more fairly. You know all that." Jim nodded, and Jack tightened his grip as Riley continued. "I was never going to be given any kind of control. I know that now."

"Because Gerald Hayes isn't your father," Jim said gently.

"He wanted to do everything in his power to stop you from getting any control at Hayes Oil. But he had a deal with your mom to provide you with the Hayes name and at least some semblance of ownership," Jack added.

Riley raised his impassioned gaze to Jack. "I *need* to stop Hayes Oil in its tracks, and the only way I can do that is to get my voice heard."

"How watertight is the twenty-two percent you hold?" Jack went to the crux of the matter, because parentage issues aside, they needed to be sure.

"Jim says totally," Riley offered simply, and Jim nodded his agreement.

"Okay," Jack responded, "let's get this thing sorted."

* * * *

Jeff sat opposite the skinny guy with the bad complexion, feeling dirty by association and wiping his hands on a paper napkin. He was like a fish out of water. The coffee in his mug was sludge, and the table was scarred and dirty. He shivered at the germs he was probably touching just by sitting in the chair. Still this needed to be done.

"The fire was an unfortunate failure," Jeff began, stilling the other man's nerves with a dismissive wave of his hand, "this is a simple observation process. Think of yourself as a private eye."

"I don't do observation."

"You do if I pay you three hundred a day, no questions asked." He watched the man's eyes light up with interest; exploitation of greed was always the best way to win a war. "I want every movement she makes off the ranch recorded and reported. I want your eyes on her and your ears to the ground for anything you can find out."

When he discovered she was pregnant... Well, this had become more than personal. He slid an envelope across the scarred top, moving his hand before the other man could touch him, and simply said, "Campbell, Elizabeth. Starting today."

Chapter 34

Riley found Jack leaning against Solo's stall, lost in thought, the sorrel mare nudging at his arm. It had been nearly six weeks since the fire, and Solo had settled into being a momma with an ease that had Jack beaming with pride. Her bay-colored foal, named Solo-Alexandra, was a beautiful breath of fresh air. Her innate curiosity with life could tempt Riley to stand and watch for hours if he had the time. Instead, Jack was working him hard on the ranch, deciding that now, in this limbo time of decisions on Riley's side, he could fulfill the whole twenty-four days on the ranch clause of the contract.

So here he was, and Riley had aches in muscles he'd never known he possessed before. Of course it didn't help that their sex life was verging on the insanely physical. With neither man able to get enough of the other, they often collapsed into each other's arms, sleeping the few hours left until dawn, unable to even move.

They had fallen into a routine. Jack always offered himself just at the point that Riley was incapable of saying anything, let alone no, and the strength and power he used to get them both off was intoxicating. In his head, there was nothing better than Jack lying beneath him, begging for more, demanding harder, faster.

Last night it had been different. Something indefinable had switched itself on in Riley, the need for *right now* being replaced with the need for forever, and it scared the ever-living shit out of him. He didn't even question how he'd gone from the poster boy for Het-city to craving a man as he craved Jack. It wasn't even just physical; he admired Jack's mind, his determination, his love for his family, his seemingly never ending need to sacrifice his own happiness for others. It shocked Riley to see the depths of passion his husband had inside him, and the erotic dreams he was having about him didn't help.

Riley wanted to be held down the same way he could hold Jack down. He wanted to know what it felt like to have Jack inside *him*. The need was becoming the only thing he could think about. Jack was strong and muscled through manual labor. He was rough and ever so slightly dangerous, as demonstrated in the bar brawl, and it sent shivers down Riley's spine to imagine submitting to Jack. Allowing Jack to take *him*, push *him* over the edge, fuck *him* into next week… Jack hadn't broached the subject. They had gotten close, but the latent alpha in Riley inevitably took control, and Jack was more than happy it seemed to let him take the lead, despite topping from the bottom with his counter pushes and his demands.

Riley had researched a bit, if you call Wikipedia and various random porn sites research. The dynamics of a gay relationship were as fraught with potholes and problems as any other kind of relationship. Thing is, in all the many one night stands Riley had enjoyed, it was always him calling the shots. They'd wanted that, these simpering girls that killed his time. He sighed. How did he go about telling his husband what he wanted? How did he get Jack so worked up that he didn't question what Riley wanted?

He stood for a moment, simply watching his husband. His jeans were worn and white in places, his boots scuffed, his denim jacket loose over a Black Sabbath T-shirt, and his thoughts clearly a million miles away. Jack was beautiful, rugged, slim-hipped, broad-shouldered, relaxed and strong; a study in cowboy if there was such a thing, and Riley shifted to relax some of the instant pressure in his jeans.

"Hey, husband," he said softly, making Jack jump and turn to face him, the sapphire in his blue eyes so clear in the early morning light, a smile lit across his face. Riley crossed to pull him into a close one-handed hug, aware he was still damp from his shower, shaking his wet hair in Jack's face playfully. Jack grimaced and punched him on the arm. "Careful, you'll spill the coffee," Riley teased, offering Jack one of the mugs he had his fingers threaded through. Jack fell on it as if it was from the gods, inhaling the bitter smell and sighing.

"Did I ever tell you I loved you?" Jack said as he sipped at the hot brew, wrinkling his nose at how dark it was compared to what he would make himself. Riley winced. They had this conversation every morning on the merits or not of black coffee. Jack drank his with milk, and Riley had his black, but with so much sugar Jack swore he could stand a spoon in it.

"Too dark, yeah?" Riley smirked.

"People have been shot for less," Jack growled low.

Riley leaned in for a good morning kiss, one of many they'd already exchanged and would carry on exchanging throughout the day. They couldn't get enough of touching, kissing, hugging, or just talking, holding hands, exploring limits for public displays of affection. Jack only ever said the love word as a joke or during sex. He never said it with meaning. Or at least not the meaning Riley was starting to want, but then Riley hadn't said it at all yet so he couldn't exactly talk. Something was missing. He knew everything had started so damn badly, with the worst plan in history, with Jack being blackmailed into marriage, but it was good now. Wasn't it? They had slipped into a routine that was hot, passionate, new, and Riley felt loved, felt needed. It was just… Would Jack ever really trust him, could he ever *really* love him?

He guessed he had a kind of love from Jack. It amazed Riley how Jack made him feel so different, almost special. He couldn't get his head around just how much Jack appeared to want him, how Jack found him sexy, praised him, and told him so often how much he wanted him.

"I'll be ten minutes," Jack offered quickly, handing back the mug and crossing to Alexandra. The poor thing seemed to be struggling with feeding this morning, and Jack had mentioned he was mildly worried that maybe Solo-Cal wasn't up to nursing her baby. Riley nodded, seeing the worry in Jack's eyes again, and a similar worry skittered down his own spine. He adored Alex and her horsey ways, something he would never have expected. In his world, horses were for amusement, for recreation.

He let his mind wander as he stared out at the Texas morning, and thought back to two nights ago when Steve and Beth sat at the table with Anna and Donna talking weddings. They planned a simple wedding at the D, in the new barn being constructed on the site of the old burned horse stables. They had a list of people to invite, a local band to do music, Jack and Josh as joint fathers of the bride, and Eden and Anna as bridesmaids. It sounded perfect, and Riley lost himself in images of his best friend in a tux tying himself to the beautiful Beth for the rest of his life, or hers.

The bridesmaids and Beth were discussing flowers.

"Can I talk to you?" Steve had asked him. Standing from the table, Steve walked to the door.

Riley snapped out of his thoughts as he realized Steve was talking to him. He grabbed two beers and followed Steve out to the porch, the night dark around them, and the haze of the Dallas lights on the horizon. Behind them the canopy of stars appeared low to the ground as the land dipped in the distance. Riley, at ease and relaxed, felt peace settle around him like an old blanket.

"Wassup?" Riley was prepared for anything now. They had done the whole "you are a shitty friend thing" whereby Riley admitted he'd been one and Steve had agreed. He wondered what Steve was going to add now.

"I have this favor to ask." Steve seemed nervous. The only other time he'd seemed this nervous was when he'd originally approached Riley for the money for Beth. That had been way back before the whole arranged marriage thing. "I want you to be my best man." Riley blinked. He hadn't expected that in any way, shape or form.

"Yes," he said quickly, his answer instant. "Jeez, I would be honored." He didn't know what else to say, blown away that Steve had asked him after what he'd done. He really couldn't ask for a more forgiving friend. Steve smiled, pulled him into a back-slapping hug then stepping away, still with the nervous looks.

"There's just one thing, Riley," he said, a hint of hesitation in his voice. "I'm being totally honest with Beth, about my past, things that I've done, people I've been with. I don't want any secrets." Riley thought of his secret-driven marriage and inwardly thought Steve was definitely making the right decision. "That starts with telling her about the money you gave me for her medicine, for the visits to the specialist when she became pregnant."

Riley paled. Jack wasn't even aware of the details of all that. Shit, promising money for Beth had been the one thing that had gotten Jack to agree to the whole arranged marriage idea— the promise that Riley would provide for all of Beth's care, putting money in trust for her.

"Shit, Steve," was all Riley could form in the way of a response, leaning back on the railing, the beer loose in his hand.

"I'm telling her tonight when everyone has gone. She *worries* about Jack and you, worries about your marriage, about you. Despite the whole fire-rescue-hero thing, I know there's something there, a hesitation in her whenever your name is mentioned. I want her to know what kind of man you really are. That you're not just some playboy Dallas prince with money to burn, but a genuine person who can be trusted." Steve looked so earnest, and Riley wanted to say it was okay, but all he could think of, albeit selfishly, was facing Jack over this. Steve squeezed his shoulder. "It will be fine, and Jack will think you even more of a hero for helping out his sister."

Chapter 35

Riley hadn't really believed that, not even as he stood toe-to-toe with Jack in the bedroom, his husband's temper so close to the surface that Riley could almost touch it.

"So," Jack said, icy calm, his arms folded across his chest, "the one thing that made me decide to do this, the money for Beth, you had already gone and done, and you lied to me."

"Yes." Riley offered nothing in defense, his voice dejected, and his heart twisting at whatever was going to happen next.

"How much, Riley?" Riley frowned at the question, and shrugged. "How much?" Jack repeated dangerously.

"Four hundred," Riley finally answered miserably.

"I'll pay you back," Jack said. "From the sale of Alex, I will pay you back the entire four hundred thousand dollars plus interest." There was determination in his voice and a hard light in his eyes, his face taut with tension.

"No, it was part of the contract anyway," Riley said quickly. There was no way Jack was paying it back. Jack took a step closer, so close that Riley could smell the horses and the sun-kissed sweaty skin that was so much a part of his husband. He flinched as Jack raised a hand, frowned as Jack gently touched his face, moving fingers to his hair and pressing his hands into the short hair that he said he loved.

"See, that is the problem, that contract. I pay you back, and then the contract is wiped. It's not like you've given any of the other money over yet, and I don't intend to take it."

"Jack, I—"

"No, Riley, if we want this to last the year then you *have* to let me do it my way from the start."

And that single sentence —"If we want this to last the year"— was where he knew he'd fallen in love with his cowboy rancher, inextricably, totally, forever in love, wanting it way past the year he had intended.

And standing here now, watching Jack deal with Solo and Alex, seeing the gentle touches he used on the beautiful new life, Riley knew what he wanted.

He wanted Jack to take control, if only once, or maybe taking it in turns, whatever. He wasn't at all sure of all the terminology, and he wanted to tell Jack that he loved him.

Jack was happy Alex was nursing okay, moving back to stand next to Riley and stealing some of his coffee, grimacing at the amount of sugar.

"Thought we could start on the barn today if you're up for it," he suggested, locking the gate and leaving momma and baby in peace.

"Yeah," Riley agreed, swiping the worn Stetson from the hook, his Stetson, the one Jack had loaned him. Feeling very much the cowboy in jeans, T-shirt and black denim button-down, he followed Jack to the site of the new barn. Josh had been over the day before, and between him and Jack, most of the debris had been cleared away before Riley had returned from a meeting with Eden and Jim and his mom. Today they were moving frames, starting to construct the barn from the ground up, and the heat was warm on their backs.

They soon stripped off their outer shirts, Riley standing under the blazing sun, sweat sliding off his skin, soaking his white T-shirt, and collecting at the base of his neck. He stretched, reaching his hands to the sky, his skin hot and his mouth dry. He turned to Jack to call a water break, wiping the sweat from his eyes with his discarded shirt, and stopped as he realized Jack was staring.

"Water," Jack said calmly, turning on his heel and moving swiftly to the horse barn, grabbing the bottle and tipping it over his head before swallowing mouthfuls of the cool liquid. Riley followed, reaching for the container. He began pouring water over his head, allowing it to soak into his hair, then pushed the thick mess of hair back off his face, gulping down the water that felt so damn good. He never saw Jack move, only felt himself being manhandled back inside the barn, far into the shade where no one could see. Riley tripped and stumbled even as Jack tried to steady him, until he found himself flat against wood, his hands scrabbling for purchase.

Jack didn't stop. Pulling Riley's head down for kisses, he inserted his body between Riley's thighs, forcing Riley to widen his legs. Bringing him down to his level, Jack forced his head back by his wet hair so he could kiss-bite his way down the sweat and water on Riley's skin. Riley was incoherent, his hands still flailing, his dick iron in his jeans before he could think, or not think, as the case may be.

Jack moved his mouth up to Riley's ear. "Do you have any idea how fucking hot you look in this?" Jack pulled at the white T-shirt, pulling it up to Riley's neck, his clever fingers ghosting over hot skin, pausing to twist at sensitive nipples, chasing the touch with his lips and tongue and teeth. Riley whimpered, finally able to catch hold of the beam above his head, gripping tight as Jack explored his body with groans and touches and desperate need and want. Jack stepped back, his eyes taking in every inch of Riley standing, legs spread, hands gripping the beam, his head thrown back, wanting. He almost whined as Jack had stood away from him, for only seconds, but it was too much.

"Jack?"

"Don't move. Okay. Don't move." And with that Jack ran from the barn.

* * * *

Only minutes later, Jack came back in, predatory, slow, pulling his T-shirt over his head and standing in front of Riley. Seeing Riley there, like he was tied in place, every muscle pushed to the limit was too tempting, and he had to touch. Caressing, slipping hands over damp skin, he found a small tear at the neck of the T-shirt and ripped it in two to reveal Riley's, his husband's, broad chest. He settled his lips just above his lover's left nipple and bit hard, causing Riley to yelp in pain, but his lover still didn't move. Jack's hands closed around the button fly on Riley's jeans, pulling at them until he could push an eager hand in to close round Riley's weeping, needy dick. With the other hand, he went into his pocket, pulling out the lube and holding it out for Riley, imagining his husband splitting him apart in the dark of the barn.

"Jack, no." Riley shook his head, stubbornly holding on to the beams. Jack was puzzled. Had he misread this? He thought that Riley wanted to make love in the barn. "I wanna know… I want you in me," Riley rasped, his voice gruff, his breathing harsh.

Jack didn't need to be asked again, didn't question his husband's words. He pushed denim down over sharp hips, following the material, passing kisses close to Riley's dick, biting into his thigh, licking the marks he had left. He helped Riley toe off boots and lose his jeans altogether until his husband stood gloriously naked in front of him.

"Turn 'round," Jack ordered. "Hold the beams, spread your legs." His voice was so broken, yet he felt so determined as Riley twisted to face away from him,

Jack again using his denim-clad legs to get Riley to spread his. "Beautiful," he breathed, his fingers in damp blond hair, pushing Riley to reveal his neck, kissing and sucking marks he knew would still be there tomorrow. He worshipped skin, whispered demands, until Riley was writhing under his hands, making his own demands.

"Please. Make me feel."

Coating his hand with slick, Jack began to open Riley, torn between being careful and taking his time, and just fucking pushing his whole hand in. Jack kept up a litany of words, "So good— I'm sorry— so fucking hot— I'm sorry— I love you", hearing Riley alternately moan in discomfort and then nearly whine with *more*. One-handed, he pulled at his own jeans until he had his dick in his hands and had slicked himself up. He pinched the base of his cock as he almost lost it over his husband's tight muscled ass, at just the erotic images in his head. After lining himself up, the first push was tentative until he slipped past the tight ring of muscle. He heard Riley gasp and felt him stiffen, knowing it was hurting him. He made to pull back, but couldn't as Riley pushed against him. Jack was moving in a small way, and then it was too much; he was lost, pulling his lover farther away from the wall, reaching around with slippery fingers to start a counter rhythm as he bottomed out inside Riley and began to thrust.

He angled to find the sweet spot, tried so hard, only knowing when he found it by the exhaled gasp and whimper of his name in Riley's throat. The rhythm he set was punishing, biting down on Riley's corded neck as orgasm started to build to the explosion point. Under him, Riley was cursing up a storm, demanding harder, wanting more, and Jack twisted his fingers around his lover's dick. He was upping the movement until Riley went rigid under him, and the feeling of heat and wetness on his hand was enough to have him coming hard into his husband. Riley's dark heat was gripping his dick as he pumped into him, only stopping when Riley all but collapsed against the wall. Jack followed him, caging him with his arms to prevent himself from landing on top of him. They stood in the intimate embrace until Jack pulled himself free, and Riley turned in the cage, his pupils blown, his face flushed.

"Jesus," he said simply.

"Jack," Jack replied, smirking.

"Fuck."

"We did." Jack leaned in to capture Riley's lips in a hard kiss, his body still vibrating with the aftereffects of orgasm. Every single point of his body was alive with Riley. He wanted to say the words, wanted to tell this gorgeous man, his husband, that he loved him. He wasn't sure if Riley was ready to hear that, but not wanting to push, he kept quiet. What would Riley say if he knew that, in his head, Jack saw them growing old together, being together for as long as they could. It was going to be torture, giving Riley up at the end of the contract year; he couldn't even begin to think about it.

Riley pulled back, resting his forehead on Jack's and curling his hands around his neck. "I love you," he said quietly, so quietly Jack wasn't entirely sure he'd heard right.

"Riley?" *Please say it again if that is what you said*.

"I love you, Jack Campbell-Hayes. I'm sorry if that makes you feel uncomfortable but I needed you to know how I felt and—"

"I love you," Jack interrupted, his head spinning with the implications of what they'd just admitted to each other.

Suddenly the year ahead of them became two years, ten years, twenty, life. So suddenly, despite the chaos outside their small world, everything seemed right. Everything seemed perfect.

Chapter 36

When Eden heard her Momma call from Jeff's apartment and found her, she slid to her knees in horror at her side and shook her head as Sandra made her promise not to say a word— "Not one word, Eden." Eden helped her to her own rooms, separate from Gerald's, got her painkillers and water, and sat by her on the bed.

"Did Jeff do this, Momma?" she had asked quietly.

"No, Eden, it was the monster we created inside him."

"Mom, you can't say that. Riley and I were brought up the same way, and however dysfunctional that was, well, we turned out okay."

"Eden, there is evil in him, even I can see that. He was never like you and Riley. He was always his father's boy, never mine."

"If he's evil, he needs to be stopped, Momma." Eden cradled her mom to her. They had never been close, but that didn't mean she didn't love her. Jeff was not getting away with this.

* * * *

Riley sat back in his seat, the final papers in front of him. Eden sat to his left, his mom to the right, each in their own way ready to make the Hayes name mean something with the scratch and scrape of a pen.

Jim stopped him, just as he reached to sign, placing a hand flat on the papers. Riley looked up startled, blinking at Jim, wondering why he'd stopped him.

"Riley, you realize what you're doing here?" Jim asked for what Riley assumed was the fiftieth time today.

"Jim, this is what we want. We wanna drag Hayes Oil up by its ears and make it accountable for its standards, we want you in as interim manager, we want you to organize a management team, and we want Jeff's power cut off at the knees for what he's doing to the company." Riley summarized each step with a tap of the pen on the papers. "Have I covered everything, Eden?"

"Jim, manager, team, Jeff, knees; I think that covers it," Eden replied.

"Mom?"

"I've waited too long, watched too many good people get hurt by Gerald's actions, and now Jeff's actions. I want it done." Riley sketched a look at his mom, still concerned about the bruises on her face that even makeup couldn't cover. He hadn't asked where she got them after she stopped his concern with a harsh *"Enough,"* and Eden had just closed her eyes and shaken her head, saying *"Leave it"* silently. Riley hated that his mom was hurt, hated that someone had hurt her, hoping to God it wasn't his dad that had done this to her, but not knowing who else to blame. And now, sitting here under the harsh light she looked tired and exhausted, but equally relieved.

Riley knew that what he was doing was exactly the right thing to do. Quickly he scrawled his signature, Riley Nathaniel Campbell-Hayes, bold and strong on the line next to his printed name on all three copies, and soon after, Eden added hers, and finally Sandra. Riley pushed the papers towards Jim, feeling as if the world had been lifted from his shoulders. He may still have a twenty-two percent stake in Hayes Oil, but from this moment on, he was a name on a piece of paper. The real control had passed to Jim and to a new management team.

Jim paused. Only his name was needed on the contract, and that was it. He could go into Hayes Oil, guns blazing, and clean house from top to bottom. He stared into Riley's eyes. Then drawing in a deep breath, he added his signature and closed the file, passing everything to the other lawyer who had been employed for this moment only. Sandra stood and left the room, and Eden made to follow her, but Riley stopped her, following instead. He wanted to be there for his mom, wanted her to believe that he was here for her, and he caught her at the turn of the corridor, with a quiet "Momma?"

She stopped, turning to face her son, tears tracking down soft cheeks, her expression twisted in grief.

"What's wrong? Do you regret what we just did?" Riley needed to know.

Wordlessly, she shook her head, her hand to her mouth, taking the single step that meant Riley had her safe in his hold.

"It's a good thing what we're doing here," she said softly, gripping his shirt and looking up. Riley looked at the bruise on her face, the mark on her neck, the exhaustion in her face, and he needed to know.

"Who did this to you, Momma?" He traced the bruise and half closed his eyes as she winced at the touch. "Was it Da— Gerald?"

Sandra shook her head. "No, he wouldn't go this far. Riley. I'm scared."

"Scared of who, Momma? Who did this?"

"Your brother." Riley stepped away from her, his head reeling. Jeff had done this?

"Mom?"

"He isn't well, Riley. We need to get him help."

"Isn't well? I've put up with his shit all my life, but to hurt you… I'll kill him if I get my hands on him."

* * * *

Riley left the office, climbing into the Hayes limo and giving instructions to cross the city to the tower. Jim was sitting next to him, his face blank, and his thoughts obviously elsewhere.

"You okay?" Riley asked carefully. He needed Jim to be strong today, to present a joined front.

Jim looked at him, blinking. "Yeah, just… your mom." Riley didn't push any further. He could see something still existed between Jim and his mom, but knew the time wasn't right yet. He didn't want to pry. He wasn't even capable of imagining the headspace Jim was in at the moment.

They arrived, and no one questioned Riley and Jim and the team of five people following them as they passed through the security and on to the bank of elevators.

No one questioned them as they appropriated Jeff's office in his absence, and shut down IT systems to be covered by new systems when they rebooted. The IT specialist was rewriting code and reallocating passwords in as many seconds as it took for Riley to back out of the office and hide in the supply room, close to hyperventilating.

The elevator sounded, and Riley peered through the frosted glass of the room's door, inhaling as he saw Jeff pass reception. He stepped out. Jeff looked at him oddly, which wasn't new, to be honest.

"Hiding in the stationery room, little brother? Is Campbell in there?" He didn't wait for a reply, just carried on to his office, stopping on the threshold.

Riley heard talking, shouting, and closed the distance to stand behind Jeff. He felt anger radiating off his older sibling.

"As of today, Jeff, the consortium controls just short of fifty percent of Hayes Oil." Jim was adamant and firm.

"What the fuck. You can't have enough shares to control. What about my family?"

"It's true, Jeff," Riley said softly, handing Jeff the contract copy. "We need to ask you to leave the premises until we get the management team in place and up and running, then we'll sort out what your position will be here." Riley tried to word it diplomatically, seeing his brother's brown eyes glaze and harden in shock. Keeping himself focused on the fact that his brother had hit their mom, he kept his heart closed to any kind of pity.

"What the fuck? This is our company, Riley." His lips tight and his voice strained, Jeff sounded like he was going to burst a blood vessel.

"It's bigger than just us," Riley replied patiently, moving to one side as two men from security flanked Jeff. Jeff shrugged off their touches.

"I'll take these papers to my lawyers."

"You do that, Hayes. I can assure you that all the legal documentation is in order," Jim said simply, and then turned his back on the eldest Hayes son,

effectively ignoring any response Jeff
might give.

"Just go," Riley said encouragingly.
"We'll talk later."

Jeff was finally escorted, swearing
and threatening, to the lobby by the
guards he had formerly employed.

Chapter 37

Jack was restlessly waiting for Riley to return from the tower, only half understanding the conflicting emotions that must be running through his husband. He wanted to help Riley, but he needed Riley to explain how he should be helping. As soon as Riley's SUV came to a halt, Jack was pulling him out of it, past the paddock and to the back to Solo's old barn, back to where he'd had Riley naked and spread for him, holding on to the beam, begging Jack to make him *feel*. Jack didn't want that now, not at this moment. He didn't need lust, or fire, or fucking— he needed to touch, to remember the good in amongst all the bad.

They didn't say anything, not even as Jack pushed Riley back into the corner, back into the shadows, and started to pull at clothing, uncoordinated and clumsy. Riley stopped Jack's fingers, pulled his own shirt off, his own T-shirt, his own boots, jeans, and boxers, finally standing naked and hard in front of his husband. Jack shook himself out of staring, realizing he was doing nothing productive but watching as each muscle moved, as each inch of golden skin was exposed to his gaze. Slowly he stripped off his clothes, finally standing as naked as Riley, his hands reaching to touch. Riley stopped him, grasping at his hands and bowing his head.

"Riley?" Jack's voice was liquid gold, Texas slurred, and wary. Was this so wrong to need Riley now? Did Riley not want this?

"I never expected to love a man," Riley said softly, raising his head, his face tired, his eyes red rimmed, and his lashes spiked and thick with tears. Jack could see he was stripped bare, literally and figuratively, and everything he had to offer was here in front of Jack. "I didn't think I could, that it was even possible," he added carefully, placing a hand flat to the side of Jack's face. Jack turned his head to kiss the palm and then pushed into the hand like a cat, his eyes half closed. "But in all the things that are wrong." He stopped. "Jack… this is right. Is that what I should be feeling? That this seems so right?"

"Riley, I can't tell you how to feel, I know that it's like I've been waiting for you all my life." He took a step forward, bare skin against skin. Jack could taste Riley's tears on his lips, taste the dark heat of him as he deepened the kiss, his hands moving to trace hip bones, and around to Riley's lower back, resting on the dip, one hand stopping there, the other moving to brush across hard nipples.

Riley sighed into the kiss. They didn't have long, but Jack needed this gentle reminder of what he had more than breathing.. The sharp cut of passion and need made him move, subtly at first, and then with more insistence against Riley. They had nothing here, no slick, no plans for making love in *their* barn.

Riley began to drop kisses to Jack's neck, biting and sucking small blooming marks into his skin, using his hand to tilt Jack's head to one side, following the kisses to his pulse and down to the hard nub of his left nipple. He used tongue and teeth to worry at the small mound, his hand twisting and stroking its mate. Jack pushed into the exquisite pain-pleasure of the small bites. He was lost to the sensation, his head thrown back, his dick hard and weeping, wanting to fall to his knees and suck Riley dry, wanting… everything.

It rocked him to the core when it was Riley who moved to his knees in the straw, drawing Jack out of his fantasies at the tentative touch of Riley's mouth, just circling the tip, licking the pre-cum and sucking gently.

"Ri— fuck," was all Jack managed to push out, leaning back to grab one-handed to the stall side, the other hand twisting in Riley's hair. Gently he pulled his husband's head back, the hot mouth leaving his dick, and Riley's suddenly uncertain face looking up. "You don't hafta," Jack said on a breath, trying to be noble, trying to give Riley the chance to back away, but Riley didn't. He simply repositioned, sliding his hot wet mouth as far down as he could, the difference in length made up by Riley's clever fingers, jacking his lover as he sucked him in rhythm. Jack was a pleading incoherent mess as Riley moved his fingers back to trace Jack's heavy balls, moving attention from his dick to draw them individually into his mouth, softly rolling the weight of them and wetting his fingers at the same time. He may not have done this before but, fuck, Riley was a quick learner. He was following what Jack normally did to him, his hands cupping and rolling, his mouth tight on the hard length of his lover, suction tight, movements faster, deeper, and he stroked fingers against Jack's ass, finding the spot he needed, pushing, rubbing, insistent.

Jack couldn't look down, because seeing Riley's lips stretched obscenely wide around him would be enough to finish him. He was on that precipice where he wanted to come, but the sensation was too damn good to come. He didn't want to lose it; he wanted it to last forever. He started to talk, trying to settle his orgasm even as it curled in the pit of his stomach and the base of his spine.

"God, Riley— your mouth— your   Riley— nuuhhh— I'm gonna come— Riley." He tried to pull Riley away by his hair, but his husband was having none of it. If anything, he just sucked harder with the counter rhythm of his hands and his fingers sending Jack higher. With a strangled groan, he shot into Riley's mouth, sharp, hard, his hands tightening with a frightening grip, hearing Riley whimper around his dick, but not being able to stop himself.

Finally Jack released his hold, pulling Riley to stand, looking up into a face smug with pride, and it was too much. Jack just pushed him back, flat to the wall, grabbing Riley's hard straining dick and setting a rhythm of twisting and pulling, Riley's expression of pride changing to one of *fuck— jeez— now* in the blink of an eye. It wasn't going to take much. He was already so close, and as Jack closed his hard teeth around the corded muscle of his neck, it was enough to send Riley tumbling over the edge into oblivion with a muffled shout, swallowed by a hot sticky cum-slick kiss. He panted into his release, his orgasm washing over him in waves, hard sweat-sheened skin sliding against him, murmured praise against freckles and bite marks.

"I want a real ceremony. I want real words." Riley was insistent.

It was Jack that said it first, but Riley repeated it, a litany of confirmation, that they were in this together, that there was nothing they couldn't do if they were together. *I love you— I love you— I love you...*

Chapter 38

Jeff found Gerald on the sixteenth hole.

By the time they were at the eighteenth hole, Gerald was the picture of enraged father, but inside he just knew Jeff wasn't strong enough, with his temper and his sexual perversions, to guide Hayes Oil. The photos he'd found on his desk last night, carefully arranged so he couldn't miss them, showed him that. Maybe he should have put his money on the bastard son instead. Perhaps it wasn't too late.

"Dad?" Jeff sounded almost petulant at what had happened, demanding that Gerald sort it out, that Gerald get on Jim and get him his role at Hayes Oil back.

Gerald just turned around to his eldest son. "Why in the Sam hill did I waste my time on you?"

* * * *

Jeff was left standing, his mouth open in shock as his dad stalked to the eighteenth hole, catching up with his golfing buddies. He was losing control here. He hadn't found out where Lisa was with the kids, and his brother had turned on him. As for Elizabeth Campbell, well, she needed to learn a lesson. He adjusted his pants as he half hardened at the memories of her whimpering under him. Now Elizabeth? He had control over her.

* * * *

Beth was fighting to keep herself sane. She was sure she was being watched. It felt like eyes followed her everywhere, and it was starting to get to her. She was normally so level headed, pragmatic, calm, but for some reason just now, she felt scared and vulnerable. As she replaced the fuel nozzle on the pump, she cast a final look around the gas station and hurried into the shop to clear the bill. When she came back out it she found a familiar figure leaning against the driver's door, his arms folded across his chest and a wry smile on his face.

"Miss Elizabeth," he said, nodding and tracing a look down her body. He stopped on the obvious bump that she curled her arms around to protect.

"Get away from my car." Beth managed to form words despite the cold ice in her heart and the fear spiraling up her spine that left her unable to move.

"I hear you may have some news for me."

Beth reached into her bag, fingers hesitating over the pepper spray and instead closing around her cell phone, pulling it out and scrolling for a name.

"I have nothing to say to you," she managed to half whisper, terror clutching at her as he moved away from the door to stand toe-to-toe with her. Craning her neck, she looked up, images from the party digging like knives into her eyes. Fear and terror, tears and pain, so much pain. She saw his hands move, hovering an inch above her bare arms, the static hissing around her as she imagined his touch.

With a smile that Beth could only describe as evil, he leaned down to whisper six words in her ear, bringing bile from her stomach.

She couldn't move, couldn't talk, wanted to scream, push him away, even knowing how solid he was and that he could probably lift her and throw her to one side. Chuckling softly, he sauntered back to his car, climbed in, and, with a wave, drove off in Dallas direction, leaving her shaking and terrified. Pressing the button she had selected, she started to cry even as Steve's voice came on the line.

"Beth?"

"Steve, help me."

"Beth? Where are you?" She managed to blurt out where she was, shivering the words in haphazard mindless chaos, and she heard him say things, important things. "Stay where you are. I'm coming."

Her fingers were shaking so badly she dropped the cell, clutching her stomach with one hand, the other resting on the scar that twisted across her chest, her breathing shallow.

Six words.

"I'm gonna come for what's mine."

* * * *

Steve made it in ten minutes, his heart in his mouth, his head spinning with thoughts. The baby, she was losing the baby. Her heart, she was dying. He wasn't going to make it in time. She was going to die. He had the presence of mind to shout his fears over the phone to Jack, who didn't even reply, Steve knew he was on his way, knew Beth could need both of them.

He arrived at the gas stop to see a large man leaning over Beth, who sat huddled on the ground next to her car, arms around her legs, rocking and sobbing. Steve immediately pushed him out of the way. "What the fuck are you doing?"

The large man stepped back, his hands raised. "I work here. I was just asking her what's wrong. I saw it from the window. Seriously, dude, I was just looking out for her."

Steve wasn't listening. He dropped to his knees next to her, listening to her repeat over and over, "He can't have her, he can't have her, he can't have her." Desperately, he pulled her hand away from her knees, encouraging her to sit up, and she jerked upright, a scream in her throat, terror in her eyes, scooting away from him even as she seemed to realize who it was. She then fell sobbing into Steve's arms.

"Beth, God, what happened?" She couldn't answer. She was sobbing so loudly it must have hurt.

"I saw some guy, real tall, talking to her, and then he left, and she just kinda collapsed," the attendant said quickly. "You want I should phone 911?"

"No!" Beth cried desperately, clawing at Steve's arms as he tried to soothe the tears. "Take me home." Steve didn't hesitate. He scooped her into his arms and hurried to his SUV. He helped her into the passenger seat, buckling her in as she clutched at him to stay. "Don't let him take her."

Steve shook his head. "Who, Beth? Who?"

"The baby, he wants her and says he's coming for what is his." Steve suddenly understood exactly what she was trying to say. She hadn't told him who the father of her daughter was, saying he was nothing, saying he was meaningless to her and her daughter, but Steve needed to know. He couldn't fight a ghost.

"Who, Beth? Tell me."

"I can't. He said he would— I can't. Don't hate me, Steve, please." She looked so lost, small, so convinced he would want nothing to do with her, want not to touch her.

"Beth, I could never hate you, I love you," he said simply, filing away the hate and the need to kill for much later.

Jack barreled into the station, jumping out of the truck before the engine really died, and was at Beth and Steve's side in seconds.

"Is it the baby? Beth, is it your heart?"

"It was him," Steve said, "the father of the baby."

Jack looked confused, reaching in past Steve to touch his sister, making sure she was okay. She just looked at him blankly.

"Beth?"

She couldn't speak at first, couldn't even look her brother in his eyes. She lowered her eyes, clutching at Steve's hand. "He says he wants my baby, says he's gonna come for her."

"Who, Beth? Who?"

"He said I couldn't tell; he said he'd hurt me."

"He can't hurt you, Beth, because we'll keep you safe. Talk to me." This came from Jack, her big brother, half of the big brother team that looked after her. Steve knew Jack kept her wrapped in safety, and she could tell him everything.

"I didn't want it, Jack." She clutched at his hand, looked up at the brother she adored. "You gotta believe me, I didn't want to. He wouldn't listen. I said no." Jack rocked back as he clearly recognized the implications of what she was saying.

"It's okay, Beth, it's okay. Tell me."

"Jeff— Jeff Hayes."

Jack staggered back, anguish distorting his features.

He looked at Steve, and they exchanged heated looks, and Steve gathered a weeping Beth in his arms.

Leaning into the car, Jack reached out and touched his baby sister on her cheek.

"I love you, Beth, it will be fine. Everything will be fine. Don't worry, he can't touch you. I won't let him. *We* won't let him."

Steve said he was taking Beth back to the ranch to Donna, shut the car door, and turned to Jack. Steve knew where Jack was going now that he was sure Beth was going to be safe with his mom and Steve.

"Should you get Josh as well?" Steve asked.

"No, not today," was all Jack said in reply, his voice even. Dangerous.

Steve wanted to stop him, not out of fear for Jeff, but out of fear for how much trouble Jack could get into. Half of him wanted to go with Jack to *see* Jeff.

"Promise me, Jack, that you'll remember your family, your husband. What you have. Remember."

Jack nodded, crossed to his truck and left. Steve watched him go, his heart heavy. His head still numb with shock, he climbed into the car, leaving Beth's car at the pump, promising someone would be over to get it soon.

He arrived back at the D, handing Beth over to Donna, who suggested that Steve give them a while. He paced the kitchen, murder in his heart, and with a final decision, he grabbed his keys and within minutes was on the main road, heading back the way he'd just come.

* * * *

Jack turned into the Hayes mansion, not stopping for security at the gate. He had murder in mind. He was going to strip the skin from Jeff's body an inch at a time for what he'd done to Beth. Seriously. Inch by red bloody inch. When he screeched to a stop outside the main door, he didn't leave the truck parked straight, or worry about blocking anyone in; it was pure adrenalin and passion that pushed him in through the front door, shouting Jeff's name. Turning on his heel he saw Jeff appear from the breakfast room, his tie perfectly tied and his suit just so, his hair carefully groomed and looking like butter wouldn't melt.

"Good morning, brother-in-law," he said calmly. Jack just let the red mist descend. He didn't give Jeff another chance to speak as his fist contacted with Jeff's jaw in a satisfying crunch and forcing Jeff's head back. Following it through with another punch to his temple, another to his neck, then his chest, he pushed the taller man, countering every hit that Jeff tried to make back, until his fists throbbed with pain and blood splattered in haphazard marks on the pristine walls. Someone grabbed his wrist and forced him away from the whimpering bleeding man lying on the floor, and Jack turned to his new attacker, Riley. Pulling his arm from Riley's grip, he pushed past him to land a couple more blows, this time closing his hands around Jeff's neck, feeling the life under his fingers weak and pathetic. Riley used his entire body to force him away from Jeff, prizing icy hands free from Jeff's neck, and shouting at Jack, shouting something Jack couldn't hear over the beating of his heart, over his complete and utter fury.

"Jack, stop! What the fuck?" Jack snapped out of it, pushing back and away from his husband, sickness inside him as he looked at the man lying on the floor.

"He raped Beth. Your brother raped my sister. Now he's threatening to take the baby from her. Tell me I can't kill him, Riley."

* * * *

Riley was horrified, sickened at what Jack was saying, shock making him turn back to his brother. He was bleeding on the floor, trying to crab-walk backward away from them, terror in his eyes. He didn't want to believe that this man he called brother was capable of rape and of hitting their momma. He didn't want to believe it. Couldn't. Then he turned to Jack, who leaned on the wall, blood on his face, his shirt, and the utter loss in his eyes was damning.

"No," he said, just one word, not a word of disbelief but one of denial. Jack straightened against the wall, his eyes bright with temper.

"Fuck you, Riley," he spat, throwing open the front door and half running to his truck.

"Jack! Fuck, wait! I didn't mean—Shit." He caught up with Jack as he reached the door of his truck, pulling at his arm and forcing him to wait. "Jack, he nearly killed my mom. He beat her unconscious. You think I don't want to kill him myself?" His words stalled; he wasn't sure what he was trying to say. In his head, it had sounded better. "But killing him is not the way. Jack, please. We need to talk to Beth, see what she wants to do."

"He touched my sister. Riley, we need to call the cops. My beautiful sister." The last was a plea, a plea for Riley to see why, to see what was bringing Jack to his knees.

"We'll go home, Jack. We'll talk to Beth. Please listen to me. If we get the cops involved now for any of this, then Beth is dragged through the papers and her life becomes open to all. Jack, you have to let me deal with this inside the family. For Beth. For my mom."

Jack bowed his head, took a deep breath, and climbed into the truck, starting the engine. "I'm gonna go for a drive, get my head straight. I'll be at the D in an hour."

Riley nodded, watching as the man he loved drove away, then he turned to face the mausoleum of ice, wondering what the fuck he needed to do now.

* * * *

Jeff half crawled to his apartment, passing a maid on the stairs who simply looked at him in horror and then turned tail and ran. Jeff knew that there were only three staff here today, that at least one of them had probably heard the whole thing, and that he would have to dig deep into his pockets to keep that one quiet. No sense in people knowing *how* Beth got pregnant, just that he was a daddy, and he would have the baby when it was born, fucking fag brother in the way or not.

He shouted down at the small woman, "Go home, all of you, just go home! I want this house empty in ten minutes." She nodded, scurrying off to God knows where to carry out his bidding, and the familiarity of ordering his staff around felt strangely settling.

He watched as they left in their cheap cars, going home to their shabby houses, and then he washed off the worst of the blood in the bathroom, the water running red, then pink and then finally clear. It seemed most of the damage was internal. His breathing was harsh, his chest heaving with pain. Fucking bastard Campbell. He was gonna pay for this.

Steel shot though his spine as he straightened, and in his head, he started to consider ways in which Jack could meet an untimely end, maybe with brother dearest sitting next to him when it happened. Maybe a car accident? Another fire?

A noise behind him made him turn, and he looked in disbelief at the barrel of a gun, and the person holding it.

"You?" he smirked, disbelief giving way to certainty that the weapon would not be used.

The bullet entered high on his chest. He was unconscious before he hit the floor.

Chapter 39

Riley couldn't bring himself to go onto the ranch. He stopped his SUV at the gate, under the twisted D's, and rested his head on his hands. How was he going to be able to face the rest of the Campbells? After what Jeff had done, how could he look Beth in the eye ever again? Jack had been destroyed, had murder in his hands as he tightened them around Jeff's neck, and God knows, Riley just wanted to let him finish it. That would have been the coward's way out, to have let someone else deal with Jeff. No, he needed to deal with all of this himself. He had managed to get Jack to hold off, to leave it, and what they needed to do now was talk to Beth, talk to Donna, understand what Beth wanted to do. Shit. How was he ever going to be able to have Steve call him friend when his brother had done so much wrong?

Grief knifed through him, and he couldn't stop it from manifesting into the utter blackness that was consuming him. He was slow to anger, always had been, but what Jeff had done —how could he?— Riley couldn't begin to understand. Beth was so small, so delicate and so damn young and now pregnant. He was going to be an uncle again. Maybe something could come from this, something positive, seeing Steve so happy, so in love. The child may have been conceived in hate, but all it would ever know was love.

He sighed. That was of course all dependent on whether Beth and Steve, and Jack, would even let him be part of the little one's life. He caught the flash of metal out of the corner of his eye. Steve's car pulled into the D, not stopping, just going straight past Riley with single focus, and in a singular moment of decision, Riley turned on the engine and followed his best friend to the main house. He arrived as Steve climbed out to stand looking up at the sprawling ranch house, something akin to shock on his face.

"Steve?" Riley said carefully, but Steve didn't turn. "Steve?" This time Steve turned on his heel to face Riley, his skin pale, his eyes staring and scarily empty.

"Sorry, Riley, didn't see you, man," he said, running a hand through his short hair and sighing. He looked devastated, lost, in shock, and Riley reached out to touch his friend. Steve moved out of reach at the last moment.

"Steve, I'm sorry."

"What for?" Steve seemed genuinely puzzled. "It wasn't you. It was your brother, your half-brother." With that he left Riley standing in the sun, climbing the steps to the front door and going inside. Riley stood for a while longer. What he was waiting for only became obvious when Jack's truck came to a stop next to his SUV and Jack climbed out, his face as white as Steve's. Riley didn't move. Jack didn't move. They just looked at each other. Jack leaned back against the door of his truck before bowing his head, his shoulders shaking with grief. Within seconds Riley was there, holding his husband, being strong for him when Jack couldn't be strong for himself. He held him for a long while until Jack could breathe properly, knowing they needed to go inside, knowing they would be needed.

* * * *

Beth wouldn't look at Steve, wouldn't touch Steve, and Donna just stood, loosening the grip her daughter had on her. "I need to go and find your brothers," she said quietly, cupping her daughter's face and looking into liquid blue eyes. "Talk to him, baby, he loves you."

Steve sat down on the bed next to her, his hands clasping at hers. "Beth?" She tried to pull her hands away, but he held them firm. She wasn't going to hide; he wouldn't let her.

"You made me feel loved, beautiful again, and now all I am is ugly," she forced out, her body heaving with anguish, her hands on her belly. "And now I have this thing in me," she spat out, then almost immediately raised wide eyes to Steve. "Oh God, I didn't mean that, Steve. My baby!"

Steve pulled her in close, his hand over hers. Joined over *their* baby. "You are so beautiful to me, and our baby is just that. Ours."

"Can you forgive what happened?" *Can you forgive me? Can you love me still?*

It was almost as if Steve could read her mind, sense the unspoken words, as he began gently kissing his love onto her skin, each kiss punctuated by whispered words, "I love you— I love our baby— We'll be such good parents and make her life so good. We'll be fine."

"I want so much to believe that's true."

"Believe it. Believe in us."

* * * *

Jack phoned Josh, telling him to just get over here now, not telling him anything else, and then he sat, stony and quiet, listening to his mom and Riley talking softly. They were discussing what Beth should do, what they all should do. Would Beth want this dragged through the courts? How else could Jeff pay? Jack looked at his bruised knuckles, remembered the feel of his fingers around Jeff's neck, the sense memory as hard as his heart, pushing blackness where emotion should be. He felt numb, only wishing Josh was here to help him. The two of them could… No, what would that do to Beth, to have her brothers in prison for murder?

Josh brought the Texas day in with him, in suit and tie, a briefcase in his hand and a frown of concern on his face when he saw Jack as still as death and his momma in Riley's arms.

"Is it Beth? What's wrong? Is it the baby?" No one said a word.

"Josh, we need to talk." This came from Riley, who suddenly seemed to be the only one capable of rational speech. "It's Beth. We know who the father of her baby is. It's Jeff, my brother Jeff." Riley pushed it all out there in one breath, Josh widening his eyes in shock and looking to his brother for confirmation. Jack closed his eyes, inhaling a deep breath, not wanting to push this on Josh, but knowing he had to be told. "It wasn't consensual, Josh," Riley finished.

Jack released a breath he didn't even know he'd been holding, waiting for Josh to react. All Josh did was leave the room, making for the study. Jack followed and saw his big brother unlocking the gun case, pulling out the rifle, and grabbing at shells.

It was the same impulse to kill that had cut through Jack. It wasn't right; he had to make Josh see. "No. Josh, please." He blocked Josh, tried to get the bullets off him, tried to stop him, and finally stood in the doorway, the only way out of the room, Riley a hulking presence behind him.

"Out of my way, Jack," Josh said calmly, looking over his brother's shoulder at the brother of the man he wanted to kill.

"No, Josh, we need to talk to Beth."

"Out. Of. My. Way." He pushed past Jack and Riley.

Josh almost made it to the door, almost made it out to the daylight with murder in mind, but Beth was there, standing in the kitchen in the sunlight, tiny and pregnant, with her spine straight and her shoulders back.

"Josh, no," she said simply. It was enough. It defused his anger immediately.

Steve moved to stand next to her, his arm around her protectively, and she leaned into him for strength.

"Josh, I'm sorry," she offered quietly, closing her eyes. Josh froze for a mere second, then took that step forward, the rifle clattering to the floor as he released his death grip. Pulling her away from Steve, he gathered his sister into his arms. "Don't you say that, Elizabeth, don't you ever say that *you* are sorry."

Jack reached blindly for Riley's hand, holding it so damn tight it had to hurt. Riley seemed to sense the need for touch, bumping his shoulder gently. Finally Josh pulled back, cupping Beth's face with his hands. "Is the baby okay? Are you alright?"

"I'm fine, Josh," she replied, "and the baby is fine." Taking Josh's hand, she placed it on her belly. She smiled softly. "She's here, and she's fine." She looked at Jack, at their mom standing in the doorway, age and worry creasing her face, and then back at Josh.

Where would they go from here?

* * * *

The 911 call was anonymous,
made from a payphone in the city.
"There's been a shooting. Jeff Hayes is
dead." That was it. The entire message.
Delivered in a monotone, no emotion
there at all. A woman's voice.
      When dispatch sent the
paramedics, they found the body of a
tall man, his face and torso red-raw with
bruises and cuts, obviously beaten and
beaten hard. They found a bullet wound
that had missed the heart by the breadth
of a hair. They found a man very close
to death.
      Unconscious, but still alive.

* * * *

Beth didn't really have an awful lot
of friends outside of her family. Years of
hospitals and doctors isolate even the
most gregarious of people, and so, when
Eden arrived at the D, it lifted Beth's
heart to see her. She arrived with
concern marking her face. "Riley called
me and said you needed me."
      Beth just burrowed deep in her
arms. It was heaven to have a friend not

much older than her who seemed to instinctively know what to do, holding her close and just stroking her hair. She could see Riley at the table, knew he was struggling, knew she should reach out to him as well and tell him she didn't blame him, but the nerves inside stopped her. He was so tall, like Jeff, so strong, confident, imposing. He wasn't Jeff, but she didn't have the emotion left in her to make that distinction with any clarity, even though she knew she was making it worse for him. He sat in the kitchen, a picture of misery, of anger, of murderous intent, and Eden encouraged Beth to sit, still holding her hand. Steve hovered expectantly while Donna boiled water in the kettle and busied herself to keep focused.

"Can anyone tell me what's going on?" Eden asked, confused and frowning. No one said anything. "Guys?" Finally, it was Riley that spoke.

"Jeff is the father of Beth's baby. He…" Riley paused for a moment, then said, "He took advantage of her." He clenched his hands into fists, knuckles white with tension. Eden paled, turning to Beth.

"Rape— He wouldn't— he— oh my God."

"Beth, did you call Dallas PD?" No one said a word. Beth could see that everyone seemed to be avoiding looking at Eden. "Riley?"

Riley flinched and saw Jack frown and open his mouth to speak, before shutting it again and subsiding into more brooding.

"I don't want to tell anyone," Beth said firmly. "I don't want my little girl to grow up seeing reports that she— I'll tell her," she clasped Steve's hand, and he crouched down next to her, "We'll tell her what we can, when we can, but I won't take it any further now." At this Riley made a choked-off sound, pushing his chair back and stalking out of the kitchen, the door slamming behind him. Jack made to stand, but Beth stopped him, pushing herself to her feet and squeezing Steve's hand. "I'll go. It's my demons he needs to face."

Carefully she made her way down the steps to the front of the ranch house, seeing Riley leaning against the fence, watching Solo and her foal in the open paddocks. He was hunched over, his hands supporting his head on the wooden frame, and Beth had never seen him look so beaten.

"Riley?" Startled, he looked up, stumbling as he straightened and catching hold of the white wood to stop himself from falling, embarrassment on his face.

"I couldn't stay in there," he said, "I'm sorry, I couldn't look at you— no— that wasn't it. I couldn't let you see me." He sounded confused, disorientated.

"Why couldn't you look at me, Riley?" Beth leaned into him, her small frame warm against his arm. "Am I different to you now?"

Riley looked horrified at the thought. "No, God, just— No— What Jeff did…" He started and then stopped, choking. It seemed he wasn't sure where to start.

"It wasn't you, Riley, and it wasn't Eden. It was your brother, a man that you really only have biology in common with."

"He's not a man," Riley spat out immediately, "he's a monster." Beth just nodded in agreement, kind of slipping under Riley's arm, and gripping his T-shirt. Riley looked down at her.

"Promise me one thing, Riley?"

"Anything. Whatever I can do." Riley sounded so broken.

"Be a good uncle to this little one and, above all, love my brother as he deserves to be loved." Riley pulled her in tight.

"Both of those things are easy to promise, Beth."

Chapter 40

Detective Tom Stafford arrived just as the paramedics were leaving. His partner was already there, scribbling notes and talking to the CSIs who were hovering.

"Thought he was still kicking," he said, indicating the scene investigators, who only turned up to corpse cases.

John Lafferty turned to him. "The call we got said he was dead. CSI got the heads-up from DPD there was a 10-87, hence their beating your lazy ass here."

"So, bring me up to speed."

"Jeff Hayes, shot once, through and through chest wound, beaten badly, unconscious, but very definitely alive when he was loaded onto the meat wagon."

"Who called it in?"

"Downtown payphone."

"Security cameras at the phone?"

"On it already. Message not recorded."

"Okay, do we have family here, witnesses?"

"No one, house is empty, staff missing. We have a call out to his wife." John led his partner up the stairs, Tom noting the blood splatters on the hall wall, on the wooden floors, and a bloody smudge halfway up the stairs. They finally turned into some sort of set of linked rooms, decorated in muted blues and grays, a man's suite.

"Forensics have closed the room he was found in, but we have blood in a sink and blood on the floor where the body was found."

"So he gets attacked, beaten, hence the blood in the hall and on the wall of the stairs, then he comes to his room to wash off the blood, and his attacker follows him." Tom paused, looking at the entrance to the sprawling apartment, and gauging possible angles. He held his hand held out in front of him like a child pretending to shoot a gun. "One shot, to finish him off."

"Sounds plausible I guess. Question is why would someone take the time to beat him, wait for him to then clean himself up, and then shoot him?" John indicated the Rolex on the table just inside the door, the cufflinks and a wallet. "Looks as if robbery wasn't the motive, despite the rich pickings."

"So, crime of passion then, scorned lover, wife, girlfriend. Revenge maybe?" Tom offered. In summary, it was just the kind of case he usually loved— intricate, with a web of reasons why someone might have been attacked. What he didn't need was a case that was going to hit the papers before he even had time to breathe. John answered his cell, nodding and responding before sliding it closed. "Nada on the wife, T, but we have a contact for his brother. The mother's details show she owns this mausoleum so no trace there."

"Brother it is then; put a call in, then we visit the hospital."

* * * *

Beth gave Riley one final hug.

"I'm gonna go in and let Jack know you're okay. He's in there worrying like a mother hen, an' I'll send him out."

That brought a smile to Riley's face, and he relaxed back against the railing to wait. As Beth disappeared in to the house, his cell started to vibrate in his pocket. He brought it out and slid the case up to answer the call, listening to the words from the caller, even as he watched Jack jump down the steps to reach him.

He said little in response to the caller, acknowledging his identity and nothing else. Carefully he ended the call and slid the cell back in his jeans, horror growing in the pit of his stomach and beginning to spread out through his body.

"That was Dallas PD," he said, sounding deceptively calm even to himself. Jack frowned.

"About Beth?"

"No, no…" Riley felt the horror reach his heart, the disbelief of what he'd just been told, of what Jack might have done. "It's Jeff. He's been shot— Tell me, Jack, Please tell me it wasn't you."

Chapter 41

As soon as the words left his mouth, he wanted to pull them back, seeing how Jack stiffened in shock. He didn't think Jack had done it, but everything that had bombarded him in the last few days, everything with his brother… He thought he'd known his brother and look how that turned out. This shooting was just one more thing being thrown at him, and it was all he could do to keep functioning on the autopilot he seemed to be on. His father wasn't his father, his brother was a rapist, and to top it all, he'd fallen in love with a man. And now, to add to this whole steaming pile of crap, his brother had been shot. He simply had nothing left to react with. He just felt numb, as if his head had decided for him— no more.

Riley tried desperately to concentrate on one thing. He wanted to understand, to figure this out, but it was as if all he had in his head was white noise. His heart felt heavy and all he wanted was someone to deal with this, to take it away, and then Jack was standing there in front of him.

Please don't let him be involved. He isn't involved; it wasn't him, but I can't lose him.

The cracks were starting to show, and he couldn't stop them. He was shaking; he knew he was, and he could feel the sickness rising in him. The complete shock at what they'd told him started to trickle down his spine as he looked helplessly at Jack, waiting for him to speak. His head couldn't make sense of any of it as he relived Jack's hand wrapped around Jeff's neck, choking him, temper and violence whipping around him like a storm.

Just tell me it wasn't you. Please…

Riley realized at that single moment that he really didn't give a shit about how Jeff was. On being told he was alive but unconscious, Riley didn't even want to go to the hospital. Why should he be responsible for a man that was nothing more to him than a relative by blood. His thoughts immediately turned to Jack, how Jack could be accused of murder, how his blood would be on Jeff, how Riley had seen the fight and was a witness. Confusion crashed over him. Shouldn't he be more worried about his brother? What was Eden going to think?

* * * *

Jack said nothing at first, processing what Riley had said, hearing the worry and fear in his question, the complete shock, the pain, the questions and the anger. Knowing it would destroy his new husband totally to lose Jack to prison on top of everything that had happened, he knew Riley didn't speak out of belief, but out of a desperate hope to not lose Jack.

"I didn't do it, Riley," he said, his voice completely devoid of pretense or guile. He said it calmly, his hands out flat in front of him and in peace.

Riley just nodded. "I know, I know, but Jeff… he's at Mercy. They're going to see, going to know what you did. They'll have your blood, your DNA… it's all over him and—"

Jack stepped forward, cutting off Riley's scared words with a finger to his lips. "I'll be honest, and I'll tell them what I did, and I'll tell them I didn't shoot Jeff. It's the truth."

"But Beth… you can't tell them why you…" Riley's voice tailed off. Beth didn't want to press charges, didn't want it made public. Hysteria started to bubble inside him, out of control, and he couldn't concentrate on one thing out of everything in his head. He was losing it; losing hold of his sanity, inch by painful inch.

"Okay," Jack started firmly, his hands on Riley's upper arms, giving him a small shake as he spoke. "We get Eden, we go to Mercy, we see what has happened, get the facts, see who's been assigned to this case. I'll come clean about what I did and get my wrist slapped. Simple." Jack lowered his hands, grasped Riley's tight, the cell hard between them. "Riley, listen to me. Stay here, okay? I'll get Eden."

* * * *

Riley felt himself nodding allowing Jack to help him, needing Jack to help him.

When Eden stumbled down the stairs, Jack trying to support her, Riley held himself straight, watching as Donna and Josh hovered by the door, not knowing what to do. She ran the small distance to the fence, and Riley just opened his arms, pulling her in and holding her close.

"He isn't dead, Eden," he kept repeating, not sure why he was saying that. He thought he caught her saying "When will this end?" He hugged her tighter, knowing exactly how she was feeling. When would it all end? This nightmare that he seemed to be caught in, the nightmare Eden was in along with Beth, Jack, and so many others, was hurting people again and again in the name of Hayes.

"Do we have to go and see him?" She sounded so very young as she clung to him, and as if she was a feather, he picked her up and sat her atop the fence, lifting her chin to look into eyes so like his own, his mother's legacy he guessed. They were swimming with tears, and he sensed Jack handing over tissues, standing at his side, a calming presence.

"Do you want to go and see him?" Riley asked softly.

"Is he unconscious?"

"They said he was being taken into surgery; that the bullet was near his heart—"

"He doesn't have a heart," Eden interrupted quickly, a sudden mask of determination on her face. "I don't want to see him."

Riley nodded. He hefted his cell phone and flipped the cover, redialing the last number received and waiting. Eden looked confused and Jack made to speak, but Riley hushed them with a raised hand until finally the call connected.

"Riley Campbell-Hayes. No, we decided not to. Nope, we don't plan on it. I'll contact Jeff's dad. No, if you need that then we're at the Double D—the Campbell ranch off of— Okay." He closed the cell, leaning in and burying his face in his sister's hair, looking for something normal, a familiar smell, a familiar touch, just looking for peace. "The detective in charge, Tom Stafford, wants to speak to us all. He's bringing his partner, and we should expect him in about an hour." He spoke calmly, glancing over at Jack, who just nodded, closing his eyes and sighing.

"I'm gonna go keep Beth company," Eden said softly. "You gonna be okay, Riley?" To an outsider, it might have looked odd, this tiny slip of a girl looking up at her brother, broad in the shoulder and a good foot taller than her, asking him if *he* was going to be okay, but to Riley, it meant everything. He smiled softly, using his thumb to wipe away the tears on her cheeks. She was his sister, and she was his to look after, but she had an incredible strength in her that was sometimes his only anchor to the real world.

"I'll be fine." He linked hands with Jack. "We'll be in soon." Eden reached up on tiptoes, placing a small kiss on her brother's stubble-rough skin.

"Love you, big brother."

"Love you, little sister."

Chapter 42

It was a tense two hours interviewing Riley and Eden, and then finally moving on to Jack Campbell-Hayes, who sat quietly at the table and explained exactly what he'd done.

Stafford made notes. Riley Campbell-Hayes, brother of the victim, no alibi, the last person known to have been with his brother; Jack Campbell-Hayes, the husband, who for some reason, Tom knew, wasn't being entirely honest about why he'd beaten up Jeff Hayes. Again, Jack, no alibi, was driving, no witnesses, both men had access to guns, both licensed to carry. And then there was Eden, clearly distraught, but constantly looking to her brother for strength.

Interesting.

He made notes on the family dynamics, knew enough about the Hayeses from news items as to who was missing from here. Gerald Hayes, father, missing. Sandra Hayes, mother, missing. Lisa Hayes, wife, missing.

He also recalled Riley's phrasing during the phone call— Jeff's father, a slip that maybe a less observant man wouldn't have caught, but he had caught it. He turned to his partner, closing the notebook, his eyes carefully scanning the individuals standing in the kitchen.

"I'll need you to come downtown tomorrow and make a formal statement," he said to Jack, who nodded and pressed his lips together in a tight, frowning face. Tom knew he needed this on record. If Jeff woke up after the operation then he would probably want to press charges. His badge was telling him now to take Jack, who had no alibi and blood already on his hands. But his gut feeling was telling him that there was more to this story. "It's simple enough to check through traffic cams. If you can detail your drive as closely as you can."

Jack's heart sank. He had been mostly driving on instinct, not really with any destination in mind. "I'll try to remember," he said finally.

Tom stood, turning to Riley. "I need to speak to your mother, your father, and your sister-in-law. Do you have any ideas where they would be at this moment?"

"Try the eighteenth hole at the Oaks for Gerald. I have my mother's cell number. I've left a message, and you have the number now. Lisa…" He shrugged. "She left Jeff. Mom may know where she went."

"If you should hear from any of them, I need to know," Tom finally said, before thanking Donna for the coffee, and indicating John should follow him out. It was only when he was outside that he breathed a sigh of relief, his head pounding from an intense headache right across his eyes.

"You okay?" His partner looked concerned.

"So many secrets," he said. "The Dallas aristocracy and their freaking secrets."

Chapter 43

The knock on Jim's door was unexpected and very loud in the stillness of his apartment, and it was with not a small amount of irritation that he opened the door, ready to sound off at the drop of a hat. If it wasn't one thing, it was another, if it wasn't his son's brother being in the hospital unconscious, it was Gerald freaking Hayes demanding his presence at everything from meetings to golf games.

Gerald knew Jim was Riley's dad. Jim didn't need to say a word. There was too much water under that particular bridge to even go there. They would, in the same way as they'd done for over twenty-five years, ignore the elephant in the room every time they spoke. Jim had made promises, and he intended to keep them, but he wanted to know his son. More than the closeness he already shared with Riley, he wanted a family connection.

"What?" he bit out as he opened the door, wincing as Eden Hayes launched herself at him, gripping at his shirt, her head buried against his chest, sobbing uncontrollably. Pushing the door closed, he eased her back from him, seeing grief so deeply etched in her face it scared him.

"Eden, what is it? Is it Riley?" She couldn't speak, couldn't get words past her need to gulp air, and she shook her head. He knew he wasn't going to get sense out of her, so he guided her to sit on the sofa, disentangled her hands and fetched her water before sitting on the coffee table in front of the sofa and waiting.

Finally she seemed to calm and looked at Jim, her eyes steady. "I need you to help me. Can you help me?"

Jim frowned. Of course he would help her. She may not be his daughter by blood, but she was every bit as much his as Riley was in every way that mattered. "Help you with what, babe?"

"When Jeff…" She stopped, her teeth worrying her lower lip, her expressive eyes filling with tears again, but this time without the shaking he'd seen in her.

"When Jeff what?"

"I was there… in the house."

"You were there? Did you see something? Eden?"

* * * *

The day of the shooting

How was it Jeff had the capacity to hurt her so much? She was Eden Alyssa Hayes, heiress, socialite. She was confident and her own woman, but with a few well-chosen words, her oldest brother could make her feel like a spoiled brat. She tolerated him, just this side of hate. He'd always been the perfect pseudo-Gerald with his sly, intolerant, elitist mannerisms and his icy uncompromising grip on everyone's life, including hers.

"What's up, Eden? Someone piss in your Jimmy Choos?" It wasn't much, but it was enough to push her to snap back with a simple and effective "Fuck you." She had been staring listlessly out of the window at the manicured lawns beyond, her mind turning over Beth being pregnant, her new friend positively glowing with the evidence of what had happened to her, and Steve was so completely in love with her, so attentive.

It sent knives of envy through her, and she had found herself simply standing, wishing Jeff would just leave. He knew which buttons to press, which words to use that made her quick to temper, and it was best to leave. She pushed past him and out of the front door. Maybe a walk in the garden would stop her melancholy.

She had spent a little while with the roses, breathing deeply of the scent of freshly cut grass, and then returned to her room. She would shower and return to the Double D and visit with Beth. She enjoyed it there. She heard the shouting coming from downstairs, and it grew louder. She couldn't make out much, but she heard thuds, grunts, and the sounds of fists on flesh. She crept to the landing, her hand over her mouth as she saw Jack beating Jeff, almost killing him, and Riley running in, trying to pull his husband away.

"Jack stop! What the fuck," Riley shouted, holding him back, looking down at Jeff, gripping Jack tightly.

"He raped Beth. Your brother raped my sister." Jack's voice was broken, and Eden nearly ran down the stairs. "Now he's threatening to take the baby from her. Tell me I can't kill him, Riley."

"No," Riley said, and she heard Jack reply "Fuck you" before stalking from the hallway. Riley ran after him, leaving Jeff a bloody mess on the floor.

She wondered what she should do. Should she call 911? She was a witness to what Jack had done… but Jeff had raped Beth? And he was threatening to claim the baby? Eden heard a whimper, and saw Lisa stumbling back to the rooms closest to her, her momma's rooms. Eden thought to follow but then Jeff moved, pushing himself to his feet, and she ran back to her own rooms, hiding in the bathroom, her cell in her hand.

She crept to the door, hearing Jeff dismissing staff, coming to her room, calling her name and then the noise of him going down the corridor to his own rooms, cursing every step of the way.

Then she heard the shot. She knew as certainly as she knew her own name that Lisa had shot Jeff. She entered the bedroom and found Lisa standing over the body of her husband, the gun loose in her hands.

"Give it to me, Lisa." They needed to get out of there.

"Eden?" Lisa looked to be in shock. She was pale, her eyes empty.

"We need to go."

* * * *

The Present
Jim leaned forward. "The gun, Eden. Where is the gun?"

She seemed to shakily snap back to the here and now. She reached into her purse, pulling out the weapon and dropping it to the floor as though horrified by the feel of it.

"Hell. You were carrying it with you?" Jim couldn't believe what he could see in front of him, couldn't even begin to comprehend what Lisa had done, what she'd been through, but Eden looked at him, hazel eyes pleading.

"Help me, Uncle J. Please tell me what to do."

Helplessly he bundled her into his arms and moved to sit behind her on the sofa, pulling her back. The midnight hour cloaked them in darkness, and he simply held her as she wept and finally fell asleep in his arms.

There had to be a way.

He pulled out his cell, thumbing contacts.

"Bailey?"

"Gerald, we need to talk."

Chapter 44

It was the tenth day since the shooting and the tenth time that Riley was the first one up. Jack was still asleep and curled on his side, though Riley knew he would wake soon and come to find him out with the horses. To be fair, Riley hadn't actually fallen asleep at all; he had too much spinning through his head. He was exchanging his vows with Jack today, with his family and friends around him, a much better man than he'd been mere months before. He felt no nerves, only an incredible sense of peace that started in his belly and ended up curled around his heart. He was promising his life and his heart to Jack, and it felt so right he could almost weep with the emotion. He sensed Jack arriving behind him before his husband even said a word.

"Hey," Jack said as he slid into the circle of Riley's arms, offering him coffee and smiling almost shyly.

"Hey," Riley replied softly, capturing Jack's mouth in a soft kiss then pulling back to look into blue eyes, soft and warm with sleep.

"It's a big day," Jack observed carefully, wondering why his husband was standing so alone out here as the

Texas dawn painted the sky with muted hues.

"A day we'll remember for the rest of our lives," Riley said. "I couldn't sleep earlier and I wondered if what we're doing is right, With Beth pregnant and Jeff in the hospital and Lisa missing, should we be—"

"If you ask should we be looking into renewing our vows then I may have to beat you into submission." Jack smiled at his own joke, pleased when Riley smirked back, shadows lifting from his eyes.

"Like to see you try," he offered, and laughing, they leaned into each other and looked out over the land that was the D, lost in thought and contemplating the day ahead. It was Riley who saw the lights heading inexorably towards the ranch house. A car. Both men moved to greet whoever it was, Jack frowning as Detectives Stafford and Patterson climbed out of the car, weapons drawn, looks of determination on their faces.

Riley half smiled, saw the gun, saw the purposeful look in Stafford's eyes, then the next was a blur. Strong arms pulled Jack away, pushing him against the car. Stafford's partner cuffed Jack, words spinning in the morning air.

"Jackson Robert Campbell— Right to remain silent— Right to an attorney— Do you understand these rights?" What was happening here? Why were they doing this? The single moment was crystallized in front of him, Jack resigned, quiet, Stafford's partner dragging Jack away, Stafford standing between him and Jack and stopping Riley from stepping forward.

"No, wait!" Was that his own voice? Riley couldn't tell Jack was watching as he was forced into the back of the car. "No!" Jack finally shouted, pushing forward, but Stafford stood firm, gripping Riley's arms, his face calm and understanding.

"I'm sorry, Mr Campbell-Hayes… Riley. Please work with me here. I can't stop this. Your brother is awake."

Riley stood rooted to the spot, shock and disbelief cutting into him like knives, then in a sudden lunge, he made to wrestle Jack away from the other cop. He slipped past Stafford in a practiced move, his hands almost reaching Jack before he was body checked, Tom pushing him hard against the front of the car, shouting at him.

"You are not helping Jack here, Riley. Leave it, follow us to the station."

Riley struggled, desperation giving him the edge, heaving and twisting until he turned the situation and Tom was now the one pinned to the car. It was Jack's voice, loud and clear from the car, that stopped him. "Riley, no! Call Josh. Call Jim. It will be okay."

The fight left Riley as quickly as it had started, and he released his hold on the detective, his thoughts scarily blank. "He didn't do anything," he said simply as he looked into Tom's face. He saw a flare of understanding there before it was pushed behind the mask of a man doing his job.

"Riley," he began, "your brother gave us a name. He identified Jack as the shooter."

Chapter 45

It was a new dawn when Gerald arrived at Jim's apartment. The dark of the hallway and the silence of the block was unnerving. To get a call from Jim in the middle of the night, he guessed it must be something to do with the whole Jeff situation, and he wondered if Jim was going to admit to having shot Jeff himself, although for the life of him, he couldn't fathom any reason *why* he would have done anything like that. He knocked on the door, only having to wait mere seconds before Jim ushered him in and closed the door behind them.

"What is so God-fired important you got me here at 5 am?" Gerald blustered, decided the best defense was an offense, turning suddenly in shock at a small voice behind him.

"Daddy?"

Gerald couldn't believe his eyes. His Eden here, in Jim's apartment, sleep mussed and red-eyed. His mind went suddenly blank. Was Jim making a statement somehow by sleeping with his daughter?

It was as if Jim could read his mind, hurrying to reassure him. "Eden was upset, and she came here for help."

"Here? She came *here* for help?" Gerald felt sudden remorse stab through him that she couldn't have turned to him for help— but help with what exactly?

Eden seemed terrified, looking from Jim to him and back again. "Uncle J, why is Dad here?" Her voice was shaky, and it took only moments for Gerald to piece it together. The energy to stand left his body in one sharp exhalation of breath.

"Eden?" he said, suddenly afraid of what he wasn't hearing. He watched as she moved unconsciously towards Jim, pressing into his side, letting herself be led to the sofa, and he waited.

"Sit, we have some things we need to tell you."

Gerald listened, he learned, he stood, he sat, but he couldn't stop himself from shouting, then from apologizing, then feeling sick to his stomach. Gerald finally sat on the sofa next to his daughter, an arm around her protectively, encouraging her back to bed. "We will take care of this Eden. Lisa will be okay, but you must promise to never breathe a word of this to anyone."

When she was in the bedroom, Jim stood, his eyes narrowing as Gerald asked him for the gun.

"Why do you want the gun?"

"I want it away from Eden and Lisa."

* * * *

Jim looked down at his cell as it vibrated on the table, Riley's name on the screen, and he dismissed the call quickly, not willing to let Gerald leave as he seemed to want to.

"How do we fix this?" Jim said softly as Gerald shrugged on his jacket, seeing the man's face carefully blank, lined and gray. "You are losing Hayes Oil. The scandal will be enough too, if it gets out that Lisa shot her husband and Eden witnessed the shooting." Jim stopped, he didn't know what else to say.

Gerald took a deep breath. "I think I've wronged you in this life, Jim, for nothing more than money and the need to win. But, know this, I respect you. You've been a good employee, although I know you only stayed to watch over your son, and you have been a good friend to him. Without your influence, with just his brother and me as role models… Well, he would have been just another Jeff, with his vices and his vicious manipulations. I won't let Eden or Lisa get hurt in this. I won't let my grandchildren suffer."

"How can you stop them from tracking down Lisa?"

"With all the money I have, I still can't buy time," he said enigmatically. Jim looked alternately blank and then confused, but Gerald pressed on. "I'm not getting any younger. You promise me, look after Eden and Lisa, Jim... and Riley. You make sure they stay safe and well, and leave me to deal with what's happened in the time I have left."

"Gerald, this is stupid talk."

Gerald just half-smirked that familiar Hayes smirk and walked to the door, the gun safely in his jacket pocket. He turned to face the man who was going to have everything now —his family, peace— and he wondered for a moment what he could say. *I cheated Alan out of everything, I lost Donna, I didn't love my wife, and I drove my children away.*

"Gerald." Jim had one last question, suddenly taking in how frail Gerald seemed since the last time he saw him. "Are you okay?"

"I don't need long. I just need enough time to make it all right."

Chapter 46

Riley was out of his head with worry. He couldn't contact Jim, and he was following the cop car to the station across the dead landscape of downtown Dallas, empty of its usual rush and purpose and eerily silent. Josh had left immediately when he'd heard from Riley, saying he'd meet them at the station, emphasized with more curse words than Riley had ever heard come from his brother-in-law's mouth.

When he arrived, he wasn't allowed through the same entrance. The door closed in his face, and his last image was that of an impassive Jack being led down a corridor, his hands still cuffed behind his back. In a fit of anger, Riley smashed his fist against the heavy wood door before turning and leaning back, trying to figure out which way to go. By the time he got to the front of the station, Stafford's partner was there waiting, a look of expectation on his face, his stance solid and guarded.

"What the fuck is going on?" Riley spat out.

"If you'd like to take a seat, we'll be out to talk to you when we can," Patterson said calmly. He probably dealt with irate husbands every day, Riley thought bitterly, crossing his arms and mirroring the same calm stance.

"I'll wait," he said carefully, "but you have gotta know, my husband did not shoot my brother."

Patterson inclined his head and nodded, dismissing Riley's words and indicating a room marked for waiting. He turned on his heel, pushed past the doors marked *Secure Area*. Briefly the flash of an idea hit him, an idea whereby Riley pushed the door whilst it was still open, found Jack and dragged him out, an idea dismissed as soon as it formed. Instead, he started to pace outside the room, counting the time until Josh would arrive. He was a lawyer, and he'd know what to do. Damn it all to hell, where was Jim? Ignoring the *No Cell Phones* sign, he dialed Jim again, leaving another voice message and hanging up as Josh barreled in through the front doors.

"What the fuck, Riley?"

* * * *

Gerald stood for a moment next to his car, looking up at the sign for the private wing— the Hayes wing. It was a donation from way back. He turned the gun over in his pocket and held it tight. He had no real idea of what he was doing, or what he was trying to achieve, and he had to steady his breathing before he could move. The early morning air felt welcomingly cool on his hot skin.

Finally he simply walked in, nodding briefly at the nurse on duty and the security guard who sat at her side. No one stopped him; no one would dare to. It was *his* wing, and he was visiting *his* son.

"Mr Hayes, we have been trying to contact you. It's good news, sir. Your son regained consciousness for a short while earlier."

"Excellent," Gerald heard himself say, turning to the room, not wanting to hear anything else.

"Sir, the police who were with him left, saying you should call them when you can. Your son managed to talk to them, and the case has taken a turn for the better." She was obviously reading from notes, not realizing the pain that was knifing into Gerald as he listened. Was he too late?

Straightening his back, he just nodded and pushed open the door to the litany of beeps, his eldest child deathly white against the sheets, tubes and machines pumping nutrients and painkillers into his system. How easy would it be to dial up the morphine, or maybe pinch the tube for the oxygen? He'd seen it done in movies, subtle murders, but he had the gun. The gun that was cold and hard and very real in his pocket, an ideal solution, one bullet direct to the heart, no missing, no thoughts—just instant death. It took only moments for Gerald to close his hand tight and start to take the weapon from deep inside his jacket's hiding place. There was no decision to make other than the right one, but how long he stood there he didn't know. An hour— two— The nurses bustled around him, attending to his son even as he tried to get the courage together to bring this whole thing to an end.

The noise in his head was harsh, the confusion around him quick and deadly, as suddenly Jeff started to convulse, arching and twisting on the bed, alarms in the room alerting staff. Gerald just stood there, the rush of nurses and doctors around him, pushing him back out of the room. "Give me ten of— Charging— I need—" and he stood outside the door, listening to the sudden silence inside as everything was as still as death.

"I'm sorry, Mr Hayes, he was just too weak. We tried— Time of death? Oh, eight twenty two. Sorry—"

Gerald left in a daze. What had just happened had made it so easy.

He slid into his car, sliding the gun onto his lap and carefully wiping it of all fingerprints, Lisa's, Eden's, his own. Then gently he held the gun as if to shoot, pressing harder, pushing his prints and his prints alone onto the weapon. Finally he wrapped the gun in a T-shirt from his gym bag and placed it on the passenger seat.

He had only one other thing to do.

* * * *

The interview room smelled of coffee and sweat, and Jack was uncomfortable in the hard seat. Stafford hadn't said much, simply repeating the Miranda, and then passing Jack coffee before he sat down opposite him.

"You have indicated you don't wish to have a lawyer present."

"I don't need a lawyer. I haven't done anything that warrants one."

"At oh seven-thirty this morning, Jeffery Gerald Hayes identified that you, Jackson Robert Campbell-Hayes, shot him at close range," Stafford summed up briefly, and then stopped, simply leaning forward in his chair and grasping his coffee in his hands, a thoughtful look on his face. "Talk to me," he added, almost gently.

Jack didn't know what to say, so he said all he could. "I didn't shoot my husband's brother."

"He says you did," Tom pointed out, "and let's be honest here. You have already admitted to grievous bodily harm, and you have no alibi as to your whereabouts after you left the Hayes mansion."

"And I say again, I did *not* shoot Jeff Hayes."

* * * *

Tom sat back, his face carefully blank, looking at Jack's steady hands and the shell-shocked but grim determination on his face. "So," he began carefully, "Tell me why you attacked him in his own home, why you beat him up."

Jack shuffled in his chair, clearly uncomfortable. "We already did this," Jack answered finally, a stubborn set to him that Tom was worried he wouldn't break through. Damn idiot was hiding something.

"Not under Miranda we didn't," Tom shot back, a glint in his eye as he leaned forward, seeing those words impact the prisoner, seeing his full lips tighten, and his blue eyes darken.

"I have nothing to add," Jack finally said, "we had a falling out, a *family* disagreement. It was an explosion of irritation that got out of hand."

"He came off quite bad." Tom opened a file listing the damage to the older man. "Facial bruising, finger marks on his neck, a couple of cracked bones, a broken nose." He didn't list everything, just left it hanging. "That must have been some argument when all you came away with was bruised knuckles." Jack dropped his hands to his lap. "A lot of passion. Just what exactly was the argument about?"

"He didn't like me marrying his brother," Jack offered.

"And for that you beat him, and… wait," he glanced at the notes again, "you tried to strangle him."

"What do you want me to say? We sorted it, and I didn't shoot him."

Tom collected together the papers, pulling out photos of the unconscious Jeff, of the crime scene, the blood from under him, and turned them to face

Jack, who looked everywhere except directly at them.

"Let's start at the beginning, shall we? Or do you want to wait for your lawyer?"

"I want my lawyer," Jack spat out. Tom sat back. He stood, about to ask Jack for details, when his partner entered the room, indicating Tom should step outside.

It was a few words, but it was enough for Jack Campbell-Hayes to be in the clear. He walked back in, and gestured to the open door. "You *will* need to appear here at a later stage for the assault charge, but for the moment, you are free to go." Jack scrambled to stand, disbelief on his face. He followed Tom, passing other rooms. Tom caught Jack's expression, the younger man's eyes widening to see Gerald Hayes sitting at a table in an adjoining room. The man glanced up at him, nodded almost imperceptibly, and then lowered his gaze. In an obvious state of confusion, Jack just followed Tom to the booking area where Jack's brother and his husband waited. Jack almost fell into Riley Campbell Hayes's strong hold, gripping him tight.

"What is going on here, Detective?" Riley demanded.

"Someone has just turned themselves in for the shooting and murder of Jeff Hayes," Tom said softly. "Mr Campbell-Hayes is free to go for the time being."

"Murder?" Riley sounded shell-shocked, holding tight to Jack's jacket.

Tom turned to Riley. He had to be told, but it was never news he liked to tell. "I'm sorry for your loss, sir, but your brother died just over an hour ago."

"Who turned themselves in?" Jack asked softly.

"I'm afraid I'm not at liberty to say," was all Tom replied, nodding to Josh and retracing his footsteps to the secure area, leaving the three men in various states of disbelief, the lawyer questioning, Jack confused, and Riley clearly in the beginning of shock.

* * * *

"Gerald is here." Jack said, pulling back from Riley. "Gerald is in one of the rooms." Riley looked blank, scared, confused, and couldn't even form words. His brother was dead, his dad was here. Gerald here?

"Riley? Riley?" Jack's voice seemed a long way away, distant, tired, concerned, and it was all Riley could do to clutch at him. He needed Jim. He might know what is happening. "Riley, Jim is here. Riley?"

Riley turned to his friend, his father, the one person who could sort this out, could help him, level him, maybe keep him sane. It wasn't grief he was feeling. It couldn't be; he hated his brother for what he'd done to Beth, to Jack, to his mom—

"Gerald Hayes is here because he's admitted he shot Jeff. He has the gun. Riley can you hear me? Riley?"

"I've got you," Jack's voice penetrated through the haze, and his hands held him upright. "We need to get him out of here, get some air."

"I'm staying for Gerald," Jim replied carefully. "Take care of Riley."

"Riley, come on, man. Let's get you out of here and get our heads clear." Riley felt arms holding him, Jack, Josh, but his head was full of noise, panic, confusion, questions, and he allowed himself to be led out to the warming morning air, the thick of it hard against his air-con-cold skin. The morning had changed. The noise of the city was around him as he was led to the back of the station, where there was shelter and peace.

He shook his head, trying to clear it, blinking and leaning against Jack, "Josh, I need to see Gerald. I need to know what's going on."

* * * *

He said it was against his better judgment, but Stafford gave Riley five minutes with his father.

Riley couldn't speak, didn't even know where to start, glancing up at the detective who was leaning against the doorframe just watching them.

"What you're doing for Hayes Oil was a good plan, Riley. I'm proud of you," Gerald started. "Jim will be good for Hayes Oil, better than Jeff would have been."

"Is that why you killed Jeff? Tell me, because I don't understand this." Riley was suddenly insistent. He only had five minutes with this man he'd once called Dad, and he needed to know—

"Yes," Gerald said simply, and Riley slumped back in the chair, disappointment running through his veins like ice. "You can never understand, Riley. I don't expect you to."

"You killed your son!" Riley shouted, watching for emotion, for a sign that Gerald felt anything, but there was nothing, only silence. He sensed the detective coming closer, probably worried Riley was going to lose it.

"Riley, I want you to know that I'm happy for you and your husband. I need you to talk to your momma, tell her Lisa is safe now, tell her she can come home, that they can bring my grandchildren home," Gerald said finally as the detective cleared his throat and indicated time was up and Riley needed to leave. Riley just stared at Gerald, his head swimming with grief, confusion and hatred. He turned his back and left.

There was nothing to say.

Chapter 47

Riley knew he wasn't doing very well. Every time he thought about everything that had happened, it was as if there was a surge in his heart rate. He would find himself sweating, edgy, jumpy, feeling constantly on guard. It was driving him mad, and he discovered the best way to deal with it was to avoid thinking at all. Every time someone asked him a question or alluded to the events of the last few days, it was easier to just switch off, to steer clear of places or people who reminded him of the Hayes family.

He realized this was wrong. He wasn't stupid, but he was losing interest in everything, feeling more and more distant from Jack. Sometimes, when he looked back over what happened, it was as if he could almost erase some parts of what had happened, and he knew he was developing far from healthy coping strategies. Added to that, he wasn't sleeping, was irritable, and couldn't concentrate. He decided the only way to not entirely destroy what was left of his life was to stay away from everyone. Jim asked questions, Jack asked questions, Donna just hugged him every time she saw him. Lisa had visited, and Riley had held her as she wept. Eden took to following him around, her hazel eyes inevitably full of tears, her face permanently tear-stained and pale.

Beth couldn't look him in the eyes, and he knew why. He had let everyone down, not *seen* what was in front of his eyes. If only he'd been vigilant then Jeff might never have gone that far, never hurt Beth. His mom had visited, told him to pull himself together, that he needed to be strong for everyone. He thought she probably assumed she was helping, handing over the mantle of man of the family to him, but she wasn't. He couldn't say that, although he wanted to scream at her, tell her he wasn't the right person to be looking after everyone else.

And then there was Jack. He loved him, but Riley knew he didn't deserve to be loved back, not when his brother had wronged the Campbell family so very badly. He wondered how Jack could even look at him. All the time Jack would touch Riley with concern and half smiles and whispered promises of love, and it was all Riley could do not to run in the opposite direction. To think they'd almost renewed vows, well, that was laughable. There was no way he was going to force Jack to tie himself to

Riley for any longer than the prescribed year. In fact Riley had researched the whole contract scenario. The contract could be easily made null and void. A divorce would be simple enough, and Jack could then find someone who wasn't so damn broken and pathetic, someone who didn't have the name Hayes carved into their soul.

He needed air, needed space, and after snapping at something Jack had said and having to look at pity-filled blue eyes, he saddled up one of the quarter horses, the movements familiar and soothing. The smells of the old barn served as a reminder of what he could have had, and he hurried the task until he finally stood outside in the Texas heat, his eyes fixed on the horizon, on the need to test those far off limits, to escape.

"You wanna wait, Riley? I'll join you." Jack's voice was careful, but Riley could hear the questions in it. He didn't reply. He inserted a foot in a stirrup and swung his frame onto the horse's back, stilling the shift in the animal's movement with a firm pull on the reins.

"If it's all the same to you, I'm best off alone," Riley said, and heard Jack sigh.

"Riley, you can't keep doing this."

"Doing what?"

"Running. You need to get this all out so we can deal."

Words hovered on Riley's tongue. Was Jack not seeing that now was the time to back off? Riley didn't need touchy-feely crap, and what Jack needed was to just fucking run away from Riley and the remainder of the Hayes family as soon as he could. He didn't say what he wanted to say— My brother was a rapist, and he's been murdered by the man I called father for twenty-seven years, I'm organizing my brother's funeral, dealing with Dad in a cell… I don't have time to talk. Instead he said nothing. He applied light pressure to the mare's sides and guided her out of the barn area and past the paddocks. He was heading away from the ranch house and into the oblivion of his own confused thoughts.

* * * *

Eden watched as her brother rode off and sighed, her heart twisting at the pain that must be inside her brother.

"He's not doing so well, is he?" she asked softly. Jack turned to her. She'd been here almost solidly since Jeff's death, because she couldn't face the

Hayes mausoleum. He pulled her into a close hug.

"He's hurting, and he won't talk to me."

Eden couldn't help the tears in her eyes or the mind-numbing pain in her head, and she just burrowed into Jack's reassuring strength for support. She needed to tell Riley what she had done. It didn't matter what she'd promised Jim and her dad. Riley was her brother, and he deserved to know. But how could she tell him? How could she even *begin* to explain what had happened? If she left it as it was, with Riley thinking Gerald had killed Jeff for nothing more than the family name and for money, then she was scared there would be nothing left of the brother she loved, the brother who had seemed to finally be getting a life he could enjoy.

She waited at the barn until evening pulled in, wishing she could just get this over with, standing from her nest among the hay bales when Riley finally jumped down from the saddle. He hadn't seen her in the half gloom, and his face was open, grief carved into it, and his shoulders hunched. She knew he was at the edge of a cliff. Would talking to him, telling him what she'd done, be enough to push him over or be enough to pull him back? She needed him, he needed Jack, and she knew what she had to do.

"Why are you shutting Jack out?" she asked, Riley jumped, startled at the voice, and he whirled to face her.

"Jeez, sis, you scared the shit outta me."

"Tell me why you won't talk to Jack."

He paused, uncertainty crossing his face. "Has he said something?"

"No. You know he wouldn't do that. It's stuff I see. You avoid him, won't touch him, walk away when people start talking… Tell me."

"It's nothing that needs tearing open."

"You're wrong. It's the very thing that needs opening."

"You wouldn't understand," Riley began. "Hell, everyone expects so much from me now. I have a lot to process is all." He sounded ultra-defensive. "I can't handle any more talking, least of all cozy meaningful chats with another man."

"He's your husband, Ri, and you need to talk to him."

"I don't *need* to do anything."

"I'm scared. Can I talk to you? Will you listen? I need to tell you something,

something that may…" Eden stopped. May what exactly? May drive her brother to be angry with her? She stepped back away from him, and he looked confused for a moment. He wasn't Jeff; she knew he wouldn't hurt her. She kept telling herself that even as the words tumbled from her mouth. "It was Lisa that shot Jeff. I know because I was there."

Riley blinked. "What?" Disbelief echoed in his tone, and his eyes widened in shock.

"I don't know how it happened. There was just so much hate in her, and she was scared for the kids… And she just…" Her voice broke on a silent sob. "Riley, I told you I was there. I know." Riley said nothing, dropping the reins of the mare, and taking a step towards her, his hands wide in front of him, begging for her to take it back in body language that was screaming denial.

"Lisa?" His tone was confused. "But Gerald—"

Eden raised her eyes, reaching out a hand, almost touching Riley's but not quite.

"He's protecting her, and me. I handled the gun." Her whisper dripped with fear; she could hear it in her own voice.

"Fuck. Eden." Riley's voice was broken. "I don't believe you."

She shook her head wordlessly. How could she make him understand what she'd done when she couldn't understand it herself. Reaching out, he grabbed her upper arms, shaking her, switching from fear to temper. "You had the gun? What have you both done?" She started to sob in his hold, even as his fingers dug into her arms.

"Riley, you're hurting me, let me go, please." It was the *please* that pushed through to him, and seemingly startled at his own strength, he released her, causing her to stumble and fall back, breaking into tears.

"Christ, Riley, what the fuck?" Jack was there, reaching for Eden, pulling her away from the fence, his eyes wide in shock. Riley stared back.

"I didn't mean to— Shit— Ask her," he managed to push out on a breath, but Eden couldn't speak as she leaned on Jack, sobbing.

* * * *

Detached, Riley watched, the ice in him starting to crack… He wasn't like them —anymore than she was— so what could make his beautiful sister-in-law turn a gun on her husband and pull the trigger? What was so bad that she could kill for it? Suddenly it was like an unknown force was pushing him back to her, pulling at Jack's hands until she stood alone, vulnerable. "Eden, what did he do? Did he touch the kids?" *Abuse them?*

Jack looked at Eden's eyes, and probably saw the same thing Riley did, the fear, the total shock. Riley heard her wordless gasp of horror, as he tried to connect the dots. *Fuck*, what was he missing here? "He didn't, Riley, he didn't. Lisa said he hadn't, but it was women, and some girls not much older than sixteen." Riley staggered back, his hand at his chest; he'd thought it was a business deal gone wrong, revenge, nothing to do with Lisa.

"What do we do?" Riley murmured, his head spinning.

"Jim says we should say nothing, that daddy knows what he's doing."

That point there was make or break, that last piece of information that sealed the decisions he'd make next. He turned and walked away.

* * * *

Jack made a split second decision, releasing Eden, and striding after Riley, catching him and turning him round in a pull of muscle. "Don't you dare," he said abruptly, spitting the words fast and hard. "You go back there, and you talk to her. She is your freakin' sister, for God's sake." Riley was shaking his head.

"I can't hear any more about him and what he did," he replied, trying to pull his arm from Jack's grasp.

"You don't get to decide when to stop listening, Riley. He's obviously hurt Lisa. Just listen to what Eden has to say. It will be okay."

"Shit, Jack, when will it ever be okay to hear this shit?"

Jack crowded his husband back against the barn wall, not caring who might see.

"Listen to me, Riley." He placed his hands either side of Riley's face, made him look down at him, and captured his gaze. "You go back, you listen to her, you be a good brother, and when you've finished, you come find me and we'll deal with this. Okay? Together." Riley nodded. "I mean it," Jack continued firmly. "You find me, and I will take care of you. This has gone on long enough."

* * * *

Jack released his hold, and Riley stayed leaning against the barn as Jack headed for the house. His husband didn't look back, evidently trusting him to do what needed doing.

Pulling himself together, gathering every ounce of reserve he had left, Riley returned to Eden. She hadn't moved, but her head was down and she was crying silently. Carefully he closed in and pulled her into a hug, startling her enough to look up, fear in her eyes, fear that he'd helped to put there. It was fear of what he was going to say.

"Tell me, Eden," was all he said.

So she did.

Chapter 48

Jack waited, sitting quietly on the side of the bed, his eyes focused on the two dark suits hanging on the back of the door, and the black ties and crisp white shirts ready for the funeral the next day. He was trying to stay calm, trying to be the strong one. The phone wouldn't stop ringing. Newspapers, reporters, society pages, they all wanted the Hayes story. Yesterday they even had people driving onto the D to get photos, turning back only when met by a rifle-toting Donna in full-on momma bear mode. It was front-page news — *Father kills son, the fall of Hayes Oil*— all blown up, untrue statements and demands, and the guilt layering up on Riley was visible. Every time the phone rang, or a paper landed on the doorstep, it was as if Riley was taking a step back. Jack had heard him last night, tossing and turning in what little sleep he was having, disturbed by dreams and nightmares.

Idly he opened the closet and looked at his suit, pulling at the one tie he owned and curling it around his hands, the feel of the expensive silk soft against his work-roughened skin. It would do for the funeral, unless Riley wanted him to wear something different— not that Riley would tell him. His husband wouldn't talk to him, wouldn't share any of it and was closing himself down more and more as each hour passed. He said it wasn't right for him to share it with Jack. Said that it was up to him to sort this out because it wasn't Jack's family. On and on, he threw stuff like that at Jack, and to be honest, Jack was starting to get a little pissed.

He looked up as Riley came into the room, his skin pale, and his eyes wide and filled with shock.

"Is she okay?" Jack asked softly, startling Riley out of his thoughts.

Riley nodded and crossed to sit next to Jack. "Thank you for making me go back."

"Are you going to tell me what she said?" Jack asked carefully, sighing when Riley just closed his eyes and shook his head.

"I don't know what to say," he started, opening his mouth to continue then shutting it just as fast. Jack stood, trying to tamp down the fury inside him for what Riley's family had done to his lover, closing him off and making him unable to deal with his emotions. It was dangerous. Fucking dangerous.

"Do you trust me, Riley?" Jack asked softly, unwrapping the tie and leaning back on the door to their room. He carefully slid the lock. Riley wasn't even aware of; it was as if he wasn't even in the room. Jack crossed to him, lifting his lover's chin with his hands, and staring into hazel eyes. "Do you trust me?" he asked again and saw Riley nod. "Lie back and shut your eyes." Riley looked confused, his face creased into a frown. Jack just laid a firm hand on his shoulder. "I'm not asking Riley, I'm telling."

They were frozen that way for long minutes until Riley scooted up the bed and lay down, closing his eyes as he'd been told.

Carefully Jack slipped away Riley's T-shirt and jeans, cutting off his protests with a harsh "Shhhh", leaving no room for argument, until Riley lay clad only in boxers. Carefully he grasped Riley's hands, lifting them above Riley's head, wondering if he should trust Riley to leave them there.

"Are you gonna move 'em?" he asked, his drawl Texas-long and insistent.

"Shit, Jack, I don't wanna fuck. I—"

Jack stopped the words with a hand over Riley's mouth, deciding that no, Riley was unlikely to keep still. With deft movements, he slipped a knot around Riley's hands, the silk ties soft against his skin, and looped the end over the middle bed post. Riley would be unable to move his hands all the time Jack straddled him. It took Riley's brain a few seconds to catch up on this, finally bucking up, trying to dislodge Jack.

"Keep still." Jack ordered softly, just using his own body weight to hold Riley down, until at last he obeyed. Jack was making it very clear that *he* was leading this.

"Jack?" It was a question, a plea.

"Tell me… Did you know what was happening with Jeff?" It was kind of a huge question to lead off with, and Riley squirmed under him, but Jack held strong and just leaned forward. He began kiss-biting a trail from cheekbone to nipple, drawing the hard nub into his mouth and biting softly, hearing the mewl of pleasure-pain in the man strung out under him. He lifted his head. "Did you know?"

Riley lifted his head and spat out, "No!", then said more softly. "No." He lay back down. "He hit Lisa, I didn't know."

"Why, Riley? Why did he hit his wife?"

"I don't know. He had evil in him."

"Do you have that same evil in you?"

"I don't… Jack…" His voice tailed off as Jack moved to the other nipple, pulling on it, worrying it with his teeth, and unbidden Riley rocked his groin up, seeking resistance, hardening without even realizing it. "I'm not like him," he rasped.

"If you were, what would you have done? Would you have helped Jeff?"

Riley's eyes widened. "No! Jesus— No!"

"What about Beth?"

"Beth?" Riley asked helplessly as Jack moved lower, sucking marks of possession into skin stretched taut over hipbones.

"Would you have hurt her like Jeff did?"

Riley's eyes widened even farther. "No, no! Fuck, Jack!"

Jack nipped his inner thigh, and Riley was thrusting into air, trying to force Jack's mouth *there*, whining as lips touched the folds at the base of his dick, gently laving at his balls, just this side of pleasure-pain. Jack drew one then the other into his hot wet mouth.

"I don't want to think. Don't make me think— please Jack."

Jack lifted his head, looking direct into hazel eyes blown with need, with want, seeing the confusion there. "You ever hit your momma, Riley? Your mom with her sad lonely life and her ghost-like existence… You ever want to slap her to get her to live? Maybe push her around?"

"No, Jack! Fuck! I haven't ever… I wouldn't!"

Jack's lips touched the crown of his dick, licking gently at the evidence of his arousal, gentle, very gentle, his hand moving up to twist hard on a nipple and then he leaned back slightly.

"Are you a bad person, Riley? Have you ever had your hands around someone's throat, willing them to die? Like I did in the hallway with Jeff? Closing the fingers tight, waiting for the fragile pulse to just stop under your hands?"

"No, Jack, it wasn't you, it was Jeff." Riley's voice subsided into mindless babble as Jack closed his mouth around Riley's dick and swallowed him whole in seconds. He bottomed out against the back of Jack's throat, and Jack moved his tongue just how he knew Riley liked it.

It went on and on, Riley so close, and Jack kept him at the edge.

"I left Eden with Beth, should be there with her. I should be seeing Gerald, Momma needs me, Lisa, and the company, I need to bury Jeff…" Riley kept talking, a confused jumble of noise.

But Jack didn't let up. He kept taking him close, pulling off, his hand jacking Riley slowly, then he'd move up to have his mouth a breath away from Riley's. He could see Riley was so close because he knew the signs.

"You are not your brother, Riley. Don't carry his guilt." He twisted his hand, that clever twist he knew would finish Riley, and within seconds, his broken husband was coming hot and wet across his hand, harsh sobs tearing from his chest. Jack didn't hesitate. He pulled at the tie that held Riley, leaning into his strong body and just holding him as he cried, listening to the words that tumbled from his lips.

"How could he do all that, hurting Lisa? He deserved to die. How can I say that? How can he leave me to deal with it all? What do I do? I didn't see Lisa, I didn't see what had happened. I didn't see what Jeff was doing to her, and I didn't stop what happened to Beth. I didn't stop him hitting Mom."

Then Jack heard the worst thing of all. "Why didn't I see all that?"

Chapter 49

When Riley woke, it was to dawn creeping in through open curtains and to a headache that wrapped around his head like a steel band. He rolled onto his side, groaning with the pain in his eyes that only crying could leave, and buried his face deep into soft cotton, flushing red with the embarrassment about what had happened the night before. Jack was warm and strong against him, deep in sleep, his breathing a rhythm to count heartbeats by, and Riley tried to inch away. He wasn't sure he was up to talking after what had been pulled from him in the dark.

"Where ya goin'?" Jack's voice was slurred with sleep, his arms reaching up above his head to touch the wall, exposing his chest to view, honey-toned skin and tracks of freckles just there to see and to touch. Riley suddenly forgot he needed to run, or that he'd cried like a freaking baby for hours the night before. He totally ignored the headache that had forced him awake. Turning back to face Jack, not knowing what to say, not knowing how to say thank you, he did all he knew how to do. He pressed his hands on Jack's, holding them above his head, and leaned in to rest his head against Jack's pulse and his bed-warm skin. Who could resist touching a naked Campbell-Hayes in their bed?

Not Riley for sure.

* * * *

Beth poured more chocolate into Eden's mug. After what Eden had just told her, and given Beth wasn't drinking alcohol, chocolate seemed like second best. They sat silently for a good ten minutes.

"What did Riley say when you told him?" Beth finally asked, watching as Eden hunched over her mug and took in deep breaths of the fragrant liquid inside. She didn't ask again, just waited as Eden quietly sat and contemplated.

"He walked away," she started, lifting her head quickly at Beth's indrawn breath. "No, not like that. He came back; Jack made him come back. I know he didn't mean to walk away. He's just overwhelmed, and he was… I guess he was in shock."

"So he came back."

"And we talked, and I told him everything, even when I wasn't sure I should tell him."

"Why wouldn't you tell him? Why keep Lisa's secret?"

"Why did you not tell Jack or Josh about the baby?" Eden said simply, almost as if that was answer enough.

"That was different," Beth said quickly.

"When you told Jack and Josh, they wanted to kill someone; they had it in their blood. That urge to protect you, kill for you. I knew Riley would do that if he found out Jeff was hurting Lisa, and that it would destroy our family. I wasn't brave enough to do that. I wanted peace, and I wanted to forget."

The girls sat in silence. Steve walked in wearing boxers and a T-shirt, his hair mussed from sleep and his eyes worried. He took one glance at her and Eden and turned back to Beth's room with a simple nod of understanding. Eden looked at Beth's smile.

"You love each other very much," she said almost wistfully.

"Yes, Steve is…" Beth didn't know how to explain, how to put into words what her and Steve were. "The other half of me," she finished, half wincing at the cliché but knowing Eden understood. "He loves our daughter, and that is such a big thing for me, for us, to be the three of us."

* * * *

Riley felt like a voyeur watching his sister and Beth from the doorway, neither knowing he was there. He couldn't hear what they were saying, but he heard his name mentioned and wondered what they were saying. He felt strength inside him, thanked Jack for what he'd done, snapping Riley out of the downward spiral of denial and distress enough to make him see what was happening to his family.

"Hey," he finally said, pushing away from the door and crossing to pour himself coffee. They both glanced up at him, Beth with a smile, Eden looking uncertain, worried. She plainly didn't know what to say to Riley. It was almost as if the ball was in his court, and it was his turn to reassure her that everything was going to be okay.

Riley found it hard to start. He wanted to just say everything that was inside his heart— sorry, and thank you, and everything will work out. He wanted to talk to her about what they should do next. He tried, he really did, opening his mouth to at least say one thing, just one damn thing, but nothing was happening and the atmosphere was turning cold, icy as Beth seemed confused and angry, Eden unsure, and Riley simply unable to talk.

Eden stood, shakily holding onto the back of the chair. "Thank you for the chocolate," she half whispered, but she didn't get far. He hooked her with one hand and gripped her tight into a hug, tucking her head under his chin, his hands locked behind her, his arms around her, holding her.

"Good morning, Missy Eden," he said gently, using the nickname he'd given her as a young child. "Did you manage to sleep some?" She didn't answer, just snuggled closer holding onto him tight.

"Did you?" she finally asked. Riley chuckled.

"Jack made sure of it," he said, then added the proviso that he thought she should hear. "Didn't stop me worrying about you, or Lisa." It was the concern of a brother that was the last straw, and hot tears started to track from her eyes, burning into Riley's skin.

"I'm sorry I didn't tell you straight away," she whimpered softly, seemingly unable to stop the flow of tears.

All Riley did was pull her tighter, rocking her gently, supporting her grief. "I love you, Eden. Shhhh, we'll find Lisa, and everything will be okay now. I've got you. It will be alright."

They stood for a long while, Riley carding his hand through her hair, just being strong for her, tears in his own eyes, as if they needed to cry together to wash away the hate and the misery. He felt stronger just having her there in his arms, stronger with Jack looking out for him. Just stronger.

Chapter 50

The helicopter whirled overhead and finally hovered in one position, the noise of it a distant reminder of the paparazzi that stalked them all on a daily basis. The group huddled around the open grave was silent, stoic. Riley stood between his mom and Eden, his arms around both of them, each lost in thought. Lisa and the children were huddled at the head of the open grave, Lisa pale and drawn and the kids crying. He seemed to be listening intently as the minister intoned the eulogy, the words familiar and reassuring. Steve stood with Beth, Jack, and Donna to one side.

Jim kept himself slightly apart, his features carefully blank of anything, his head a million miles away.

He'd known exactly what he should say when he had arrived at the D earlier that morning, knew Riley needed to know the whole truth. He owed it to his son and to the woman he wanted to call daughter. He sat them down, shuffled paperwork, legal documents, letters of intent, medical records, and he knew exactly where to start.

"Your dad is dying," he began, realizing he needed to qualify that statement. "Gerald is dying. He has maybe two more months and is refusing treatment for cancer." Riley had looked up quickly, and Jim knew what Riley's question would be. He'd want to know if that was the reason Gerald had organized the whole Hayes Oil presidency thing, to tidy his house before he died. "No, I didn't know before the night Eden revealed what she'd heard and then, only after I called your father… Gerald, and he told me what the doctors had said."

"Is that why he's taken the blame for the murder?" Eden had asked. "Because he knows he can't be tried for it? Has he turned down the treatment for his cancer because of a *need* to die?"

"The treatments open to him would prolong his life for maybe an extra few weeks," Jim hurried to say, knowing immediately what Eden was implying. "He has signed a DNR, and the authorities that have him are aware and know there will be no trial. They have a signed confession, and that is enough for them. I think Stafford would like to dig further so we need to remain cautious, but yes, in the main, this is the end of it for all of us."

Jim stood quietly, remembering their conversation, his eyes on Lisa. She was now leaning into Riley for strength, and he willed her not to lose it and blurt something out as she looked over at her father-in-law. Gerald was dressed in a suit and cuffed to guards on either side of him. He'd been allowed out on special leave, but bail had been refused in light of his admission of guilt, and he'd been bound over. Now he was here at Jeff's funeral, a broken man, old before his time, but somehow, now the master of his own fate.

Jim watched as Lisa and Riley approached Gerald. Lisa in tears, Riley white-faced but calm.

Riley nodded. "Dad," he said simply.

"Son," Gerald replied, nodding in return, leaning into the hug that Lisa was giving him and then being pulled back by the guards.

* * * *

It was three weeks to the day after Jeff's funeral that Riley and Eden buried Gerald Hayes in the family tomb, his name to be inscribed next to his son's.

There was only one thing Riley could say, and it was important. He pulled Jack to one side. "Promise me, when I die, that you won't put me in there with them."

Jack just held him close, promising him he wouldn't. "Nah, Het-boy, you'll be with me."

* * * *

Beth rolled onto her back, her head and neck propped up by pillows, her daughter practicing gymnastics in her belly and Steve snoring softly at her side. She had woken up from a graphic dream. Her daughter was telling her goodbye, and Eden was sobbing softly at Jeff's grave. It brought so much pain that it forced her awake to face the midnight hours on her own. She could get up, wander out to the kitchen, and see if anyone was awake, Jack maybe, Riley, Eden, or she could lie here and look at the ceiling for a few hours until she was too tired for her body to remain awake any longer.

Steve made her decision easy, his sleepy voice asking if she was okay and if she needed anything. Ever since she'd passed the seventh month mark, her skin stretched tight across her belly and her back arched to support the weight, he'd worried and fretted and followed her around, intent on missing nothing.

She smiled in the dark, her hand finding his and lacing her fingers tightly through them.

"You," she finally whispered into the night that invited secrets and shared desire. "I need you." Steve leaned up on one side, focusing on her in the dark, and he traced a line of small kisses from her neck to her lips. He couldn't seem to get enough of her, of the taste of her, touching her, her and the child inside her. They were to be married in three days. That was Steve's idea. He wanted to be married before their daughter appeared. Beth had tried to argue. What if something happened? What if she died? Then Steve would be saddled with a daughter that wasn't his.

That had been one of their only arguments, and it had been harsh and hard. Steve had ended it swiftly. "You're afraid I would leave our daughter if you died? Is that what you think of me?" She had the grace to blush, because yes, it was what she'd thought. She'd assumed Steve wanted only her. Surely he couldn't truly want the daughter that had been created in anger and hate. He made her see she was wrong.

"I love you," he whispered against her skin, moving to kiss her belly, laughing softly as he felt the kick inside, and slipping her tight grip, he used his fingers to touch each freckle that marked the trail to her center. "Three days is too long. I want my ring on your finger now." She arched into his touch as warmth began to pool and spread out through her body, and her breath hitched at his words. He had the power to push her over the edge with just the softest touches, and she curled into his arms, letting him take control, letting herself relax into him.

* * * *

Riley was equally as restless but for different reasons, not least of which was the fact that Jack currently had him pinned to the bed with his lips wrapped tight around his dick and his hands getting creative in matching rhythm.

"Jack." He couldn't voice his needs any more coherently that just random words of begging, despite being at the back of the ranch and away from everyone. He was trying to keep it quiet, and it was so damn difficult. He wanted to demand more, harder, there, more, harder, and Jack damn well knew it, teasing him, pushing him to the edge and then retreating, until Riley was a writhing mess of want. He arched up, pushing harder, and Jack moved back, the fucking tease, actually taking his mouth off and chuckling low in his throat.

"You sure look pretty, needy and begging under me."

"Fucker."

* * * *

"What d'you want, Riley?" He shifted himself and scooted up the bed, encouraging Riley to move with him until they lay side by side, heads on soft pillows, legs twined together, Jack hard against his lover. With his hand closing around Riley, he found a rhythm and finished him off with no more than a few twists and pulls of his clever fingers. He didn't give Riley time to say a word, or even to breathe. He wanted to come when he was kissing Riley, wanted to lose it as he tongue fucked his husband's mouth, his need for touch and taste overwhelming. He didn't know what was pushing this. Even as he felt Riley finally come, arching hard and stiff against him, hot and wet between them, he wanted to taste and rut and feel. He heard Riley's breathing in his ear, harsh, quick, and words of love and thanks, and he lost it, coming so damn hard he saw stars. Riley reached for the towel he'd been wearing after his shower, wiping them and pulling Jack back close to cuddle.

"I know something is on your mind. Talk to me," Riley demanded softly.

Jack groaned inwardly. He was so going to come out of this sounding like some huge girl.

"We didn't arrange to renew our vows," Jack finally said. Great, he'd said it now, it was out there, and yes, he did sound like a girl, all kind of hurt and worried. Riley, for his part, was silent, and Jack lifted his head, expecting to see Riley's wide grin and reassurance in hazel eyes. Instead he saw a face twisted in a frown and closed eyes. "Riley?" he asked. This really wasn't going how he expected it to go. Riley slid out from his grasp, moving to sit on the side of the bed, twisting and pulling at the sheet that pooled around him and then slumping in defeat with a huge sigh. "Riley?"

"We don't have to, you know," Riley finally said, his shoulders stiffening as Jack embraced him from behind.

"What do you mean?" Jack asked softly, even though he knew damn well what Riley meant.

"You *can* change your mind, you know. We can leave it at the year," Riley finally offered.

"I knew that was in your head, Riley, and I say again, I love you, I want this to go past a year, two years, ten years, twenty, even more if we're lucky."

Riley looked up, a hopeful light in his eyes "So we could do it properly."

"Properly?"

"Us. That's all we need, the family, and words we mean— maybe out by the paddock with your land laid out in front of us, at dusk?"

Riley sounded so wistful, and it was all Jack could do not to smile a sappy smile in return to his husband's words. He didn't need to say anything else. He hoped Riley could see he wanted this and could see the remainder of his life spread out in front of him with Jack in his life.

"Beth and Steve get married in three days," Riley finally said. "I want to renew our vows sooner."

"Sooner?"

"Tomorrow."

Chapter 51

Beth and Eden sat side by side in front of the mirror, Eden desperately trying to tame her long hair, and Beth trying to cover the bags under her eyes with concealer. Both were chatting and laughing and discovering things about their respective brothers that they knew would make awesome blackmail material at future family parties. It was natural, it was real, and it was a friendship that went way past family. Simply put, it was two women together, at ease, as they discussed being little sisters, Beth being pregnant, being scared and being happy. Steve did try to sit with them. He lasted ten seconds, blanched at the word tampon, and left the room to, in his words, "find some men".

Beth shifted in her chair, the smile slipping from her face momentarily as her back twinged horribly, sending sharp pains up and down her spine and into her legs. To add insult to injury, her daughter decided to join in, kicking her hard and pushing, as if to say "Down here. I'm down here."

"You okay, Beth?" Eden asked, frowning.

The pain in Beth's back had started at breakfast, and Eden had voiced her concerns as to how Beth was not only going to make it through their brothers' vow renewal ceremony but to her own wedding.

"Yeah," Beth finally said. "I phoned the doctor. She wants me in tomorrow, just to check. Says it's probably just the baby turning, sitting on a nerve." Beth smiled softly, resting a hand on her swollen belly. "Only four more weeks, and I get to meet her."

Eden placed a hand over Beth's, squeezing gently. "I can't wait," she said simply, and Beth looked into her friend's expressive eyes, knowing that her daughter's aunt was going to play a huge part in the baby's life. Feeling suddenly and overwhelmingly sentimental, she leaned as much as she could, ignoring the twinges in her back, to pull Eden in for a hug, which Eden returned with a similar affection. They pulled back, both blinking tears. Then just as easily turned back to the mirror and resumed their beauty ritual.

* * * *

Sandra accepted the coffee from Donna, sitting at the scarred kitchen table, her head spinning and her eyes wet from tears. Donna didn't know what to say, but she felt she should maybe say something, anything.

"Thank you, Donna, for taking in Riley and Eden," Sandra finally said. "They needed a home, and the D is a better home than they ever had with me."

"I don't want to hear that, Sandra. You aren't the kind of person who just thanks people for apparently giving your kids a better life than you did. That's bullshit." Sandra's eyes widened, as Donna continued. "You can play the fading southern rose card all you want, but know this, Sandra Hayes. You survived. You had things piled on you that no normal person could have endured, and out of all of that, Riley and Eden are kids you can be proud of."

"But—"

"No buts, Sandra, drink your coffee, swallow the southern genteel crap, and get some backbone. We've got candles to arrange."

* * * *

Jim hovered at the kitchen door, listening to Donna giving Sandra the sound advice the woman he loved needed to hear. He wondered if he could love Sandra any more than he had when he was younger. He wondered if he would ever tell her that he still loved her, that whatever happened, however many years had passed, he always would.

* * * *

Dusk was starting to draw the evening in, and the entire ranch was lit with the glow of the setting sun in hues of red and gold. Donna and Sandra had gone all out with the candles, creating a flickering backdrop for Riley and Jack, who stood by the paddock with the people in their life they loved standing around them.

It was Riley who wanted to speak first. The words he had in his head now were very different from those he'd planned the first time they were to renew their vows.

"Despite how this started," he began softly, "I want you to know that over the past few months, ever since you came to the Hayes Oil tower to see me, my heart hasn't really belonged to me anymore. We fought, and I resisted, we loved, and I resisted, but you didn't let me stay away. You opened your heart, your life, and offered your family to me, and I finally accepted." He swallowed, seeing the dusky colors reflected in Jack's eyes and seeing them suspiciously bright. "I promise you that you will *never* regret the gift you gave me. I swear it, Jack." He reached for Jack's hands, clasping them tight. "On our wedding day, I pledged many things to you and, said words that made little sense to me at the time. But today, the first day of the rest of our lives, here in front of our family, I want to make sure you know how much I love you. I, Riley Nathaniel Campbell-Hayes, love you, Jackson Robert Campbell-Hayes. I promise to love you more each day than I did the day before. "

Sighing deeply, hesitating only momentarily, he continued, "I read something somewhere, and your eyes, your beautiful changeable blue eyes, made me remember it. Someone once wrote this, and I hope I can remember this right. 'The world, for me, and all the world can hold, is circled in your arms; for me there lies, within the lights and shadows of your eyes, the only beauty that is never old'. I will trust you and respect you, laugh with you and cry with you, loving you faithfully through good times and bad, regardless of the seemingly incredible obstacles life puts in front of us. We will face it together. Jack, I love you, and I give you my hand, my heart, and my love. Forever."

Riley was lost in the words, meaning every syllable, aware of little more than the pressure of Jack's hands in his, of the smile that was on Jack's face, of each freckle he could see on his skin.

* * * *

It was Jack's turn to respond, and he drew every ounce of emotion from his heart. "When we said we would renew our vows, I had this whole speech prepared, but today I find myself just asking these two questions. How do I explain how I love my husband and how has our love changed since we exchanged our wedding vows? And I have a simple answer. I didn't love you when we exchanged our vows. I couldn't have. I'm sorry I lied to my momma, but that is the truth here and now. I didn't know you as anything other than the son of our family's nemesis. Just a name is all you were to me. So today I stand here, with new promises, learning from every single thing that has happened over the last few months, and from crisis to crisis, my love has grown. My new promise, and yet maybe not so new, is that I love you, and I will continue to hold you in my heart and my mind and love you for as many more years as God allows. I, Jackson Robert Campbell-Hayes, take you, Riley Nathaniel Campbell-Hayes, as my partner, loving what I know of you, and trusting what I do not yet know to be just as amazing."

He smiled. "I am so damn excited to have the chance to grow together, to get to know the man you will become, and fall in love with you a little more every day. Know this, Het-boy, I promise to love you always. I don't have the poetry in me to give to you, Riley, but I have the love for my family, my land and my horses, and I want to share every single part of it with the man I call husband. I love you, Riley."

There wasn't a dry eye as they moved to embrace, kissing away any doubts they had before they exchanged these new vows, to the applause and catcalls from their family. It was a moment not one person present would ever forget.

* * * *

Steve was dancing with Eden, and the party was in full swing, the Hayeses and Campbells laughing and reminiscing and crying and just forging simple bonds that would last many generations. It was odd really that it took so long to notice Beth was missing. After all, she'd been the center of attention for so long that for no one to see she wasn't in the tangled mess of noise and confusion would be something that would haunt him for the rest of his days.

He was suddenly aware that the drink Beth had gone for had taken at least ten minutes, and concerned, he went to find her. He grew more concerned when he couldn't find her in the kitchen. Maybe she'd gone to lie down in the bedroom? Eden caught his arm as he passed by. "Is Beth okay?" she asked.

"I think she's lying down; I'm going to go check on her."

So he did.

But she wasn't lying down; she was in the bathroom, and he pulled her into his arms, shouting for help… She looked so pale, so lost, her eyes closed, skin gray, and blood— blood everywhere. Steve lifted eyes filled with horror and disbelief, to Jack, to Josh, to

Donna who had arrived to answer his shouts.

"Help us" was all he could say.

Chapter 52

Two weeks later

Jack continued rocking little Emily who was fast asleep in his arms, her tiny rosebud mouth slightly parted, her hands in fists as she slept the sleep of the innocent. Looking at her peaceful face, no one would ever guess how much drama had occurred before the cesarean that had brought her into the world. She was just beautiful, a miniature Elizabeth, eyes still the blue of a newborn but hair thick and dark and in curls around her face. She moved her lips in that all familiar sucking motion, half opening her eyes and then closing the lids again, sleep outweighing the need for food. She had been born at a good weight for a preemie, five pounds of mewling, squealing need that Jack cradled in his large hands because she was the most precious thing he'd ever held.

Steve had named her Emily Elizabeth, Beth had wanted Emily all along, he'd said as he cried tears of pride over his tiny daughter, and Riley had just hugged his friend close as Jack picked the baby from the bassinet and cooed over her delicate features.

"You are so loved," he whispered down at his niece, humming the words to a lullaby and continuing with the rhythmic rocking and singing as he protected her from the world. She tensed in her sleep, pulling her legs up to her stomach, and he lifted her gently, rubbing her back and resting her head on his neck, against his pulse, his chin resting on her soft curls, the baby smell so sweet and soft. He kept singing, low and soft, the rumbling in his chest soothing her as he massaged her back, and finally, she stilled again, so much so, he had to listen hard to make sure she was breathing.

She was dressed in pink. Everything was pink, from her sleep suits to tiny hair bows, from her bottles to the teddies that sat outside her crib. In fact, Jack thought he had never been surrounded by so much pink outside of Beth's room when she was little. He remembered holding Beth as he did Emily, being trusted by his mom and dad to hold his new sister and, feeling like he was the most important person in the world. It felt the same way still.

Riley had just left, to get coffee he said, but really Jack knew he wanted to find Steve. He worried about him and wanted to make sure he was okay. The suddenness of what had happened the day they renewed their vows had shocked everyone to the very core, and he knew Steve was being hit the hardest, blaming himself for not noticing Beth was ill, that things were going wrong. Everyone had said they too should have noticed, but Steve had excuses for them all, leaving only himself as the one person that should have been there for Beth at the moment it counted. Riley had been Jack's rock, silently supportive, silently loving him, organizing, helping, signing forms, handing over money like there was no tomorrow, buying the best at the drop of a hat, willing it to be enough.

It had been the longest two weeks of Jack's life, the only single point of light curled into his arms at this moment. They had christened her —just in case— but Emily Elizabeth Campbell-Murray was a fighter. Regardless of her early arrival, she was determined to live. Other than slight jaundice, she was well, healthy, and a good weight, with an exceptional set of lungs when the stubbornness of a Campbell broke through. Jack looked up at the clock; it had been an hour since Riley had left. He wondered if he'd found Steve yet, wondered even as the door opened gently and Riley let himself into the room, closing the door behind him and leaning back against it. He looked pale, shocked, and Jack felt grief twist inside him. He imagined his husband was going to tell him that Jack's beautiful sister would never regain consciousness despite fighting for so long and had finally died.

"Jack, she's awake." Riley's voice was broken, and Jack looked down at Emily, unable to speak, fat tears collecting in his eyes and choking his voice. He tightened his grip on Emily, feeling her murmur and snuffle against his skin.

"Let's go see your momma," he finally said, drawing a breath, trying to stop the tears, stumbling to stand with his niece in his hold. Riley was there, supporting him, pulling him into a quick hug then leading him to the door. They exited the nursery into the long white corridor, and to the left where Beth's room was, where she'd been since she had fallen into a coma when her baby was born. The room was quiet, Steve leaning over Beth. When he heard the door, he leaned back, a grin on his face, revealing Beth, so pale but so peaceful. Gently Jack handed Emily to Beth, watching as Steve helped her to hold her daughter and whispered soothing noises as she began to cry looking down on what she had created.

Beth looked up at Jack, to Steve, and then back down to her daughter. "Emily Elizabeth Campbell-Murray," she said softly. "Hello, little one."

Chapter 53

Sandra was pacing, and despite both Riley and Jim trying to calm her down, she kept walking from kitchen to hall and back. Finally she stopped as the realtor reached the bottom of the stairs. He shook hands with the couple that stood with him then waved them off to their car.

"And?" Sandra said simply.

"Seems like murder pays." The realtor smirked, stepping back at the look of irritation in the son's eyes. He looked at Sandra. "They want you to drop two mil, then it's a deal."

"Done," Sandra said without hesitation, leaning into Jim as he held her carefully. Riley nodded at the decision. Jim was glad Riley agreed. They didn't need the money, and they just wanted this symbol of what the Hayes family had stood for gone from their lives. Jim smiled inwardly, loving the feel of Sandra in his arms, tightening his grip, and feeling her relax into his firm hold.

"I'll stay with your mother," Jim offered. He knew Sandra had said she had some items to sort out at the house, and he knew Riley was eager to get back to Jack.

They watched the realtor leave, watched Riley leave with a final hug for his mom, and then they stood in the hall of the place that held so many bad memories. Sandra turned in Jim's arms and sighed. Jim sensed her hesitation and knew she was holding back.

"What's wrong?" he asked gently, knowing that she could reply with anything, from worrying about Eden to thinking of Riley, from remembering Jeff to losing her husband. What she finally said rocked him.

Very carefully, she touched his cheek, her eyes strong and clear and determined, and said, "Can you help me forget?"

It was a decision that was very easy to make, and he pulled her into his arms, the kiss between them as hot as the days he remembered. Maybe, just maybe, their son would have his parents together again.

Jim could only pray.

* * * *

The day of Beth and Steve's wedding was Texas hot and clear, the ceremony itself full of tears and laughter and the cry of a newborn needing attention. Beth looked as beautiful, and as stunning as a princess in ivory and lace. Steve looked ridiculously handsome in his dark suit, and the minister who guided the service was like a proud papa as he joined the two young people in marriage. Sandra and Jim held hands, a fact that wasn't missed by anyone, and Josh and Anna chose that day to announce Anna was pregnant again and another Campbell was to join the world in five months' time.

Jack watched the wedding with pride for his sister and pride in his husband as he stood smiling at Beth and Steve, so obviously in best friend "I did that" mode, it made Jack laugh. They danced and partied until the early hours of the next day, Beth half resting and half dancing, until finally everyone started to drift away to various rooms in the D, the beautiful old ranch house lit with a thousand white fairy lights.

He leaned back against the fence, looking at the house, imagining every person in each room, then turned to face the paddocks, empty of horses but fresh with the promise of a new day. He felt partly sad, partly happy, and he allowed the events of the last few months to drift through his head. From the contract to the vows, from Beth to

Jeff to Gerald, to his own momma, who stood tall and happy as she saw her only daughter wed to the man she loved. It was heaven to stand here, with Texas stretching way into the distance and his land beneath his feet, and when Riley came up behind him, wrapping his long arms around Jack in a tight hold, it was a heaven that was complete.

"Hey, Mr Campbell… you okay?" Riley said softly, leaning to leave a small kiss on Jack's neck.

Jack turned in Riley's arms, raising his own hands to cup his face. "That's Campbell-Hayes to you, Het-boy," Jack returned with his customary smirk. "And yeah, I'm good."

"I love you, Jack."

"I love you, Riley."

"I got this idea," Riley said with a smirk, capturing Jack's lips in a heated searching kiss and then pulling back. Whatever idea he came up with it seemed Jack was on board if his eagerness to carry on kissing was anything to go by.

"Yeah?" Jack finally prompted.

"Wanna go find another bar fight?"

THE END

About RJ Scott

RJ Scott lives just outside London. She has been writing since age six, when she was made to stay in at lunchtime for an infraction involving cookies and was told to write a story. Two sides of A4 about a trapped princess later, a lover of writing was born. She loves reading anything from thrillers to sci-fi to horror; however, her first real love will always be the world of romance. Her goal is to write stories with a heart of romance, a troubled road to reach happiness, and more than a hint of happily ever after.

Email: rj@rjscott.co.uk
Webpage: www.rjscott.co.uk
Facebook: https://www.facebook.com/author.rjscott
Twitter: https://twitter.com/Rjscott_author
Yahoo: http://groups.yahoo.com/group/rjscott/

For an up to date list of available eBooks by RJ Scott and where to purchase them please visit www.rjscott.co.uk

29515251R00248

Made in the USA
Charleston, SC
15 May 2014